Her heart pounded...

Breath came only in short, shallow gasps as she ̵ ̵ ̵ ̵ ̵ ̵ ̵ ̵ ̵ ̵ ̵ her hand. The killer had sent ̵ ̵ ̵ ̵ ̵ ̵ ̵ ̵ ̵ ̵ ̵ ̵ he was?

Brenna jumped and spun around to see Nick mere inches from her. As he reached for the letter, his chest brushed her, and she gasped, stepping back from him and the smell of leather and aftershave.

"Want me to open it?" He came even closer and the air left her lungs, making breath and speech impossible. Not when he was so near, all she had to do was exhale and their bodies would be touching in ways she'd only dreamed.

"No, I can do it." She lowered her eyes so he couldn't see how affected she was. Or how afraid she was for the job she had to do.

He pushed a strand of her hair back behind her ear and traced her jaw with a soft fingertip. "You don't have to be strong all the time, Jensen."

The urge to lean into him assailed her and she pulled away just in time. "Yes, I do. I'm a cop, Nick. I don't have time to be scared." Of killers...or tall, gorgeous FBI agents.

ELLE JAMES

DAKOTA MELTDOWN

HARLEQUIN®

TORONTO • NEW YORK • LONDON
AMSTERDAM • PARIS • SYDNEY • HAMBURG
STOCKHOLM • ATHENS • TOKYO • MILAN • MADRID
PRAGUE • WARSAW • BUDAPEST • AUCKLAND

Like the heroine in this story, I was burned severely as a child and suffered the insecurities of being flawed on the outside. This book is dedicated to my father and mother, Charles and Phyllis Hughes, who've always loved me unconditionally and treated me just like my siblings—normal—the best thing they could have done for me. Without their love and support, I wouldn't have grown into the confident woman I am today. A special thanks to my mother- and father-in-law, Janell and Jerry Jernigan, for giving us a home while we were in transition and for making it possible for me to continue writing. Their support helped make this book happen.

RECYCLED PAPER

ISBN-13: 978-0-373-22938-3
ISBN-10: 0-373-22938-0

DAKOTA MELTDOWN

Copyright: © 2006 by Mary Jernigan

www.eHarlequin.com

Printed in U.S.A.

ABOUT THE AUTHOR

2004 Golden Heart Winner for Best Paranormal Romance, Elle James started writing when her sister issued the Y2K challenge to write a romance novel. She managed a full-time job, raised three wonderful children, and she and her husband even tried their hands at ranching exotic birds (ostriches, emus and rheas) in the Texas hill country. Ask her, and she'll tell you, what it's like to go toe-to-toe with an angry 350-pound bird! After leaving her successful career in information technology management, Elle is now pursuing her writing full-time. She loves building exciting stories about heroes, heroines, romance and passion. Elle loves to hear from fans. You can contact her at ellejames@earthlink.net or visit her Web site at www.ellejames.com.

Books by Elle James

HARLEQUIN INTRIGUE
906—BENEATH THE TEXAS MOON
938—DAKOTA MELTDOWN

CAST OF CHARACTERS

Nick Tarver—An FBI agent determined to stop the killer before another life is lost.

Brenna Jensen—Letters from a serial killer draw her into a search for the man terrorizing her hometown of Riverton.

Stanley Klaus—Brenna's successful brother-in-law, the mark her mother goads her to aim for.

Alice Klaus—Brenna's perfect sister. Will she be a target of the murderer?

Chief Burkholder—The Riverton police chief on the verge of retirement, determined to catch a killer.

Victor Greeley—The philandering married man who duped Brenna once. Is he just a cheating husband, or a killer?

Bart Olsen—A man convicted for sexual offenses, he hates Brenna for putting him in prison.

Jason Connelly—The young computer wiz who stalked one of the would-be victims.

Chapter One

The killing's only just begun. Watch them drop now, one by one.

For the past seven hours the words echoed through Brenna's head. No amount of loud music or talking to herself erased the sound, repeating like a mantra again and again.

When she finally slid her Jeep Cherokee into the driveway of the police station and parked on a hump of ice, she sat for a moment, letting the heater blow warm air in her face. If she'd had any strength left in her arms after the grueling drive, she'd have shaken a fist at the sky.

Yesterday, she'd been fooled into believing spring had arrived with sunshine melting through the mounds of solid ice piled four feet deep outside her town house in Bismarck.

With a sigh, she switched off the engine, pulled her gloves on and wrapped a wool scarf around her face before she stepped out into the storm. The storm that had raged since midnight had dipped its subzero blast as far south as Des Moines.

A native of the northern prairie, she knew better than to count on spring arriving any sooner than April and usually not until May. Her eyes stung and she pulled her scarf higher up over her nose to ward off the bite of the icy wind. Still wired by her hair-raising drive from Bismarck in whiteout conditions, Brenna stomped loose snow from her insulated boots outside the door to the Riverton police station.

The weatherman had predicted snow flurries. But one thing North Dakotans could count on was unpredictable, harsh weather. A trip that normally took her three and a half hours had taken twice as long at half the speed.

In any other circumstance, she'd have waited to make the trip until the storm had passed and the road crew had worked its magic clearing away the foot of snow already accumulated. The forty-mile-an-hour wind hadn't helped, either. She'd struggled to see the road through the heavy snowfall and fought the gale-force gusts buffeting her four-wheel-drive vehicle all over the interstate highway. But she'd made it.

Stepping through the two sets of doors, Brenna entered the police station. The reviving scent of brewing coffee filled her senses as she divested herself of the scarf and draped it over a hook, followed by gloves, stocking cap and finally her heavy parka. Even the short walk from her car to the building necessitated full snow gear unless she wanted frostbite. The coffee smelled even better without the filter of wool around her nose, and she yearned to wrap her stiff fingers around a hot cup. But first she needed to find Tom.

She planted her hands on the counter and leaned toward the curious young police officer. "Hi, I'm Brenna Jensen. Where can I find Chief Burkholder?"

"That you, Brenna?" a deep voice called out from a doorway beyond the front desk.

Her smile lifted upward as her mentor and old friend Chief Tom Burkholder stepped into the lobby.

When she held out her hand to shake his, he brushed it aside and engulfed her in a bear hug that forced the air from her lungs. God, it felt good to be home, even in such tragic circumstances.

Chief Burkholder set her away from him and stared down into her face. "Did you stop by to see your mother and sister yet?"

"Are you kidding?" She tipped her head to the side and back to loosen the muscles tensed in her shoulders and neck. "As soon as they assigned me to the case, I headed straight here."

"You're just like your father—all about the job. We sure miss him around here."

Her father had died of a massive heart attack two years after Brenna had joined the Riverton Police Department. He'd been so proud of his daughters' accomplishments, especially when Brenna had chosen to follow in his footsteps. Never once had he bemoaned the fact he didn't have a son.

She missed her father. They'd understood each other and he'd loved her unconditionally.

"Heard you're up for a new job in Minneapolis," the chief said.

"Yeah." A twinge of guilt nudged at Brenna as if leaving North Dakota was the equivalent of a sin, when so many young people fled the state to find jobs. In her case she had a job, but the new one meant an increase in pay and responsibility, with the downside of being farther away from her family.

"When do they make the final selection?" Tom asked.

"In a week and a half."

"I'll keep you in my prayers for the job and this

case." He hugged her again. "You deserve the break." The chief dropped his hands, shoved them into his pockets and stared down at his feet. "In the meantime, things been happenin' around here."

"Did you find the women?"

The chief shook his head, his skin almost as gray as his hair. "No. We had dozens of state police and local citizens combing the countryside all weekend, but the storm...well, *you* know what it was like. We pulled them in as soon as the weather got bad. No use losing anyone else in that mess out there."

"Find anything in the victims' homes?"

"Nothing yet. Only thing we got to go on is—"

"What the good ol' U.S. Post Office delivered directly to me," Brenna finished for him. Her mouth set in a bleak line. "I don't know what to make of it. But I sure as hell plan to find out."

"One other thing." Chief Burkholder tugged at the tie already loose around his neck.

Brenna recognized the signs. Chief had more bad news he didn't want to tell her.

Her lips twisted into a faux smile and she patted his back. "Might as well spit it out."

With a shake of his head, Chief Burkholder stared hard at her. "We had another woman from town go missing last night."

As if a heavy clamp pinched her lungs, Brenna fought to breathe normally. "Then the note is coming true. You sure she didn't go somewhere and forget to tell anyone?"

"No. Her car was still in her garage, her purse on the counter in the kitchen." The chief chewed on his lower lip. "And, Brenna, since victim number two was from East Riverton on the Minnesota side of the Red

River, we notified the FBI. They're taking charge of the investigation."

"Great. Let's hope they don't hamper our search like the last team they sent." She walked toward the coffee urn on the side counter and helped herself to a foam cup full of liquid resembling sludge. "I'm beginning to see what ol' Red McClusky meant when he said, 'We don't need no outsiders muckin' around our neck of the woods.' I just hope the hell they don't slow us down."

"I'm sorry you feel that way," a low, rumbling voice sounded over Brenna's left shoulder.

She froze. Then a wave of heat rose from beneath her turtleneck to fan out into her face. Inhaling deeply, she steeled her nerves and willed her cheeks to quit burning before she faced the voice. "Do you always sneak up on private conversations?"

"Only if it has something to do with the case I'm working." The man in front of her could have stepped out of an ad for an action-adventure cop movie. In his black leather jacket, black hair falling across his forehead and eyes an intense emerald-green, he was too perfect to be true. The addition of a five-o'clock shadow only made him look better. A perfect male specimen, from a scientific viewpoint.

Science be damned. Brenna didn't need a perfect man making a mess out of this case. She didn't need distractions when women were being kidnapped and more than likely murdered in her hometown.

"Nick Tarver." He held out his hand without smiling or baring his teeth to soften the sharp lines of his face, only those intense eyes staring straight into hers. "I'd hoped for an amicable relationship with the locals while working this case."

"Special Agent Brenna Jensen, North Dakota

Bureau of Criminal Investigations." *Not* nice to meet you, she added without voicing. Maybe she was a bit touchy about the subject, but she didn't need another case screwed up by the FBI or another physically fault-less person in her life. Having her sister and her sister's husband thrown in her face at every chance her mother could get was already enough to make her want to scream. Why couldn't the FBI send a really ugly, ca-pable agent instead of Nick Tarver?

As NICK SHOOK HER HAND, he observed the way Brenna Jensen's forehead settled into a permanent frown. In-stead of making her less attractive, she appeared like a fierce kitten ready to pounce on a wolf. And he was the wolf. He almost laughed until a pang of awareness reg-istered in his libido.

This woman who barely came up to his shoulder, with her straight sandy-blond hair and blue eyes, was like the girl next door. Fresh, clean and wholesome. Too small and vulnerable to be a cop. She was the kind of girl a guy could take home to meet his mother. Someone he might have liked knowing, if he hadn't already sworn off women. And as a potential victim, Brenna Jensen pre-sented more of a liability than an asset to his case.

"Mind if I keep that?" She glanced down at the hand he still held and back up at him, her brows rising. "I'm sort of attached to it."

He jerked his hand away and stepped back, for a moment off balance and not liking it.

Brenna tipped her head toward the doorway leading to the rear of the building. "Show me where you're set up and I'll show you my note."

"Not yet."

Her shoulders straightened and she dragged in a

deep, slow breath, as if she were preparing to go into battle. "What do you mean, not yet?"

"Before we do anything else, we need your statement."

The woman let the air out of her lungs. "On one condition."

Tarver's brows dipped into a frown. He wasn't used to negotiating his orders. He opened his mouth to say so, but Brenna beat him to it.

"I keep my coffee." She gave him a saccharine-sweet smile.

His brows met in the middle before they straightened and he nodded. She'd better not push him. He'd have her out of the building so fast—

Coffee in hand, she sailed toward the door leading to the back of the police station.

He hurried to follow her, falling in step behind her.

Before she'd gone too far down the hallway she stopped so abruptly Nick bumped into her. Her body was soft and feminine, but beneath the layers of clothing, he could feel the steely strength of well-honed muscles.

Her mouth made a small O and then firmed into a straight line as she looked over his shoulder to the man behind him. "Interview room still in the same place, Chief?"

"You betcha," Tom Burkholder replied.

"Let's go, Tarver." With a dismissive glance, she resumed her pace.

"Nick. Call me Nick." He almost smiled at the cocky little she-devil's back. He preferred a woman with spunk—but not at work. At work he liked people to follow orders. "Chief Burkholder will take your statement."

"Whatever. Let's get this interview over so we can get to work solving this case."

He stepped around her and led the way through a

bank of desks to a room located near the rear of the building. He held the door as the chief entered and Brenna followed. As she passed close enough to touch him, Nick caught the scents of herbal shampoo and fresh snow.

A strange combination of winter and spring. The unbidden impression formed in his mind from just that little whiff, and he brushed it aside. Too much detail about a witness he had no intention of keeping on his team.

Once they were inside the interview room, Nick Tarver closed the door, shutting them in and himself out. He moved down the hall and stepped into the observation room to watch and listen to the interview through the two-way mirror.

Stark and plain, the room was basically empty, with only a heavy metal table and two folding chairs in the middle of the floor. A single, uncovered lightbulb provided enough light to illuminate all four corners.

Brenna circled the room and stopped to stare into the mirror. "Hey, Agent Tarver, can you hear me? 'Cause I don't want to repeat myself later."

He fought a sudden urge to chuckle. The woman was annoying, but ballsy.

Chief Burkholder waved toward a chair. "Have a seat, Special Agent Jensen." Gone was the surrogate-father figure and in his place was the professional police officer.

She set her satchel on the floor and pulled out a photocopy of the note she'd received. "I suppose you'd like to see the copy of the note and the envelope."

He took the paper and shot a brief glance at it before setting it to one side of the table. "Let's start at the beginning. Your full name."

"You know me, Chief." She glared at the mirror, her fingers tapping a rhythm on the tabletop.

She was impatient and possibly a bit nervous knowing Nick was watching her. He sat in a chair and crossed his arms over his chest. Good. Make her sweat. He was glad he'd chosen to watch instead of interrogate. This way he could study her openly.

The chief's lips twisted in a wry grin. "For the record, please. You know the drill."

With a sigh, she quit staring at the mirrored wall and stated, "Brenna Louise Jensen."

"Occupation—special agent for the North Dakota Bureau of Criminal Investigations?"

"That's right." She shot a defiant look at the mirror.

So, she was a criminal investigator. It didn't mean she'd work with him.

The older man wrote on a tablet and then looked up at her. "Tell me what happened."

"I found this letter in the mailbox at my town house when I got home from work on Friday."

Chief Burkholder sat up straight, his pen poised in midair. "Not at work, but at home?"

Nick leaned forward. That was news. He'd assumed she'd gotten it at her office. So the kidnapper knew where she lived.

"Right."

"And there were no prints?" They knew there weren't any, but the chief had to put it in the record.

"No."

"Where was the letter postmarked?" he asked.

"Riverton Post Office." She sighed. "That's why I'm here."

"In your line of work, have you been assigned to cases involving violent criminals?"

Her chin rose as if challenging the man behind the wall. "Yeah. That's my job."

The chief scribbled her answers on the notepad before he looked up again. "And Riverton's your hometown, isn't it?"

"Yes, sir," she stated. "It's where I grew up."

The chief continued. "Has anyone from Riverton ever threatened you?"

"No," she said, her fingers drumming against the tabletop.

"Were you ever involved in an incident that would make someone consider you a threat?"

Her hand stilled. "Other than my casework?"

"Correct."

She hesitated, darting another glance at the mirror as she tucked a long strand of hair behind her ear. "No."

Was the hair-flicking a nervous gesture? Was she not telling the chief something? Nick's gut said *yes*. What secrets could a criminal investigator have?

Chief Burkholder continued the questioning without delving into her answer. If Nick had conducted the interview, he'd have questioned her further. But she was a cop and probably didn't think the information was relevant to the case.

When the interview was over, Brenna stood and gathered her satchel and the copy of her note. "Now can we get on with solving this case?"

"Eager, aren't we?" The chief patted her shoulder. "Come on, I'll show you where they've set up."

Nick left the observation room ahead of Brenna and the chief and beat them to the large conference room. It had been converted to a "war room." Completely covering one wall was a large whiteboard with a time line sketched out in black erasable marker. Three notches were marked with the names of the missing women and the times they'd been reported missing. Another spot was marked Note.

Now that he had Brenna's statement, she wasn't necessary to the case and Nick wanted her out of the station and on her way back to Bismarck.

Although she was another key to solving the case, Nick had no intention of allowing her onto his team. He liked to work with people he knew and trusted. Get in, solve the crime, get out and don't get involved. That was Nick's policy and he sure as hell didn't want to be in this godforsaken, frigid country any longer than he had to. He braced himself for the coming clash of wills with Special Agent Jensen.

The woman topmost on his mind breezed into the war room and tossed her satchel onto the conference table as if throwing down the gauntlet.

Chief Burkholder handed Nick the copy of the note he'd already seen on a blurry faxed copy they'd received around four that morning while Jensen had been en route.

Nick laid the paper on the table and walked over to Brenna. No time like the present. "Thank you for your statement, Special Agent Jensen. We no longer need your services. I advise you to return to Bismarck and lock your doors."

She stared up into his face for a long moment, her rate of breathing increasing until the air she exhaled blew in a sharp stream out her nose. Then she stepped closer to him, until her chest bumped against his. "I'm an experienced investigator assigned to this case by the state of North Dakota. I'm not running from some jerk who thinks he can pull my chain."

"Agent Tarver," Chief Burkholder said and then cleared his throat. "Jensen is one of North Dakota's best."

"I don't care." Tarver's eyes never left her face, and his expression remained unbending. "She's a liability. I can't focus on the case if I'm playing bodyguard."

Her face flushed red. "I don't need your protection. I've been in law enforcement for six years. I can take care of myself."

That she hadn't backed down impressed him at the same time as it annoyed him. "In case you haven't gotten the picture, the FBI has jurisdiction and is calling the shots now. You're off the case."

"Understand this, Agent Tarver. I *will* be involved fully in this case, with or without the FBI. I have more at stake here than you or any of your agents. This is my hometown, not yours. Nobody gets away with kidnapping or murder in my hometown."

"Agent Tarver, Special Agent Jensen is assigned from the state level. She won't be returning to Bismarck. If you don't include her on the team, she'll be working by herself to solve this case. You'd better serve the cause by including her." Chief Burkholder laid a hand on Nick's shoulder.

Okay, so the girl had the chief's confidence. He could admire that, but he didn't like being forced to accept her on his team. He shook off the chief's hand and stared down his nose into Brenna's clear blue eyes. "Get this straight, Jensen, I give the orders. Do you understand?"

For a moment, he thought she would spit in his eye and tell him to go to hell. But her shoulders pushed back and she met his gaze head-on. "I do."

"Good. Then don't get in my way."

"So does that mean I'm a part of the team?"

"I'll let you know." For a moment, Nick swam in the depths of her stormy blue eyes. Until he remembered how badly he'd been burned by a woman with blue eyes and why he'd never go there again. "Time's wasting. We've got a killer to catch before he does it again."

Chapter Two

With Nick's back to her, Brenna took in several deep breaths to help slow her pulse rate. Although she'd rather launch herself at the man and scratch his eyes out, she knew he had the right to toss her from the team. If she wanted to stay, she had to play it his way. But she didn't have to like it.

"Let's look at that letter again." Chief Burkholder crossed the room and leaned over the table to read aloud, "'The killing's only just begun. Watch them drop now, one by one.'"

A chill slithered down Brenna's spine. "Creepy, huh?"

"Doesn't sound good." The chief scrubbed a hand over his face. The lines around his eyes and across his forehead seemed so much deeper than the last time Brenna had seen him. Tom Burkholder had been around a long time. He'd taken over as chief five years ago when Brenna's father had died of a heart attack. Those years hadn't been so hard on him, but he was ready for retirement, not for a serial killer on his home turf. "Do you know what the spot is in the middle?" he asked.

"I have the crime lab looking at it. It looked like blood." Brenna drew in a deep breath, her lungs tight in her chest. "I haven't figured out why he sent me the letter."

Agent Tarver faced her, his eyes narrowed. "Think he might be a past conviction?"

"Maybe."

The FBI agent's attention jerked back to the whiteboard and he pointed a finger at the first mark. "Why now?"

Chief Burkholder offered, "Perhaps he's freshly out of jail and wants revenge."

God, she hated to think she was the reason a man was kidnapping and maybe killing other women. Nothing like a load of guilt to weigh her down during this investigation. All the more reason to catch him as soon as possible.

Nick's gaze caught hers.

Brenna looked away first, with the uncomfortable certainty that Tarver could read her thoughts.

He turned to the chief. "I want a scan on all the criminals Jensen had a hand in putting away, which ones are out on parole and those living in the area."

With a self-satisfied toss of her hair, she interjected, "I already have a colleague back in Bismarck doing just that. He should fax it any time to this station."

"So where does that leave us?" Chief Burkholder asked the room.

"Three missing women, no bodies and only speculation on motivation. And a letter that could be a hoax sent to a state criminal investigator." Nick lifted the letter. "Looks like a typical computer printout. Could be anyone."

A blond man Brenna didn't recognize entered the room reading from a clipboard. "Victim one was a psychiatrist. She disappeared sometime between last Wednesday night and Thursday morning, when she didn't show up for work. Missing person number two disappeared sometime Friday night. Her family notified us Saturday morning when she didn't make a date with her mother." When he glanced up, he lit the room with a grin and held out his hand to Brenna. "By the way, I'm Agent Paul Fletcher."

Brenna couldn't help but smile; it was a natural reaction to the sparkle in the man's light gray eyes. "Brenna Jensen."

His eyebrows rose and he squeezed her hand a little tighter. "Ah, the lady with the psycho pen pal."

With an uneasy laugh, Brenna pulled her hand from Paul's. "That's me. Lucky, huh?" She liked Paul instinctively. Unlike his partner, the dark and brooding Nick, he was warm and personable.

"Hang with us." He winked. "We'll keep you safe."

"Move over, Romeo." A woman almost as tall as the other two FBI agents pushed through the doorway behind Paul and held out her hand. "Melissa Bradley, part of this motley crew."

"Nice to meet you." Before the words completely left Brenna's mouth, Melissa had dropped her hand, slid another sheet on top of the clipboard Paul held and walked to the whiteboard. "Victim two was identified as Dr. Deborah Gomez, from across the river. Single female, lives alone. Victim three Michelle Carmichael, also single. Does it ever warm up around here? I think Texas is looking pretty good about now."

"All single women who live alone?" Brenna mused aloud. "Yeah, Texas does sound great."

"Two were doctors," Paul added. "The psychiatrist was Dr. Janine Drummond. But I didn't think you liked Texas, Mel."

She snorted. "I'm liking it better than the Arctic here!"

The rest of Paul's response was lost on Brenna. As

the name Janine Drummond sank in, Brenna's stomach dropped as if she'd hit a major dip in the road. "Did you say Dr. Drummond?"

"Yeah." Paul's head came up. "You know her? She was an older woman who had a practice here for over twenty-five years."

"I know Dr. Drummond. She's a very nice woman. I can't imagine anyone wanting to hurt her." Brenna had been one of her patients. Dr. Drummond had helped her deal with the emotional side of being scarred. But the others didn't need to know that yet. Maybe never.

The doctor had been someone she could talk to when no one else had understood. Who would do such a thing? Brenna forced the tears back. She couldn't show emotions with this bunch. Especially Nick Tarver. Emotion was a sign of weakness. She gulped past the lump in her throat and worked at a casual tone. "Dr. Gomez must be new to the area. I don't recognize the name. Do you know anything else about her?" Brenna asked. "What kind of doctor is she?"

"Professor at the university. She specializes in quantitative physics." Melissa shrugged. "Paul and I were about to go out and question her staff."

"Carmichael is into real estate, also lives alone," Paul said. "We'll stop by her office as well and see if anyone knows anything."

"Good. Any sign of forced entry?" Brenna asked.

"No," Nick said. "Either our perpetrator entered through unlocked windows or the victims opened their doors for him. We did find one of the windows where the snow and ice had been scraped away."

"Any fingerprints?" Brenna knew from the letter the guy was careful. He wouldn't risk leaving a sloppy fingerprint.

"Not one." Paul shook his head. "The places were clean. There was evidence of a struggle around Dr. Gomez's bed with bloodstains on the carpet. We'll have it analyzed to verify."

Brenna tapped a finger to her lips. "Have you pulled names of registered sex offenders in the area?"

"Done." Nick pulled a list from beneath a tack on the wall and handed it to Brenna. "One pedophile, Timothy Johnston, known for indecent exposure with grade-school kids, and one other, a convicted rapist, Bart Olsen, out on parole for the past month."

Paul pulled a sheet of paper off the clipboard and handed it to Nick. "Just got a report from Johnston's parole officer. Said his parolee has been in Tennessee visiting relatives for the past two weeks and they have eyewitnesses that place him in Nashville at the time of the abductions. That puts him out of the picture for now. No one's seen Olsen, and his parole officer hasn't heard from him in a week."

"Not good. When they catch up with him, I want to sit in on that interview," Brenna said.

Nick frowned. "No."

Brenna blinked. "No? Not even, 'let me think about it' or 'maybe that's not a good idea'? Just 'no'?" She planted her fist on a hip. "I'm investigating this case, too. If I can't interview potential suspects, I can't do my job."

"You can watch from behind the mirror." Nick's jaw set firmly. He wasn't budging. "I don't want you in range of this guy in case he is the killer."

"You're assuming the note writer is the kidnapper and the missing women are dead."

Nick nodded. "Based on the note, the blood found in the Gomez house and the smear of what looked like blood on that paper, yes."

"I'll let you do the interview this time." Brenna held up her hand when Nick opened his mouth to speak. "But don't pull this on me again. I'm a trained investigator. I know how to conduct an interview." Before he could say another word, she spun on the heel of her black leather boots and marched down the hallway.

"If anyone asks, I've gone to the Riverton Inn. Otherwise, I'll be back in an hour," Brenna said to the officer at the front desk.

"Shouldn't you clear it with Nick first?" Melissa Bradley leaned in the doorway, her arms crossed over her chest.

"Since he doesn't consider me part of the team, I don't have to inform him of my whereabouts." Brenna needed to get away and clear her head so she could concentrate on the case. And she had a short social visit to make. Emphasis on *short*. "If it means anything to you, I'll clear it with him when I get back."

BRENNA STOOD IN FRONT of her sister's spacious two-story home on West Nodak Street. The road was lined with dozens of similar homes—tan, white and gray siding as far as the eye could see, each sidewalk and driveway adrift with the new-fallen snow. The longer she stood, the colder her ears grew with the wind beating against her cap, penetrating the double layer of yarn. Facing the wine-colored door, she had two clear choices: go in and face her family, or stand here and freeze. Funny how freezing seemed the lesser of the two evils.

The wooden door opened and her sister, Alice, peered through the frosted glass of the storm door.

Okay, so now she was down to one choice and it was made for her.

"Brenna? What are you doing standing out in the cold?" Alice pushed the storm door open wider and waved toward her. "Get in here before you freeze."

"Hi, Alice." Brenna stepped in on the all-weather mat and immediately removed her boots and outside clothing. "Where's Mom?"

"Nice to see you, too." Alice hung her jacket on a peg and then held out her arms. "Don't I get a hug from my favorite sister?"

Feeling ungracious and unloving, Brenna tried to cook up some enthusiasm for the sister she hadn't seen in a month. "I'm sorry, of course you get a hug. I've missed you," she said.

"Liar." But Alice hugged her anyway. "Mom's in her room. Come on back and say hello."

Quick to establish expectations up front, Brenna blurted, "I can't stay long. I'm here on business."

"I heard on the news." Alice's pretty face crumpled into a worried frown. "Isn't it terrible? Two women missing in just a few days."

Make that three. When Brenna opened her mouth to respond to her sister's concern, she was interrupted with a loud, "Alice!"

"That will be Mom. You'd better get back there and say hello."

"Is she with us today?" Brenna asked.

Alice held her hand out palm down and tipped it back and forth. "In and out."

"Great. Isn't there anything they can do for her?"

"We've got her on rivastigmine tartrate, but it doesn't seem to be helping."

Brenna's heart ached with the mental loss of the only parent she had left. "I wish we had her back."

Their mother had started showing signs of Alzheimer's two years ago and her progression had been swift and painful to her family. Once an active woman who enjoyed volunteering at the hospital and the Salvation Army thrift shop, Marian Jensen had her driving privileges revoked and was forced to move in with Alice and her husband so they could make sure she didn't wander out into the cold and die of exposure.

"She shows up on occasion, maybe she'll be with us today."

"Let's hope." With a deep breath, Brenna pushed her shoulders back and followed her sister down the hallway. "Are you sure you're okay with this arrangement? We could look into a nursing home."

"No way. Mom's only sixty-eight and she gets around just fine. We need to save the money for a nursing home when I can't help her anymore."

"I feel bad this is all on your shoulders. Just let me know what I can do to help. Maybe I can watch Mom and the kids one weekend so you and Stan can take a trip or something."

"That would be great." Alice smiled. "I don't know the last time Stan and I had time alone."

"Of course it'll be after we solve this case."

"Oh, I hope it's soon. It's so scary knowing there's a psycho loose in our town. This is Riverton, for God sakes, not Minneapolis or Chicago."

Alice led the way into a well-lit room with a double bed on one side and a small couch positioned close to the window. Their mother sat on the couch, a colorful afghan draped across her lap and a crocheted shawl around her shoulders.

Brenna bent to press a kiss to her mother's cheek. "Hi, Mom. It's me, Brenna."

Marian Jensen glared up at her. "I know who you are."

Brenna suppressed a grimace and forced a smile for her mother. "I love you, Mom."

"That's more like it." Her mother patted the couch cushion next to her. "Come sit by me."

Brenna scrambled for something to say as she settled on the seat next to the woman who was becoming less her mother and more a stranger every day. "How've you been, Mom?"

"When are you going to get married, Brenna?" Ever since her mother had started showing signs of Alzheimer's, she'd fixated on Brenna's marital status. She'd forgotten so many things about her past, but it seemed she clung to the dream of seeing her daughter married as her last hold on reality.

"I don't know, Mom." Brenna squirmed in her seat, never comfortable talking about marriage or relationships.

Her mother patted her knee. "There are a lot of lonely men out there who can love you despite your scars. You've just set your standards too high."

Alice rolled her eyes while Brenna braced for the lecture.

"That's what's the matter with you, Brenna. You can't expect to have the perfect marriage, like your sister. You're not perfect, God love you, and you know I love you, too. But the truth is, you're damaged goods. You have to lower your expectations."

As her mother went on and on, Brenna tuned out. If she didn't, she'd go crazy. For the past two years, her mother had presented her with the same argument. *Settle, Brenna. Don't waste your life looking for perfection. Alice has it, but you're not Alice.*

As her mother droned on, Brenna's jaw tightened until she felt as if she'd ground a quarter inch off her back teeth. When her head reached the explosion point, she stood. "I have to go."

"You just got here." The nagging woman disappeared leaving a lonely old lady who relied on her family for her care. Her mother, the woman who'd loved her unconditionally until her mind had begun to fade. "Stay awhile with me. You know how much I love having both my little girls with me." She reached out to clutch her wrist, her grip surprisingly firm for a woman who might weigh all of ninety pounds dripping wet.

"I love you, Mom, but I have to go to work." She leaned over and kissed her mother's cheek. "I'll be back soon."

"They feed me cooked carrots. You know I hate carrots."

"I'll see what I can do, Mom." Brenna nodded toward her sister. "Alice, perhaps you and I can go discuss the menu?"

"Of course." She tucked the crocheted blanket around her mother's knees. "Mom, I'll be back in just a minute."

"Carrots." The old woman snorted. "Rabbits eat carrots. I want steak and potatoes."

Brenna stepped out into the hall. Leaning against the wall, she let the stress drain from her pores.

Alice followed, easing the door closed behind her. After the latch clicked gently in place, she reached out and pulled her sister into her arms. "Mom doesn't know what she's saying anymore, sweetie. Don't let her words hurt you."

"I don't." *Yeah right.* Then why couldn't she catch her breath or swallow past the lump in her throat? She pressed her eyelids closed. Hell, she was the cop in the family. The one to carry on her father's legacy. Cops don't cry.

"Brenna?" Alice gripped her shoulders, forcing her

to stare into her eyes. "You're a beautiful woman and you don't have to *settle* for anyone. The right man just hasn't come along."

As she stared into her sister's face, an image of Nick Tarver superimposed over her mind. Nick, standing next to the whiteboard, his black hair a dramatic contrast, those green eyes so intense with dedication to the job at hand. Perfect in every way, except one. He was too perfect. Like her honey-blond-haired sister with flawless skin that showed no sign of wrinkles nor scars to mar the precision of her beauty. Her husband loved her, doted on her and had given her two beautiful little boys and a house in the right neighborhood.

Her mother treated Brenna to endless diatribes on how well Alice had married. *Why can't you be more like your sister?* Alice—the all-American cheerleader, top of her class and homecoming queen her senior year.

Too often Brenna had to bite her tongue to keep from screaming, *Because I'm not Alice. I don't have a home, family and husband. And I don't have a perfect body to attract a man.*

Why she let it get to her, Brenna didn't know. The trip from Bismarck had taken its toll. Exhausted and in need of a shower, she stepped away from her sister.

"Alice, it's good to see you. Since I'm on assignment, I don't know when I'll get by to visit Stan and the boys. Will you say hi for me?"

"Sure." Alice laid a hand on her arm. "You will be careful, won't you?"

"Yes." Brenna lifted her sister's hand. "And the same goes for you. Make sure you lock your house and don't let anyone in. So far, the kidnapper is targeting single women. But we don't know if he'll go after married ones as well."

"I heard Dr. Drummond was one of the missing persons. I'm so sorry. I know you used to see her." Alice's forehead creased in a frown. "Do you think he's killing them?"

Brenna inhaled and let the air out slowly. "We don't have proof and we may not find them until spring, but my gut tells me it's not good."

Alice's face blanched. "Wow. Here in Riverton? A killer in our midst." She gave a mirthless laugh. "Makes me want to go pick up my kids from school and keep them inside."

"You do that. And lock your windows. If you have a security system, make sure it's on."

"Seems strange taking orders from my baby sister. But you were always the strong one." Alice squeezed her hand. "Just like Dad. Mom and I leaned heavily on you when he died. Must have been hard for you. You and Dad were so close."

"I didn't mind." Liar. She'd missed her father so much after his death, but she couldn't fall apart. Her mother and sister needed her to be strong. So she was. "Besides, I have to keep it together. The kidnapper sent me a note after the first woman disappeared."

"No!" Alice's eyes widened and her face paled. "He could be after you next. Do you think it's someone you know? Oh, Brenna, you're a single woman. Are you safe walking around on the streets? You should come stay with Stan and me. Speak of the devil…" Alice directed a smile over Brenna's shoulder. "There's Stan now."

As Stanley Klaus stepped through the front door, Brenna turned to face him, a friendly smile of greeting pasted on her face. The man was every bit as tall as Nick, but not quite as broad in the shoulders. His sandy-blond hair was pleasantly ruffled by the wind. Brenna understood what Alice had seen in Stan. He was a good-looking man.

The right side of his mouth quirked up in a half smile. "Brenna, good to see you." He reached out and engulfed her in a hug. "What's it been—a month since you were here last?"

Brenna endured the embrace for her sister. No matter how hard she tried, she never felt as though Stan was family and she didn't like being hugged by anyone but family and very close friends. Somehow, Stan didn't fit into either category.

"I'd stay and catch up, but I just stopped for a bill I left on my computer." Stan left the women standing in the hallway, an awkward silence stretching between them until he walked back through the house with a paper in his hand. "Got it! I might be late for dinner." With that parting comment, he sailed through the door and was gone.

Alice's gaze followed him until his car left the driveway, a small frown crinkling the middle of her forehead. "Nice to see you, too, dear," she said softly. When she finally faced Brenna, her lips twisted into a wistful smile. "That's the life of an old married woman."

"You're not old." Brenna wrapped her arms around her sister and hugged her briefly before stepping away. "I know this is crazy but I always get the feeling he's never forgiven me for trying to talk you out of marrying him."

Her sister snorted. "At my wedding! You have to admit that was pretty poor timing on your part."

"I'm sorry. I had no right."

"Yes, you did." Alice smiled, only her smile didn't quite reach her eyes. "You did what any sister would do. You tried to give me one last chance to change my mind. But it's been seven years, I'm sure he's forgotten all about it."

Brenna shrugged into her coat. "Well, you know where I'll be and I'll have my cell phone if you need to contact me."

"You sure you won't stay with us? We'd love to have you."

"Yeah, I'm sure. I'll be in and out at odd hours and I only need a place to shower and sleep."

Alice crossed her arms over her chest and gave Brenna her best big-sister scowl. "Let me guess, you'll be at the police station the rest of the time."

"Or out searching for clues."

"And you couldn't have crummier weather."

"Tell me about it." Brenna hated the last part of winter. After six months of snow, she and everyone else in North Dakota were ready for green grass and sunshine.

Alice sighed. "At least at the police station you're surrounded by other cops. And they say warmer weather is at the back end of this storm."

"I hope so. Look, I have to go." Brenna straightened her shoulders. "Remember, be careful. If this guy is really after me, you could be in danger just by your association with me. You might consider going to stay in the Cities." Five hours away, the twin cities of Minneapolis and St. Paul teamed with traffic and their own share of crime. Yet they suddenly seemed like a safe haven compared to the small town of Riverton, North Dakota.

If Brenna did her job right, Riverton would be back on track for one of the best places to raise a family. Then she'd get her promotion and move to Minnesota and even farther away from her hometown and family.

If she didn't get killed in the meantime.

Chapter Three

Checked in at the hotel, Brenna stripped down to skin and padded to the bathroom to brush the road grime from her teeth. As she stood in front of the mirror, her mother's words returned to bounce around her thoughts.

Settle for a man who'll accept her and all her scars.

She stood back and assessed herself in the full-length mirror on the back of the door. Besides the toothbrush in her mouth, she looked pretty normal. A little on the short side, but just like anyone else. Until she turned around.

Pivoting, she glanced over her shoulder at the wide swath of scarred skin from her right shoulder down to the bottom of her right thigh. Laced across the smooth, leathery scar tissue was a mottled pattern of splotchy pink, purple and blue lines. Burned in a freak barn fire as a small child, she accepted the scars as a part of her. But children were cruel and many had poked fun at her, calling her *alligator skin* and *burned cookie* when she'd gone outside in shorts or a swimsuit. Not that she'd let them stop her. With her father's love and encouragement, she'd grown up confident and as normal as she could. Yet when it came to adult situations in the bedroom, the lights were definitely off.

The one time she'd opened herself enough to let a man into her bed—that sleazebag Victor Greeley—he'd forgotten to tell her one important fact. The jerk was married. While she'd been hiding her scars in the dark, Victor had been hiding uglier sins.

She should have known better than to date a traveling salesman. What kind of cop was she that she fell into the age-old trap of being the other, unsuspecting woman?

After she'd learned his secret, avoiding him was easy…until he'd moved his wife to town and bought a house on a street just around the corner from Alice.

Brenna's embarrassment at her stupidity, coupled with the guilt she felt for nearly ruining another woman's marriage, was sufficient motivation to leave town and the police force she'd cut her teeth on. Living in Bismarck, she didn't have to pass by Victor's house, nor did she bump into his sweet but clueless wife, Ginnie, at the grocery store.

Brenna tapped the water out of her toothbrush and ran her tongue across her clean teeth. With the weather so bitterly cold she couldn't go out to jog, she decided on a swim in the hotel pool and slipped into a one-piece black swimsuit. Grabbing a beach towel long enough to cover all her scars, she wrapped it around her middle, tucking the edge in at the top. A dozen laps ought to work out the kinks in her neck and shoulders and help her think through the problem of one maniac on the loose. Her mind worked better when she generated exercise-induced endorphins.

The drive from Bismarck had been stressful enough without arriving to find the case had been turned over to the FBI. Especially since the man in charge was entirely too egocentric, gruff and good-looking for an FBI agent. Where'd they come up with these guys? She thought agents were chosen for their ability to blend in with a crowd. Not Nick. She could spot him in the Mall of America, much less a small town like Riverton.

She'd do her best to maintain her distance from Agent Tarver. He looked as if he could chew her up and spit her out if she crossed the line. Besides, she didn't have time to play push-me-pull-you with him. A maniac was on the loose and her job was to find him before he abducted someone else.

Brenna slipped into a pair of flip-flops and padded down the hotel hallway to the glassed-in area with the heated pool. When she pushed through the doors, she was engulfed in a thick wave of humidity and the acrid scent of chlorine. She dropped her towel beside the pool and dove in.

Fifteen laps later and still no closer to a clear mind, she surfaced and grabbed the side of the pool. When she raised her hand to brush the stinging chlorine from her eyes, an iron grip clamped onto her wrist and she was jerked from the water.

Her heart in her throat and her eyes still cloudy with pool chemicals, Brenna struggled to plant her feet on the decking. Once she gained traction, she dropped into a football lineman stance and plowed into her attacker. Hit square in the gut, he fell backward to the ground.

Brenna staggered to regain her balance and stared down at Nick Tarver lying still on the hard concrete floor, his eyes closed.

Jeez, had she knocked him out?

Dropping to her knees, she stared down at his chest, looking for any sign of movement. None. Her heart beat loudly against her eardrums as she leaned forward to feel for the gentle puff of air blowing in and out through his nose.

Nick Tarver wasn't breathing!

CPR training kicked in and Brenna tipped his head back. Pinching his nose, she sealed her lips over his and blew a long breath into his lungs, turning to see his chest rise as she did.

Before she could blow another breath, his arms clamped around her and she was flipped onto her back, their lips still connected. The air blasted out of her lungs and she lay in stunned paralysis for a full two seconds. Long enough for the man to straddle her and pin her hands to the concrete above her head. All without breaking the lip-lock.

BRENNA JENSEN WAS A WOMAN with a death wish and she needed a lesson on following orders. But now, with her wet body pinned beneath his thighs, he didn't know who was teaching whom the lesson. She lay still beneath him, but she wasn't fighting yet.

He hadn't planned on wrestling her, but when she'd knocked him to the ground, his reactions had been instinctive. Now he was lying on top of a half-naked woman dripping wet from her recent swim.

What was worse, Nick's traitorous body responded to all the shiny wet skin exposed by her discreet black swimsuit. And he was kissing her now, knowing she'd be pissed as hell when she came to her senses.

Perhaps the thought of her anger made him increase the pressure on her lips and drive his tongue between her teeth to war with hers. Hadn't he come to teach her a lesson about what could happen when you didn't follow orders?

The kiss lasted only a few agonizingly brief seconds

before her muscles tightened and she gasped. Slender fingers flew from around his neck to plant firmly against his chest, shoving him backward. "Get off!" she sputtered, squirming beneath him until she realized she couldn't dislodge him and he wasn't going to budge.

"I'll get off as soon as you calm down."

When she stopped moving, he rolled off and sat on the concrete next to her, regret washing over him for his unprofessional actions in kissing her.

And all that squirming she'd done had left its mark on him—one that manifested itself beneath the zipper of his jeans. Damn this woman. She was more trouble than he'd bargained for and she'd get herself hurt if she wasn't careful. "You didn't check with me before leaving the police station."

"Is that what this is all about?" She remained flat on her back, her breasts heaving beneath the black Lycra. "Are you telling me I have to report every move to you?"

He nodded. "That's right."

She leaned on her elbow, her brows rising on her forehead. "I didn't think I was a member of your team. Has that changed?"

"Yes." The word flew from his mouth before he thought. Okay, so she could be a member of his team instead of stirring up trouble on the periphery.

"And if I weren't a female member of your team, would you make the same rules?"

"Yes."

"Bull!" Her glare sliced through him.

"Until we catch this lunatic, you're to report every move to me, and only me. No leaving messages with any of the rest of my team or the Riverton Police Department." He leaned closer until his face was only inches away from hers. "I *will* know your every move including when you go to the bathroom. Do you understand?"

Her mouth opened and closed without uttering a word, her blue eyes sparkling in the fluorescent lights overhead. He thought she wouldn't answer, when finally, she heaved a sigh and said, "Yes, sir."

Nick rolled to his feet and held out a hand to help her up. Ignoring the hand, she lunged for a towel and slung it around her body without turning her back to him. Her cheeks flushed a bright red, and if Nick didn't know better, he'd say she was embarrassed and perhaps a bit shy about being in a swimsuit in front of him. Funny how her embarrassment gave him a little twinge of something like endearment. Was he crazy?

Nick glanced down at his wet jeans and shirt. Now that her body wasn't pressed against him, the cooler air made the wet spots uncomfortable. "The weather's clearing and I wanted to get out and interview neighbors and coworkers of the missing women. You interested?"

"Yes, I am." She tucked the end of the towel in over her breasts before she met his gaze. "I needed the exercise to clear my head. I would have been back in less than fifteen minutes."

"Just do us both a favor, and let me know exactly where you're going. I don't want another victim on my watch." His gut clenched at the thought of Brenna's swimsuit-clad body lying somewhere in a snowbank. He was only concerned because she was his key to the killer. Nick nodded his head toward the hallway. "Get changed. I'll wait outside your door."

Without a word, she blew through the glass doors and down the hallway to her room.

Nick followed her every step of the way, admiring the sway of her hips beneath the towel and the way her bare feet in the flip-flops made her look young and vulnerable. He should have waited in the lobby.

After sliding the plastic key card in the lock, Brenna stood with her hand on the doorknob. "If you're going to wait for me, you might as well have a seat in my room."

He nodded and followed her into the dark room, scanning the interior for any clues to this woman. Her suitcase stood open on one of the two queen-size beds, the contents a jumble of clothes and toiletries.

"Pack in a hurry?" he asked, settling into a chair in the corner of the room, thinking he really should march himself back down the hall to the lobby. But he wanted to know more about this woman who could knock him on his butt and still look like a lost little girl.

"When the assignment came through last night, I only took time to throw in the necessities." She grabbed clothes and underwear and headed for the bathroom. "Give me two minutes."

Nick stood, strolled across the commercial carpeting to the window on the far side and pushed the curtain aside. The skies had cleared and the sun shone brightly on the fresh layer of snow. It made him want to go out and stand in it. Nick didn't like staying inside any more than he had to, but the weather in North Dakota forced people inside for long periods. He didn't know how they did it. Now living in Norfolk, Virginia, and having spent most of his life on the southeast coast where winter may have included a few days of snow that melted within hours, he couldn't comprehend living inside for six months out of the year.

The sound of the shower captured Nick's attention, drawing his mind away from the case to the newest member of his team. The thought of water gliding over her pale, smooth skin had his blood burning a path south. He could still feel the warmth of her beneath his fingertips, the smooth wetness of her swimsuit pressed against his clothing. And that kiss. A mistake and definitely a distraction he could live without.

If he hadn't already been burned by a woman, he might consider kissing her again. He sensed passion beneath her feisty exterior. He'd caught a glimpse of it under her enthusiasm for her job and her concern for her hometown. His body would like nothing more than to explore and discover just how passionate she was, on a purely physical level.

Nick turned back to the window. Brenna Jensen was part of his job, not his life. The last time he'd made a woman part of his life, he'd made her his wife. And what had that brought him? He'd lost his home, his marriage, his partner and best friend, but mostly his faith in women. Brenna Jensen was definitely hands-off. He had a case to solve and he had to contain any wayward attraction he might feel for the gutsy blonde.

Just as the door to the bathroom opened, his cell phone buzzed and vibrated in the belt clip on his hip. He flipped the phone open and pressed it to his ear.

Brenna stepped from the steamy interior of the bathroom dressed in a pair of black wool trousers and a formfitting turtleneck sweater that hugged the swells of her breasts to perfection. Despite her questioning look, Nick had to turn away to concentrate on who was calling.

"Nick, this is Paul. We have a body."

Chapter Four

After the investigative team had collected every bit of evidence they could, the ice-fishing shanty had been pushed aside, allowing the recovery team to retrieve the body. Brenna stood beside Nick Tarver, staring down into the drilled-out ice. The wind whipped her hair across her eyes, blocking out the horror of what she saw.

Dr. Janine Drummond's white, naked body bobbed in and out of view of the hole drilled through two feet of solid ice into Eagle Lake.

Brenna turned away, bile rising in her throat. She couldn't lose her stomach. Not in front of these people. A professional kept her cool.

This was a woman she'd known and respected for years. In past cases she'd investigated, the victims had been people she'd never met.

Dave Jorgensen and Mike Koenig stood in their insulated coveralls and Elmer Fudd hats, their faces pale and pinched, giving their statement to Sheriff Tindale.

While Mike stared at the ice, Dave did all the talking. "Once the storm cleared, we thought we'd get out here before the ice started melting. This was one of the holes we'd drilled last weekend. As soon as we saw what was down there, we got in the truck and headed to town to call. It 'bout gave us a heart attack, it scared us so bad. But we didn't kill that lady and put her down there. No, sir, we didn't."

"It's okay, Dave," Sheriff Tindale said.

A detective snapped pictures of the hole and the dead woman, the camera clicks muffled by the westerly breeze blowing across the frozen lake.

All Brenna could see were the pale arms and torso of Dr. Drummond snagged by Dave's fishing line. A quiver shook Brenna's body so hard her teeth rattled.

Agent Tarver leaned close. "You okay?"

Without glancing up, Brenna nodded. She wanted to ignore the man. Instead, she studied him in her peripheral vision.

His dark hair fell across the deep frown lines on his forehead and his ears were turning pink from the cold. The black jacket and black hair were a stark contrast to the white landscape, making him seem larger than life.

She didn't want to notice him, didn't want to acknowledge his existence. But he stood beside her, the faint scent of his aftershave wafting her way as the wind shifted. Again she shivered, although not from the cold.

Tarver nudged her elbow with his gloved hand. "Want to get out of here?"

His touch jump-started her numb brain and she realized she wasn't doing anything to solve this case by staring at a dead woman. "No."

"Since you're from around here, why don't you ask the questions? They'll trust you more."

She nodded and made her way over to Dave. "Mr. Jorgensen, do you leave your hut out here all winter?"

"Yes, ma'am. Been out here since last November. Even left the auger all locked up inside. Didn't think anyone would break in and use it."

"See any tire tracks or footprints nearby?" she asked.

"No, but then it snowed pretty heavy."

"Thanks, Dave." Brenna moved on to one of the sheriff's deputies tasked with gathering the evidence. "Make sure you brush away loose snow. If someone drove out here, there should be packed snow tracks crushed into the ice beneath the fresh snow."

He glanced up at the bright sunshine beating down on them. "If we're gonna do it, it'll have to be soon. That sun will melt the evidence, otherwise."

Already, the new snow that hadn't blown away with storm winds was soft and slushy. Brenna stared up at the clear blue sky. "If the sun keeps shining and the weather starts warming, it won't be long before the ice thins." As if to emphasize her point, a loud crack ripped through the air like the sound of a shotgun blast.

Nick jumped, his brow dropping into a fierce frown. "What the hell was that?"

"The ice cracking," Brenna answered, ducking to hide a hint of a smile.

"Cracking?" He glanced around at the others. "And nobody's worried about falling in?"

"Not yet," Dave Jorgensen said. "The ice is still thick. It'll hold."

Brenna looked up at Nick, her lips twitching. "Ready to go?"

"Ready when you are." He inhaled deeply and rolled his neck and shoulders, clearly uncomfortable out on the frozen lake. "Where to?"

"I want to talk to Dr. Drummond's neighbors."

"The police department interviewed the folks on both sides, across the street and behind them. No one saw anything."

"Then we need to ask again." She snapped her collar up to block the wind. "There's got to be something."

"For once, I couldn't agree with you more." Nick slid on the ice and Brenna put a hand out to steady him. When they reached her Jeep, he held her door. "Just can't see the attraction in ice fishing. I always thought of lakes as places you swim or boat in, not drive on in a one-ton vehicle."

Brenna climbed behind the wheel. "I never thought of it as a place to ditch a body. Makes me wonder where he's left the others. Should we be examining all the fishing holes in the lake?"

"Not a bad thought. I'll check with the sheriff." Nick walked away across the ice, each step measured and careful.

Brenna hid a smile. At least he was game to step out on the ice. Some people wouldn't dream of it. The thought of the ice cracking and dumping them into freezing waters was more than most cared to face.

As Nick climbed into the passenger seat, the image of Janine Drummond surfaced in Brenna's thoughts and she shuddered.

"Are you cold?" He closed his door and peeled his gloves off, holding his hands to the heater vent.

"No, just chilled by what we found."

"Yeah." Nick's lips thinned. "Now we know for sure we're dealing with a killer."

All the more reason to bring him in as soon as possible. She turned the vehicle and headed toward the shoreline, memories of better times flooding in.

"You act like you know your way around on the ice," Nick said.

"I used to come out here with my father to ice fish." She remembered the old ice hut he'd built with scrap lumber. As soon as the ice was thick enough to hold his truck, he'd drag the shanty out on the lake and spend many contented hours fishing for walleye and trout. Brenna joined him most of the time, relaxed by the sound of the wind wailing against the boards and a companionable silence with her father.

Not Alice. She preferred to be out and about with her friends, shopping, bowling or playing games indoors. Brenna always thought she should have been born a boy. But her father had never made her feel that way. "What can a boy do that you can't?" he'd asked, and handed her a fishing pole and bait.

"You and your father were close?" Nick's low tone broke through Brenna's thoughts.

"Yeah." The old ache settled against her chest. He'd been the main man in her life. The only man to understand her and accept her for who she was, not what she looked like.

"Must have been nice. My father was gone a lot while I was growing up." He said with no emotion, as if he were stating a fact.

Brenna pictured a little boy sitting on the front porch with a fishing pole and no one to take him fishing. She was very fortunate to have had a father as supportive as hers, who'd cared enough to teach her how to enjoy life's simpler pleasures. The cold days spent on the lake with her father would be forever etched into her heart.

But Eagle Lake had changed.

"I had good memories of this place until today. Now I can't get the image of Dr. Drummond's body out of my mind."

Nick nodded, staring out across the white landscape. "We'll get him."

"You bet we will." Her fingers tightened around

the steering wheel. "Let's just hope we do before he kills again."

"I'm afraid he already has. Question is where'd he hide the bodies?"

THE REST OF THE DRIVE back to town was accomplished in silence. Sun shone down on the snow and ice, making a smooth glaze of moisture over the top. When darkness fell, the water would freeze and make a treacherous layer of black ice.

Nick stared out the window without absorbing the scenery. Instead, he combed through what little evidence they had so far and came up with nothing.

Brenna drove straight to Janine Drummond's little cottage nestled among towering barren cottonwoods on East Thirty-second Avenue. Yellow crime-scene tape marked the exterior of the fifty-year-old white house with the forest-green trim.

As soon as she shifted into Park, Brenna climbed down from the Jeep and headed for the house on the east side of Dr. Drummond's.

Behind her, Nick admired her no-nonsense pursuit of answers and the way her hips swayed as she picked her way across the slippery, wet driveway.

After knocking several times with no answer, Brenna turned to leave.

Nick touched her arm. "Wait." He nodded toward the front window where a curtain twitched. "Sir," he called out, "I'm Agent Nick Tarver with the FBI. Could we have a word with you about Dr. Drummond?" Nick pulled his credentials out of his pocket and held them high.

Brenna followed suit.

Several seconds passed before they heard the sound of a dead bolt being unlocked and the door cracked open.

An old man dressed in wool slacks and a gray sweater peeked through the opening. "We already gave our statement."

Brenna stepped forward. "I'm Special Agent Brenna Jensen. We just want to ask a few questions," she said softly, extending her hand. "Please, sir, we need more information."

Nick was impressed with the gentle quality of Brenna's voice. How different from the tough-as-nails cop back at the station. And whatever she was doing was working on the old man.

"Dean Helmke." The man reached out and shook Brenna's hand. "I don't know what I can add to what we told the police department."

"We'll only take a few minutes of your time, sir." Brenna smiled. "We want to understand the case."

The man sighed. "You'll have to talk to me. My wife's lying down. All the excitement and worry is making her sick."

"I'm sorry to hear that," Brenna said softly.

"Come in." The man held the door wide and waved them forward. "It's still too cold to stand outside for long."

"Thank you." Brenna stomped her feet on the outside mat before she stepped through.

"Although, the way the sun's been shining, won't be long before the spring melt." Mr. Helmke moved aside to make room for them. "Hope it doesn't do it all at once. Sure don't want a repeat of the flood of ninety-seven."

"No, we don't." Brenna kicked off her boots and hung her jacket on a coat rack. Then she nudged Nick in the side, staring pointedly at his boots, before she padded in her stocking feet to the living room.

Nick removed his boots and jacket and followed, glad he didn't have holes in his socks.

"Can I get you a cup of coffee?" Mr. Helmke asked.

"No, thank you." Nick took a seat across the room. "We'll only take a minute of your time." He nodded at Brenna. Having made the man feel at ease, she could lead the questioning.

Brenna waited until Mr. Helmke sat in a faded recliner before she launched into her questions. "Sir, when was the last time you saw Dr. Drummond?"

"Last Wednesday when she got home from work. I offered to help carry in her groceries." He dropped his head into his hands and his bony shoulders shook. "Can't believe she's gone. I should have gone by and checked on her later that night."

Brenna sat patiently until the man straightened.

"I'm sorry." The old man scrubbed a hand down his face and looked up, his eyes red-rimmed. "I keep thinking of all the things I should have done, if I'd been a good neighbor."

"You couldn't have known, Mr. Helmke. You weren't responsible for what happened to her," Nick said.

But Mr. Helmke wasn't listening. No matter what Brenna or Nick said, he'd probably carry the guilt, anyway.

Brenna patted the man's hand, a good technique for gaining his confidence. Yet, Nick didn't think she was as worried about technique as she was about the man's feelings. She had a natural familiarity with the people of Riverton, an affinity with their way of life and the loss of one of their own. She rested her elbows on her knees, clasping her hands together. "Did you hear anything, or see anything unusual Wednesday night?"

"Nothing. Absolutely nothing." He shook his head. "How could someone walk right in and steal a person away and no one see or hear anything? How?"

"I don't know, Mr. Helmke." Brenna stared straight ahead at nothing Nick could see. "But we'll do our best to catch him."

The old man kept talking as if Brenna hadn't said a thing. "It's so bad, my wife is afraid to sleep at night and afraid to take sleeping pills in case the kidnapper comes after one of us." He reached out and grabbed Brenna's hand. "I have a loaded pistol in my nightstand. Never in the sixty years I've lived in Riverton have I slept with a loaded pistol in my nightstand."

The fear in the old man's face made Nick's gut tighten.

"Oh, Mr. Helmke." Brenna brows dipped low. "Please be careful you or your wife don't end up shooting each other."

"Don't worry. We'll be careful." He squeezed her hand. "I knew your daddy, God rest his soul, and I've heard good things about you. You'll catch him, won't you? We won't sleep at night with that maniac on the loose. I don't see how anyone in this town can rest knowing they aren't safe in their own beds."

Brenna's shoulders straightened. "We'll do our best. I promise."

Damn right they would. Nick always got his man and this killer wouldn't get away without paying for his crime.

THE WINDS HAD DIED DOWN by the time they stepped out of the Helmke home into the sunshine. After the brisk breeze out on the lake, the sunshine felt good on Brenna's face, as if God were making a promise that spring wasn't far behind. The snow she trudged through on her way to the Jeep was quickly becoming a dirty, slushy mess with water streaming into the streets. "The weatherman said we'd have three full days of this, maybe more."

"This what?" Nick stood next to her vehicle staring back at Janine Drummond's house.

"Sunshine and warm temperatures." Brenna tipped her face to the sun and closed her eyes, absorbing the rays.

"You call this warm?"

Agent Tarver's voice felt like the sun on her skin, teasing her with a promise of more to come. The thought brought her back to the cold, wet earth with a splash. "It's above zero," she said. "What do you want?" She unlocked the door to the Jeep and kicked off the crusty snow from her boots before climbing in.

Tarver repeated the process and got in on his side. "Seventy and sunny would be nice."

She laughed. "Around here you learn to appreciate anything out of the minus temperatures. A person doesn't know real misery until he's stood out in minus forty-five with a windchill factor of minus sixty. That's when you think seriously about braving the hurricanes of Florida rather than a blue norther."

Nick shook his head. "Then why do people live here?"

Brenna stared at the silent white cottage where Janine Drummond had once lived and asked herself the same question. "It used to be a good place to raise a family."

Chapter Five

Brenna trailed behind Agent Tarver as he entered the Riverton police station's conference room.

He hadn't stopped to strip his jacket, performing this function on the go as he crossed to the whiteboard.

Notes had been added to indicate the location where the first victim's body had been discovered.

The recurring image of the frozen woman floating at the bottom of two feet of ice wouldn't be erased from Brenna's mind any time soon.

"Any news on Olsen?" Nick asked.

"The police haven't been able to put a finger on him yet." Paul sat at the computer in the corner with his back to the room, pounding away at the keys. "He's not where he's supposed to be and no one's seen him."

When Brenna entered the room, she felt the heat of Nick's gaze following her as she circled the table and stopped in front of the whiteboard covering the east wall.

Melissa perched on the edge of the conference table, a clipboard and pencil in her hands. "We got the list of Special Agent Jensen's convictions from Bismarck." She dipped her head toward Brenna. "Impressive. Paul's running a scan to see if any of them are out on parole and if so, whether or not they're in this area."

"I should have a cross match in the next two or three minutes," Paul said over his shoulder without looking up.

"I'm going to get some coffee." Nick glanced at Brenna. "Want some?"

She shook her head.

When Nick left the room, Melissa's gaze darted from Brenna to the empty doorway. "Did you see that, Paul?"

"With my back to the room? Uh, no." His fingers didn't slow on the keyboard.

"The great Agent Tarver actually asked someone if they wanted coffee."

"Is that unusual?" Brenna asked.

"For anyone else, no. For Nick, hell yeah."

"Our man Nick is known for his dedication to the job," Paul explained.

"Dedication, hell." Melissa snorted. "He *is* the job."

Brenna didn't like talking about the man while he wasn't in the room to defend himself. She feigned interest in the documents scattered across the table and, without looking up, said, "I don't know what you mean."

Melissa stared down at the list in her hands, a smile playing around the corners of her mouth. "Ever since Nick's divorce, he's been a driven man."

So, Nick Tarver had been married? Brenna wasn't surprised. A man with such a wicked combination of black hair and deep green eyes couldn't stay single long.

"For the past two years, he hasn't stopped to consider others need food, sleep or even coffee." Melissa tapped her pencil on the clipboard.

"Until today." Paul looked around and stared at Brenna as if seeing her for the first time. His eyes narrowed. "Until you."

"Think the ice is cracking on Nicky?" Melissa tilted her head to the side as her gaze wandered over Brenna.

Brenna squirmed beneath the intensity of their perusal. As if Nick Tarver had any interest in her! She was a criminal investigator, not her sister of the golden-blond-cheerleader perfection. What would he see in her?

Nothing.

"I don't know. Might be too soon to tell." With a shrug, Paul turned back to the monitor. "But my money's on Special Agent Jensen."

Melissa pushed away from the table and brushed past Brenna. "I'd keep my eye on him if I were you, sweetie. Nick can blow hot and cold in a matter of seconds."

Melissa didn't have to waste her breath. Brenna already knew Nick was trouble. The only difficulty would be within herself. The FBI agent would never fall for a woman like her. But any woman could fall for a guy like him.

Not Brenna. She knew better. Nick was strictly a hit-and-run kinda guy. Having survived a past hit-and-run relationship, Brenna was in no hurry to step out in front of a speeding car again.

"Got it." Paul hit a button on the keyboard and jumped up to stand in front of a printer. "The list I'm printing is a cross reference between all of Brenna's convictions and those parolees within a two-hundred-mile radius."

With a long leg swinging back and forth beneath the conference table, Melissa asked, "Did you need to go out that far?"

"We're in North Dakota, Melissa, not Virginia. People are used to driving long distances to get to little pockets of civilization out here." The printer spit out four copies of the report. Paul kept one and laid the others on the table.

Nick entered the room, the aroma of coffee filling the air. He leaned close to Brenna and lifted a copy of Paul's report.

The combination of the coffee and the fresh, outside scent of Nick made Brenna fidgety. She lifted her copy of the report and moved to the far corner of the room. Away from Nick. Then she forced herself to study the page in front of her.

"Most of these people live in Bismarck, Minot or Fargo," she said.

"There's our local, Bart Olsen." Paul pointed near the bottom of the page.

"None of them jumps out." Brenna tapped the list against her palm. "I'm going by Dr. Drummond's office to see if any of these names match current or past patients." She headed for the door, hoping Agent Tarver wouldn't volunteer to go with her. She needed distance from the man.

Nick stared at her with narrowed eyes. "Paul, go with her."

"Yes, sir!" Paul leaped to attention, a grin filling his face. "Come on, Jensen, I have my orders."

As she stepped from the war room, a bit of the weight she'd felt bearing down on her lifted. At least with Nick out of the way she wouldn't be thinking about him. He was too much of a distraction when she had a killer to nail.

"On second thought, I'll go with her." Nick stepped up behind Brenna and assisted her as she pushed her arms into her jacket.

Paul gave her a lopsided grin. "Maybe next time."

As Nick stepped through the door to Dr. Drummond's office, he shrugged out of his jacket, his senses on alert. A light scent of potpourri filled the air, much better than the acrid aroma of disinfectant he expected in a doctor's office. But then Dr. Drummond was a psychiatrist.

Brenna led the way into the doctor's waiting room,

stripping her jacket from her shoulders. "Hello, Mrs. Keckler," she said to the woman behind the counter.

"Brenna Jensen? Is that you? Oh, my Lord, it's so good to see you!" The older woman hopped out of her seat and came through the door to hug Brenna. "Or should I call you Agent Jensen? It's been a long time."

Why did Jensen know the receptionist in a psychiatrist's office so well? Were they old family friends or was there something more to the relationship? Was Brenna a former patient?

"I'm sorry it's under these circumstances." Brenna returned the hug and stepped back quickly, her movements jerky. "This is FBI Agent Nick Tarver."

"Nice to meet you." The older woman shook his hand and then turned back to Brenna. "I heard they found the doctor's body—" Her voice cracked. She snatched a tissue from a box on the counter and dabbed at her eyes. "We're all still in shock. I can't imagine anyone wanting to hurt Dr. Drummond. Who would do this?"

Smoothing a hand over the woman's shoulders, Brenna said, "Actually, that's why we're here. We need to check the patient files."

"Do you think it was one of her patients?" Mrs. Keckler twisted her hands together. "Oh my. How awful."

"We don't know," Brenna said softly. "It would help to see the files."

Mrs. Keckler sniffed and shook her head. "I can't. What with doctor-patient confidentiality laws and all, my hands are tied." She sank onto a nearby chair. "Just to think it might be one of her patients makes me positively ill. If it were up to me, I'd give you every last file."

"We understand and we're not asking you to break the law." Nick knew how important it was to obtain evidence legally. Too many criminals walked because of sloppy investigative techniques. "What we need is for you to do a cross-check of a list of names we have with the patients in your files."

"I can do that." Mrs. Keckler took the list Brenna held out and ducked back into the inner office to sit at a desk with a computer.

In the ensuing silence, Jensen stood with her back to Nick.

"How well did you know Dr. Drummond?" Nick asked.

Her shoulders stiffened. "Fairly well," she said, her words clipped, not inviting further probing.

That didn't stop Nick. Brenna was holding something back. If it had anything to do with the case, he wanted to know. "Friend of the family?"

"Not really."

Nick laid a hand on her shoulder and turned her to face him, his fingers holding her upper arms in a vise grip. "I need to know everything, Agent Jensen. If you had a connection with Dr. Drummond, tell me. It could be vital to solving this case."

She refused to look into his eyes, focusing instead on something over his shoulder. "I used to come here," she mumbled. Then her gaze leaped to his. "I used to be one of Dr. Drummond's patients. Okay?"

His gut tightening, Nick loosened his hold on her arms. "Why didn't you tell me before?"

"It's not something I advertise. How would it look for a criminal investigator to have a mental health history?"

"There's nothing wrong with seeing a psychiatrist."

She snorted. "Tell it to the reporters and the security-clearance guys who love to jump to conclusions."

"Look, it's just another piece of the puzzle." He drew a deep breath and held it a moment before he blew it out. "Promise me you won't keep anything else from me. I need to know I can trust the members of my team."

She sighed, her shoulders sagging. "Okay, I'll tell you what I know."

Nick waited, but the silence lengthened. "Well?"

"I don't know anything else right now. When I do, I'll be sure to report it to you." She glanced down at his hands on her arms and back up to his eyes. "Now, if you don't mind…"

Nick dropped his hands and stepped back, at the same moment Mrs. Keckler returned.

"I checked all the files and none of them matches the names on this list." Mrs. Keckler handed the sheet of paper back to Brenna. "I'm sorry. If you have reason to suspect one of the patients, you can get a warrant and I'll release that patient's information, but I can't just let you go through the files."

"Thanks anyway, Mrs. Keckler." Brenna hugged the woman and left the office.

Nick followed, stepping over a stream of melted snow to climb into the passenger side of the Cherokee.

When Brenna slid in next to him, she paused before turning the key in the ignition. "I started seeing Dr. Drummond when I was a little girl after I was involved in a pretty traumatic incident. She helped me get through it. I haven't seen her since I left Riverton."

"What kind of trauma?"

"I was severely burned in a barn fire at the age of ten. Dr. Drummond helped me to get past the nightmares and other issues related to the injuries." Brenna's voice was flat, unemotional, as if stating unimportant facts.

It must have cost her to say anything about an event that had such a major impact she'd sought psychiatric help. A hard knot formed in Nick's belly as he thought of a younger version of Brenna going through the pain of skin grafting. "How did you get caught in a barn fire?" He spoke in a soft voice, afraid if he pushed her too far, she'd clam up.

"I was out at my grandmother's farm along the river playing with some of the neighbor children. We were in and out of the barn all day, until one time I went in and I smelled smoke. I searched out the source and found a fire burning up a stack of green hay bales. It had grown bigger than I could manage to put out, and by the time I turned to leave, I couldn't see the door through the smoke. I couldn't get out."

Nick's heart skipped several beats at the thought of a child's terror. "What do you mean you couldn't get out?"

"The smoke was so bad, at first I couldn't see my way to the door. When I did find the door, it wouldn't open."

"Was it locked?"

"There were no locks on the inside. All I could figure was it was locked or jammed from the outside." She attempted a shrug, but her shoulders were too stiff to look natural.

"Had the door gotten stuck any other time you went in or out of the barn?"

"No."

"Sounds more like someone locked that door with you inside."

"I don't know." She rested her head against the steering wheel. "My sister and some of the other children heard me screaming and got me out."

"Did the fire department determine the cause of the fire?"

"They said that the hay in the barn was too green when it was stored. Spontaneous combustion was the cause noted on the report."

"Bull." Nick gritted his teeth. "Sounds more like arson. But who'd want to kill a kid?"

"None of my grandmother's farm workers were around at the time, so they were in the clear. Besides my grandmother, there were just us kids."

"Do you remember who was there?"

She shrugged. "What's it matter? That was a long time ago. We have a murder to solve in the here and now."

"Sometimes you have to look at every angle to solve a murder. If this guy is after you, who's to say he didn't try before?"

"I was too young to remember." She looked up at him. "Do you think it's important?"

"It might be."

"Maybe my sister, Alice, will remember. I don't. But I think you're barking up the wrong tree."

"I'd rather bark up a wrong tree than face another victim's family."

"Good point." Brenna sat back, the key in the ignition forgotten. "This guy is sick, really sick. And if he's doing all this to get back at me for something, Dr. Drummond's death is my fault."

"No, it's not." Nick took one of her hands in his. "You didn't kill Dr. Drummond. Someone with a serious problem is responsible, and we're going to catch him."

BRENNA FELT DRAINED after spilling her guts to Agent Tarver. During the trip back to the station, she sank into a silent stupor, blanking her mind from the terror of the barn fire that had almost killed her. Her chest burned as she remembered the thick black smoke that had coated her lungs and had made it so hard to see, she hadn't thought she'd make it out the door. Brenna was glad when they arrived at the police station because she needed to get out of the vehicle and breathe.

Paul met them at the information desk. "We have Bart Olsen in the interview room. They just brought him in."

"Good." Nick moved past him and down the hall.

Brenna's heart skipped a few beats as she hung her coat on a hook and hurried after him. "I want to interview him."

"I'll let you have him after I'm through."

She frowned. "I don't like it, but I guess that's okay." Without further comment, she passed the interview room and stepped into the observation area.

Through the two-way mirror, Brenna could see the man inside sitting alone at a table. His hands were cuffed behind his back, forcing him to perch at the edge of the chair. Brenna recognized his face beneath a couple days' growth of beard. Bart had been in cuffs the last time she'd seen him with the sheriff's deputies escorting him to jail to serve his six-year sentence for rape, of which he'd only served two years. Why the hell couldn't they keep men like him off the streets?

Nick Tarver entered the room and sat across the utilitarian table from him.

With Paul, Melissa and Chief Burkholder standing over her shoulder, Brenna kept her face turned toward the room. She didn't want to talk to the others. Her job was to read into the words and body language of the man being questioned. Nick Tarver had better know what the hell he was doing. They couldn't afford to waste time on the wrong suspect.

"Bart Olsen?" Nick settled into the hard-backed metal chair and leaned across the table.

"Yeah, that's me." Bart spat out his response. With bloodshot eyes and greasy hair, he looked as if he hadn't slept or washed in days. "Why the hell am I here?"

"We brought you in for questioning."

"If you wanted me just for questions, why the cuffs?"

"Let me take care of them for you." Nick stepped out the door and was back in minutes with a key. He unlocked the cuffs and slid them into his pocket. "Is that better?"

"Damn right." Bart rubbed his wrists and stared at the agent, his eyes slightly narrowed. "So, what do you want?"

In low, steady tones, Nick asked, "Can you tell me where you were this past weekend?"

"Not that you have a right to ask, but I was at a hunting cabin by Lake Grayson."

Nick smiled. "Do you like hunting and fishing, Mr. Olsen?"

Bart sat back in his chair and nodded. "Yeah, I go up to the cabin on weekends to unwind and catch a few fish." He crossed his arms over his chest. "But you didn't bring me in here to ask about fishin'."

Nick smiled. "You're a smart man, Mr. Olsen. I like that."

Brenna couldn't help admiring the way Nick appeared relaxed and friendly, but she could tell beneath the surface he remained alert, completely attuned. Bart was even relaxing and dropping his guard. Nick was good at his job. She could appreciate that in any law-enforcement official, even the FBI. But she couldn't lie to herself and say she didn't find everything about his looks attractive, from the black as night hair to the angular lines of his face. He looked as if he could chew on nails with that jaw, and the determination in his green eyes gave her no doubts that if he wanted to, he could.

But the way he made his interviewee relax and feel as though he were his friend interested her more. He'd have Olsen spilling everything he knew before long.

A thrill of awareness sped through her body, and she quickly tamped it down. Who had time for useless emotion where her team lead was concerned, or for the baser instincts of lust? She needed to focus on the suspect and solving the murder of an innocent woman, and possibly two more.

Nick leaned forward. "Do you know anyone who can place you at your cabin for the entire weekend?"

"No. In case you didn't notice—" Bart tipped his head toward the barred window "—the weather sucks around here. Not many people want to go to the lake under these conditions."

"Some do, like you." He nodded at Bart. "Did you have any friends visit at your cabin?"

"I ain't had no one visit me at my cabin or my apartment in town since I spent time in jail. I'm like the freakin' plague." He kicked the table leg and glared at Nick. "It's all her fault, you know." Bart lurched to his feet.

In one smooth, graceful glide Nick rose up and away from Bart, his stance ready for anything though he did not appear nervous.

But Bart turned and paced across the floor. "If it weren't for that Agent Jensen, I wouldn't be a suspect for those missing women. That's what all this is about, right?"

Brenna's heart slammed into her rib cage.

"What do you mean?" Nick asked quietly.

"Nothing. I don't mean nothing." Bart dropped into the chair, his brows drawing low over his eyes.

Melissa leaned over Brenna's shoulder. "Still want to interview this guy?"

"I don't recommend it," Paul said. "Not after that outburst."

Ignoring them, Brenna concentrated on Olsen and Tarver.

Nick planted his hands on the table and leaned into the other man's face. "What are you hiding, Bart?"

A chill raced through Brenna's blood. She'd probably tell Nick anything he wanted to hear if he asked her like that.

Not Bart. "I ain't saying another word until my lawyer gets here." He sat staring straight ahead, his lips pressed together. The man was done. After several trips to the courtroom, he knew the system and he'd take full advantage of his legal rights.

"I guess I won't be interviewing Mr. Olsen," Brenna said to the chief and the agents in the room. "At least not until his attorney arrives." A part of her was relieved. She should have expected the animosity Bart had for her, but hearing the loathing in his voice sent shivers across her skin. And her instincts told her Bart was hiding something. But was he the killer?

Without evidence, she couldn't be certain.

Chapter Six

After Bart Olsen was moved to a holding cell, the team of investigators convened in the war room. Brenna rifled through the file of statements the police officers had gathered so far. There had to be something there, a clue they'd overlooked.

"So, you think he did it?" Paul asked.

"Hard to tell," Nick said. "He's guilty of violating his parole, but I'm not convinced he killed Dr. Drummond."

Chief Burkholder stepped into the room, his face looking older than his fifty-nine years, his skin tinged gray. "Brenna." This was the first time since he'd introduced her to the FBI agents that he'd called her by her first name.

Brenna broke out in a cold sweat, dropping the papers in her hands to join the chief by the door. "What is it?"

He drew in a deep breath and held out his hand. He wore surgical gloves and dangling from his fingers was a plastic bag with a simple white envelope inside.

Brenna looked down at the envelope addressed to her, in care of the Riverton Police Department. She frowned. "Who would send me mail here?" As soon as the words slipped from her lips, the answer clicked in her brain. "Him."

Chief Burkholder nodded. "That would be my guess."

"What's this?" Melissa walked up next to her. "Is it another letter from the killer?"

"Let me get some gloves and a mask and we'll see." She didn't try to take the letter from the chief.

"Shouldn't we let the forensics folks open it?" Melissa asked.

"Later." Brenna moved toward the door, speaking over her shoulder. "I think we need to read it as soon as possible."

She left the room, her heart pounding against her eardrums and her breath coming in short, shallow gasps.

He'd sent her another letter.

As if in a fog, she walked down the hallway to the supply cabinet, removing a pair of rubber gloves and a mask from boxes inside. As she stood with her back to the war room, she breathed in and out fighting to stop the rise of panic, her heart fluttering ineffectively in her chest.

How did he know she was here so soon?

"You all right?" The deep voice jolted her from her daze.

Brenna jumped and spun around.

Agent Tarver stood inches from her, his forehead creased.

"I'm fine," she lied, trying to breathe normally.

"You don't look fine," Nick said, his frown deepening between sooty brows. "You look a little pale." He reached around her for a pair of the gloves, his chest brushing against her shoulder.

The shock of connection blasted through Brenna, an intense reminder of his kiss beside the pool. She gasped and stepped away from his shoulder and the smell of leather and aftershave.

"Want me to open the letter?" he asked.

For a full three seconds, Brenna couldn't make her brain function to process his question. Finally, she answered. "No, I can do it." She ducked her chin, knowing she couldn't let him see how affected she was. She wouldn't let him see any of the confusion she felt for him or fear for the job she had to do.

He leaned toward her and pushed a strand of her hair back behind her ear. "You don't have to be strong 24-7, Jensen."

"Yes, I do." A sudden urge to press her face into his palm nearly overwhelmed her. She jerked her head to the side to avoid the touch of his fingers against her neck. "I'm a cop. I don't have time to be scared." Of killers or tall, gorgeous FBI agents. Although she could honestly say she wasn't afraid of Tarver—more her physical reaction to his nearness.

"Being the target of a killer is nothing to be taken lightly." His voice rumbled low and warm in the silence surrounding them.

"True. And I'm not taking it lightly." She held the gloves in her hand, pulling at the rubber and letting it pop against her skin. The small amount of pain reminded her she was alive, this situation was real and she wasn't attracted to this man. "I can handle this." Ha! Who was she trying to fool when she was quickly sinking beneath the surface? Before long, she wouldn't be able to come up for air. "What bothers me is why."

"Why what?"

She turned her back to him and slammed shut the metal doors of the supply cabinet, tears welling in her eyes. "Why Riverton, why the women he's chosen, why me?"

"If we knew the answer to those questions, we'd probably already have our killer."

"I'm the one this guy wants, not those other women." She leaned her head against the cabinet, willing her tears to dry, the metal cooling her heated skin. "He's killing them because of me."

"You can't blame yourself, Jensen."

She pushed back and shoved her hands into the rubber gloves, blinking back the moisture in her eyes. When she turned, she had her emotions under tenuous control. "Why not? I'm the one he wants."

"He's using you." Nick breathed out a long steady breath. "Look, the guy is psychotic and would probably kill even if you weren't a convenient excuse."

"Sure." Brenna moved to brush by him, but Nick grabbed her upper arms and held her still.

"It's not your fault. I won't have you blaming yourself for a crazy man's actions."

"Why should you care? You're Nick Tarver, the FBI agent. The man who is all about the case and nothing else." Her voice broke and the tears she'd been holding in check slid silently down her cheeks. "Why do you give a flying flip whether or not I blame myself? You didn't know any of those women. I did! Why do you care?"

"Because it's my job and because I see a lot of me in you." He dropped his hands from her arms and stepped aside. "I used to blame myself when another victim was killed while I was still looking for the person responsible."

Brenna swallowed the lump in her throat. "You did?"

"Yes. Not only was it a drain on me, but also on those around me." His voice dropped and he looked through her as if seeing into his past. "Including those you should care most about…"

That look and the way his voice trailed off caught

Brenna unawares and she opened her mouth before thinking. "Is that why you're divorced?"

That faraway look turned into a hard, level stare right into her eyes.

Brenna held her breath, afraid she'd stepped over the line by prying into the team leader's personal life.

Then his gaze shifted to her gloved hands. "That was only part of the reason."

He didn't elaborate. Instead, he turned and walked back toward the war room, pushing his hands into rubber gloves.

When Brenna didn't immediately follow, he looked back over his shoulder. "Are you going to open the letter, or do you want to wait and let the crime lab do it?"

"Let's do it." Her feet propelled her forward until she was standing in the middle of a circle of FBI agents and Riverton police personnel. Paul handed her a pocketknife.

"Maybe you guys should leave the room." Nick looked around at the assembled group. "We don't know if this guy poisoned the envelope or dusted it with something toxic like anthrax."

Paul looked to Melissa. "You going anywhere?"

She shook her head. "I'm not going anywhere."

"Me, either," Chief Burkholder said.

"That goes for me, too." Nick nodded, his mouth forming a thin line. He took the bag from the chief and opened it.

"Then here goes." Brenna placed her mask over her mouth and nose and slid the envelope out of the bag. Then she sliced through the end, spilling the single, folded sheet of computer paper out into her gloved hand. Carefully, she spread the sheet open and read aloud.

"'The first could see inside my head, but now she

can't because she's dead. And you can't find my number two. Guess who's smarter—me or you?'"

Cold slithered over her body like someone had left the front door open during a blizzard. *This man hates me.* What had she done to garner that much hatred? Her gaze rose to lock with Nick Tarver's.

"This guy is going down." His words were low and dangerous.

"I'm with you," Paul said.

Nick walked over to Chief Burkholder. "Can you get on the phone with the judge and get us a warrant to search Dr. Drummond's office? Based on the wording of that letter, we have probable cause to believe he was one of her patients."

"Will do," Chief Burkholder said.

"The sooner the better," Nick said. "Lives could depend on those files."

"I'm on it." The chief left the room, his face more animated than when he'd entered.

While Nick issued orders, Brenna stood with the letter dangling from her fingers. "He's baiting me."

"Yes, he is." Nick touched a hand to her elbow.

Warmth spread from his hand up her arm and helped to dispel the chill settling over her.

He leaned close and said in a dangerous voice, "But we're going to spear this fish, not the other way around. Are you with us?"

"Yes." She carefully replaced the envelope and letter in the plastic bag and handed it to Paul. "This goes to the crime lab."

"Gotcha." He left the room at a jog, returning in less than a minute.

"So, is Bart Olsen no longer a suspect?" Melissa asked.

"Since the letter came through the mail, we can't be

sure it wasn't him." Nick paced a few steps and turned. "My gut says no. But we'll hold him the legal limit just to make sure."

"Good." Paul's mouth formed a grim line. "I'll go talk to the university and do a little nosing around to see if I can come up with something. I'd bet my favorite jogging shoes the professor is already dead based on the note."

"And I'll bet I'm the one he *really* wants," Brenna whispered.

Melissa laid a hand on her arm. "Don't let it get to you. Won't do you or the victims any good."

"She's right," Nick said. "We're in this together. We'll find him."

God, she hoped so. Before another life was lost.

Chief Burkholder reentered the war room. "Judge Tyler's with the mayor. It might be morning before we get that warrant. In the meantime I've bumped up the number of patrols for the night shift." The chief's lips pressed together in a gray line. "The weatherman predicts further warming."

The lead lump in Brenna's belly turned over. "How bad?"

Chief Burkholder breathed in and let it out slowly. "They're saying it could be like the flood of ninety-seven."

"Don't we have enough to worry about?" Brenna said. "We have a killer on the loose and we might be faced with a flood?"

She'd been a teen during the last one, but she remembered shoveling sand into sandbags to build a makeshift levy. One that ultimately gave way to the force of the rising river. Many areas of town had been evacuated, people herded into shelters with only the clothes on their backs. All they could do was wait and watch news clips of their homes being washed down-river taking with them a century of memories.

"Better prepare for the worst," Chief Burkholder said.

Nick's eyes narrowed. "No, we better catch him before it gets worse."

Reverberating through Brenna's mind was the old saying, *It's gonna get a lot worse before it gets better.*

"I HAVE TO GET A SHOWER and some rest," Brenna said as she moved to the door. "I'll be back around nine."

Nick glanced at the clock. Was it already seven? The day had flown and they were no closer to catching the killer.

"Wait. I'll go with you."

Brenna's brows rose. "I don't think so. A shower is something I can do on my own."

He withheld a smart-ass remark, deciding she'd had enough for one day. "I realize that. But I'm not letting you out of my sight until this guy is either dead or behind bars. And right now I'm leaning toward the dead scenario."

"You and me both. But really, I can manage on my own. The hotel is well lit and I'll be carrying a gun."

"Not good enough."

For a moment, Nick thought she'd argue, but she shrugged. "Fine. Suit yourself."

"Thanks. I will."

When they arrived at the hotel, Nick grabbed her arm and stopped her in front of the desk. "Do you have a suite with two rooms available?"

The night clerk closed the textbook he'd been studying and leaned over a computer screen. "Let me check."

"What are you doing?" Brenna snapped. "My room is perfectly fine."

"We'll discuss it later. For now let me handle this."

The clerk glanced up. "Yes, sir, we do."

"Miss Jensen and I will be moving into the suite."

"I'll have to charge you for all three rooms tonight since you didn't check out by eleven."

"Fine."

The stubborn look on Brenna's face let Nick know he was in for an argument. But he didn't care. How else was he supposed to keep his eye on her if she was in a different room on another floor of the hotel? This killer had already proved resourceful at getting into locked houses. Why wouldn't he be able to get into a locked hotel room?

"How many keys?" the clerk asked.

"One," Brenna said.

"Two," Nick countered.

Behind the counter, the clerk eyed them, his brows rising into a shaggy hairline. "Hey, this just doesn't look right." He turned to Brenna. "Do you or don't you want to share a suite with this man?"

"I don't."

He turned back to Nick. "I'm sorry, sir. If you don't back off, I'll have to call the police."

"We are the police." He removed his credentials from his pocket and flipped them open. "FBI to be exact. I'm Agent Nick Tarver and this is Special Agent Brenna Jensen. She and I are on the same team working a case together, and she *will* be sharing a suite with me." He turned toward her. "Is that perfectly clear, Special Agent Jensen?"

"Perfectly," she said through her clenched teeth. "Two keys, please."

The clerk looked from one to the other and finally shrugged and handed over two keys. "It's your funeral, Agent Tarver. She looks pretty mad about it."

Nick forced a smile. "I'll take my chances."

T<small>O LIMIT FURTHER ARGUMENT</small> in front of the hotel staff, Brenna bit her tongue so hard, the taste of copper filled her mouth. *I'll take my chances.* The guy had nerve and an ego.

Nick Tarver followed her to her old room and watched as she shoved her toiletries and clothing into her suitcase. Then he led the way to the suite on the third floor.

With a few choice words ready to spew, she waited until she could get him alone in the room to vent.

But when she entered the room, Nick stood at the door and pointed a finger at her. "You stay put until I get back." With that parting comment he closed the door and left her standing with her mouth hanging open. She sputtered a few unintelligible epithets and claimed the bedroom on the right. The one with the larger, more comfortable bed and the better view. A view of the slush-covered parking lot. Still, it was better than a view of the Dumpster. She bounced on the edge of the mattress. No matter how comfortable the bed and the room, she still felt like a prisoner and she'd be damned if she let Nick do that to her.

With a quick glance at the door, she slid out of her slacks and into a pair of sweatpants and a T-shirt. Although the sun had set an hour earlier, clouds had moved in, helping to retain the heat from the day. The outside temperature should be a balmy forty. A chill snaked down her back. Once she got going on her jog, the T-shirt would be sufficient.

If she hurried, she could slip out before Attila returned. She'd slapped her hair into a loose ponytail and was in the process of tying her shoes in the shared sitting room when she heard a card key slide in the lock.

Damn.

Purposely refusing to look at him, she continued tying her shoes.

"Give me a minute and I'll go with you." He nudged the door closed with his foot.

"That's just it. I don't want you with me." She needed the space to clear her brain. Nick Tarver had a way of crowding it with too much testosterone and broad shoulders. Jeez! How did he expect her to get any sleep knowing he was in the next room?

"I insist." He carried a black duffel bag into the adjoining room and turned to close the door. With his hand on the knob, he gave her a narrow-eyed stare. "Don't think of going out without me."

As the door closed behind him, Brenna's lungs pinched behind her ribs. *Oh, no.* The familiar pain lanced across her chest and her heartbeat sped up so fast she felt dizzy. Get a grip, she told herself. You can't fall apart now. She'd gone several years since her last full-scale panic attack. Why now?

All she knew was that she needed to get outside into the fresh air. She couldn't think until she had outside air against her face and filling her lungs.

She lunged for the door and was twisting the handle when an image of Dr. Drummond floating beneath the ice hit her so hard she staggered backward.

Dr. Drummond had been her salvation through the dark years following the barn fire. Years when she hadn't thought she'd ever quit having dreams of being locked inside a barn where smoke filled her lungs and flames leaped at her clothing. The good doctor had helped her through the fear and panic, helped her past the crippling nightmares. Now she was gone. And the killer was out there somewhere.

The irony struck her. Just when the claustrophobic

panic attack consumed her, making her seek the wide-open spaces, she realized she was no safer outside than inside.

Was being out in the open air worth dying for? But she couldn't stay in this room. Her lungs felt as heavy as when they'd been filled with black smoke. Brenna inhaled a shaky breath and closed her eyes, visualizing an open farm field full of bright gold sunflowers. She dragged in another breath and gasped when hands gripped her shoulders.

"Are you all right?" She could hear Agent Tarver's voice but she couldn't open her eyes. He turned her toward him and shook her gently. "Brenna, look at me."

She eased open her eyes and fell into his deep green gaze, like the green of summer wheat before it ripens into gold. A bright, open field of summer wheat in the sunshine. Brenna took a deep breath.

"What's wrong?" His hands still held her arms.

"Nothing," she said, but her body began to shake. She shook so hard her teeth rattled.

"Nothing, hell." Nick pulled her against him and she buried her face in his T-shirt.

She couldn't stop the tremors racing through her. "I'm sorry."

"For what?" he said against her hair, his hand stroking down the middle of her back.

"For being such a...wimp." She forced the words past her clenched teeth.

"You're not a wimp." His breath stirred the loose tendrils by her ear. Brenna concentrated on that feathery feeling that was so light and free it dispelled the remembered thickness of smoke choking the inner lining of her lungs.

Her hands dug into the front of his shirt and she held

on, feeling the strength of his muscles beneath her fingers. The solid planes of his body grounded her, pulling her out of the smoky barn and back into her hotel room. Slowly, her breathing returned to normal.

When her heart rate slowed to a manageable pace, she inhaled the faint scent of aftershave and leather that was a part of Nick Tarver. What was she doing in his arms? How had she come to lean on him as if her life depended on it? He was one of the perfect people, flawless in every way.

Disentangling her fingers from the jersey fabric of his shirt, she pushed away.

"Uh-uh." Nick's hands on the small of her back stopped her from falling backward. "Not until I'm sure you're okay."

"I'm fine." She forced a light laugh, pretending humor she didn't feel. "Really."

The tight grip slackened and Brenna moved away, reaching up to push the hair behind her ears, forgetting at the last moment her hair was up in a ponytail. Her hand dropped to her side.

"Want to tell me what that was all about?"

"No." She turned her back to him and walked to the center of the sitting room, rubbing chill bumps from her arms. Why did she feel cold now that Nick's arms weren't around her?

He stalked her, coming to a halt behind her. "Tell me anyway."

His body emanated warmth in such a way she was drawn to him, aching to lean against him. But she couldn't. Her panic attacks were something she had to overcome on her own. She couldn't rely on anyone but herself to pull her through. Yet, it had been nice— No, it had been a huge relief to rely on Nick's strength until the attack passed. In Nick's arms, she hadn't felt the aloneness that still haunted her from the barn fire.

"Brenna." Her name rolled off his lips like a feather's stroke. "If I'm going to protect you, I need to know from what."

"This has nothing to do with the killer."

"But if it incapacitates you again like it did now, you're open to whatever the killer wants to do. I need to know these things. Help me here. Trust me."

"Trust you?" She faced him, tears welling in her eyes. "I don't even know you!"

"I won't hurt you."

"How do I know that? If you were to tell someone on the team about my panic attack, I could be removed from this investigation and possibly from my job."

"I could remove you from this team, but I won't. And I'm not telling anyone anything." He reached out, locking his grip on her wrists. "I promise. But I can't help if you don't tell me what's wrong."

"Sure. You've wanted to help me right out the door since the start." She jerked against his hands, but he didn't let go. "And I'm supposed to believe you?"

"At least take a chance on me."

She stopped tugging at her wrists and stared up into his eyes. How could she trust him? She hadn't trusted anyone except her father and Dr. Drummond. Wrapped up in her picture-perfect marriage, her sister didn't have time for her. Besides, Alice confided everything to her husband, Stanley. And their mother wasn't in any condition to guide her. What did that leave her? An offer to trust a stranger—Nick Tarver—who would be out of her life as soon as they captured the killer. What the hell? She sighed and relaxed her arms.

Nick's hold loosened on her wrists, but he didn't let go.

"I haven't had an attack like that since I was eighteen." She drew in a deep breath. "Now I have to get outside."

"OKAY, BUT YOU'RE NOT GOING without me."

"Fine," she yanked the door open and stepped through without waiting for him.

Nick grabbed his room key and took off after her.

Instead of the elevator, she took the stairs and left the building from a side door.

The streetlights reflected off wet roads and residual snow and bounced off the low-level clouds that had moved in before sunset, giving the city an eerie glow. Without stopping to warm up or stretch, Brenna took off down the road.

Nick let her lead by a couple car lengths, giving her space while he watched every vehicle coming and going.

What had happened back there in the room?

Something had scared her enough to set her heart racing. The notes and murdered women would be enough to scare anyone, but Brenna wasn't anyone. She'd been a cop at one time—granted, on small-town streets, but a cop nonetheless. She'd witnessed murder scenes and solved several cases in North Dakota. The difference in this case was that she was probably a target and the murders were happening on her home turf. This guy knew how to hit where it hurt.

Brenna pulled farther away and Nick picked up his pace to close the distance. He jogged up beside her but didn't talk.

She was in good shape to keep up this pace for so long.

Water splashed up from their shoes, soaking through to his feet. His toes were uncomfortable and cold, and he knew Brenna's were no better. By the time they'd covered two miles, his sweats were drenched up to the knees with cold, nasty water, but he was warm from the exercise and ready to go on.

When they came upon a city park, Brenna slowed until she was walking. She was breathing hard and her face shone with a sheen of perspiration and…was that a trace of tears?

"Mind if we take a break?" he asked, even though he could have gone on for a couple more miles. Nick suspected that whatever she was running to shake loose of had shaken.

Brenna nodded and continued walking, only slowly now. "My father taught me to play baseball in this park."

Nick stared at the field still covered in a layer of half-melted snow and ice. At one end of the park was a backstop, at the other end boards had been erected for an outdoor skating rink.

"He also taught me how to play hockey and soccer and basketball."

Nick laughed. "Is there anything he didn't teach you?"

"He didn't teach me how to lose."

Chapter Seven

"And this is a liability?" Nick smiled and his eyes sparkled in the lights from the haloed streetlamps. "I see it as an asset."

"Sometimes. But it comes with its own baggage." She turned away from the impact of him in a muscle-hugging black T-shirt. Wrapping her arms around herself, she walked a few steps, the cold beginning to spread from her feet up into her arms. "Do you mind if we head back?"

"Lead the way."

She took off at a light jog, not the driven run she'd started with. The exercise had the desired effect and she was back in control, for the most part. If only she didn't have Nick dogging her every step, she'd relax and think through her panic in the hotel room and her reaction to being held in Nick's arms.

To be honest, she had needed him the way she needed a life raft in a stormy sea. But needing people always interfered with her judgment. And this case needed her full attention and sound conclusions.

As they approached the hotel, Nick pulled up along-side her and placed a hand on her arm to stop her. "Do you hear that?"

She strained to hear the faint wail of a siren. "Sounds like a fire truck."

Nick patted his side. "Damn, I left my cell phone back at the room."

"And you feel naked without it?" She chuckled. "Me, too. When I'm working a case, I like to be on top of everything."

"Absolutely. Come on." He stretched his legs into ground-eating strides.

Brenna began to appreciate how much he'd held his pace in check for her. The added exertion kept her concentration rooted on Nick's backside and the tight muscles beneath gray sweats.

When they arrived at the hotel, they took the stairs two at a time, arriving at the door to the room in a full lather and breathing hard.

With a quick swipe of his key card, Nick swung open the door. Before they took a step to enter the room, an electronic ringing sound greeted them.

Nick raced to the bedroom where he'd dumped his duffel and grabbed his cell phone from the bedside table. "Tarver."

Brenna hovered in the doorway, blatantly eavesdropping.

"Damn." He glanced over at Brenna. "How bad is it?"

Brenna fought to breathe quietly though she was still winded from her mad dash back to their suite. She wished she could hear what was going on.

"We'll be there in five." He flipped the phone shut and stared across the room at her. "That fire engine we heard outside? It was headed for Dr. Drummond's office."

For a moment Brenna couldn't respond past the lump lodged in her throat. She swallowed and asked, "Anyone hurt?"

"No, the office was empty."

"Except for any evidence we might have gathered. What are you waiting for?" She grabbed her keys and a jacket and headed for the door.

"We'll meet Paul and Melissa at Drummond's office." Looping his leather jacket over one shoulder, Nick jogged down the hallway and out of the building.

They accomplished the short drive to the doctor's office in silence.

Red, blue and amber lights flashed and the street was jammed with fire trucks and emergency vehicles. Forced to park around the corner and a block away, Brenna shut off her engine and got out. The overwhelming scent of smoke assailed her senses. Bright orange flames shot up over the top of a two-story office building still blocking their view. Brenna stood for a moment, tamping down the urge to run in the opposite direction.

"You okay?" Nick slid an arm around her waist.

"Yes. I wish you'd stop asking me that," she snapped, angry with herself for the flash of panic. With Nick beside her, she didn't have to face the blaze alone, and that comforted her.

As images of the charred remains of her grandmother's barn flashed through her memory, she prepared herself for the worst.

Brenna let Nick lead her forward and around the corner. The firemen shot steady streams of water from two directions into the center of the building. The flames were beaten down until all that remained was black smoke churning and mixing with the low-lying clouds, spreading sideways instead of dissipating into the night sky.

They stood for a moment, getting their bearings with

the people scattered around the scene. Three individuals broke away from the fire chief and moved toward them—Paul, Melissa and Chief Burkholder.

"The fire chief says the office is a complete loss," Chief Burkholder said.

"All the files are gone? Everything?" Brenna pressed a finger to her temple, the stench of wet plaster triggering a headache of migraine proportions. She fought the pain by taking deep breaths and concentrating on the chief's words.

"Chief Freund thinks this fire was set deliberately, based on the confined intensity of the blaze emanating from the office where the files were kept."

"Someone didn't want us to get into those files," Nick muttered beneath his breath.

"I'll get hold of Mrs. Keckler and find out if there were any backups stored off-site." Brenna pulled her cell phone from her jacket pocket and flipped it open, fumbling with the buttons in the sporadic light from the streetlamps and the fire. "I'm still getting used to this danged thing. The bureau gave me this phone before I left. It's supposed to have GPS tracking on it as well. Although how it works, I haven't a clue."

"So they can keep track of you at all times?" Nick's mouth curved upward on the ends. "Not a bad idea."

"Whatever." She shrugged. "Since the note came to me, the bureau decided I might be in danger. I think they just wanted to try this tracking thing out. I'm their guinea pig." She grimaced at the buttons for a few seconds and then dialed Information. When Directory Assistance asked what city, she said, "Riverton, North Dakota."

After asking for Sandra Keckler, Brenna waited to be connected. At the second ring, she glanced at her watch. Just after nine. The woman shouldn't be in bed yet. Mrs. Keckler answered.

"This is Brenna Jensen. I regret to inform you there's been a fire at Dr. Drummond's office."

"Oh my God!" Her voice could be heard yelling to someone in the house with her, "There's been a fire at the office!"

"Mrs. Keckler, I need your assistance." Brenna tried to get her attention.

"Yes, of course. What can I do? Do you need me there?"

Brenna glanced at the charred shell of a building. "No, there's not much you can do until after the fire department finishes up."

"I suppose not. So, what do you need from me?"

"Are there any backups of the patient files kept off-site?" She held her breath, praying for good news after so much bad.

"Why, yes!"

"Thank God." Brenna tipped her head back and breathed deeply, the headache easing. "Where, Mrs. Keckler? Where are the backups?"

"In a safe deposit box at the First Interstate Bank on Main Street. I make a backup of the computerized records every night and deliver it to the bank the next day."

Brenna clutched the phone to her ear. "Do you mean to tell me you might have a copy of the records at your house?"

"I know I made a backup today, but let me check to make sure I brought it with me."

Brenna heard a click as if Mrs. Keckler had laid the phone on the counter and walked away. In the background Mrs. Keckler yelled, "Honey, where did I put my purse? Never mind."

Brenna tapped her foot and stared around at the fire crew. Nick stood to the side, his gaze intent on her, making her warm all over in the cool night air. How did he do that?

"Yes!" Mrs. Keckler came back on the line. "I have the disk right here in my hand. But I'll need a court order to release it to you."

"I know." Brenna's gaze locked with Nick's. "You'll have that court order within the next hour. Don't go anywhere and don't let anyone in your house until you see my face at your door."

"Do you think I'm in some kind of danger?"

"Mrs. Keckler, until we find the man who murdered Dr. Drummond, no one in Riverton is safe."

"Oh, my." She drew in a shaky breath. "I'll lock my doors and wait for you."

"Thank you, Mrs. Keckler." Brenna flipped her phone shut and smiled for the first time in what felt like centuries. "She has a copy of the computer files. We should at least be able to get names of the patients."

"Good. Let me check with the fire chief, then we'll track down our county judge for that warrant." Nick picked his way through the crowd of emergency personnel to the fire chief.

Brenna followed.

"Chief, how soon will we be able to get in there and see if we can salvage anything?"

"At least the morning before we can get in. Has to cool down before our fire investigation team can get in and determine a probable cause."

"Thanks, Chief." Nick turned to Paul. "I want you here first thing in the morning searching through whatever's left."

"As they say in the great state of North Dakota, you betcha." Paul gave Nick a mock salute and stayed with the chief as Nick and Brenna walked toward Melissa.

"Melissa, first thing tomorrow, I want you to scan the newspapers and crime databases for arson cases in the area. And get some rest. I have a feeling there's going to more trouble before we've seen the end of this."

"Yes, sir." Melissa headed toward Paul and they walked away together.

Chief Burkholder joined Nick and Brenna. "I know where Judge Tyler lives. If you'll follow me, we can get there in less than ten minutes."

"Good." Nick shoved a hand through his hair, making it stand on end. "We need to get to the backup files before someone else decides they're fair game."

"Right." The chief stopped next to an unmarked black sedan. "I'll wait for you at the corner."

Brenna and Nick jogged the rest of the way to her Jeep and then pulled in behind the chief.

"Any idea what we'll be looking for in those files?" Brenna turned at the next street, following two car lengths behind Chief Burkholder. "We already know we don't have a match between my convictions and her list of patients."

"I don't know, but my gut tells me he's in there. We might also get Chief Burkholder to look at the information. Maybe he'll know some of the patients."

"I lived here almost all my life, but in a town the size of Riverton with a constant flux of people coming and going from the university, I may or may not recognize every name."

"I'm not worried about the ones you don't know. This guy knows you and there's a good chance you know him."

"Yeah, but I might not. God, I hope I do. I'd rather

face a poisonous snake in the open than an unknown snake in the grass."

"Precisely."

Brenna parked curbside behind the chief's sedan in an upper-middle-class neighborhood and turned off the engine. "This must be the place."

Chief Burkholder was already at the door, ringing the doorbell when Nick and Brenna stepped up behind him.

"Who is it?" a woman's voice called out from behind the wood-and-glass-paneled door.

"Chief Burkholder, Riverton Police Department. We need to see Judge Tyler."

"Oh. Okay." The bolt rattled and a classy-looking white-haired lady opened the door. "Please come inside and wait in the living room. I'll find my husband."

Brenna, along with the chief and Nick, remained standing in the nicely decorated entryway filled with antique furniture and family portraits. Still dressed in her dirty sweats, her feet cold and wet, she didn't want to touch anything.

Tall and hefty with a thick thatch of striking white hair, Judge Tyler emerged from a room on the other side of a sweeping staircase. "Tom, good to see you." He shook the chief's hand.

Tom Burkholder introduced Brenna and Nick.

Brenna shook the judge's hand.

"I knew your father. Good man." His words, like his hand, were warm and firm.

Brenna swallowed hard and nodded.

He held her hand a little longer in a light grip. "You're not doing so bad for yourself, are you? I saw you in the news…what was it, two weeks ago?"

"Yes, sir."

"Caught the Tate murderer. I'm glad you're on the

case." He patted her hand and let go. Then he turned to Nick. "And the FBI, did you say?"

Nick took his hand. "Agent Tarver, sir."

"This about that warrant to search the psychiatrist's files?" the judge asked.

"Yes," Chief Burkholder said. "Dr. Drummond's office was burned to the ground a few minutes ago."

The judge's eyes widened. "Does this mean you don't need the warrant after all?"

"On the contrary. The good doctor had the foresight to keep backups. Only I'd like to get to those backups before another house goes up in flames or we lose another citizen of Riverton."

"Another?"

"Dr. Drummond was found in Eagle Lake this morning."

"Damn. I was hoping we'd find her alive." The judge scraped his hair back from his forehead, the lines around his eyes deepening. "I knew Dr. Drummond. She was a good woman, even did some volunteer work on the city Council. Not to mention all she did through her practice for the people of Riverton."

The chief nodded. "Yes, it was a shock to us all."

"This is very disturbing. Any word on Dr. Gomez?"

Chief Burkholder shook his head. "None. And we had another woman reported missing last night. A Michelle Carmichael."

"Carmichael?" Judge Tyler pushed away from the wall. "As in the big-shot real estate agent?"

The chief nodded. "That's the one. You know her?"

Judge Tyler squinted and scratched his chin. "No, but it seems I saw something about her in the newspaper recently. Is she dead, too?"

"We don't know. But based on notes the killer sent

to Special Agent Jensen, we have reason to believe he might have been one of Dr. Drummond's patients."

The judge shook his head. "I have the warrant already signed and ready for you. I was going to deliver it in the morning, but it looks like you could use it now."

While the judge retrieved the document, Brenna thought through what he'd said. "Chief, did you happen to see the write-up in the paper that Judge Tyler was talking about? The one with Michelle Carmichael in it?"

"No, I don't recall seeing it. Why?"

"Nothing. I just wondered." She might be chasing air, but when she got back to her computer, she'd look through the online newspaper records and see if she could glean any pertinent information from the story. And while she was at it, she'd look for anything on Dr. Drummond and Dr. Gomez.

The judge returned and handed the warrant to the chief.

Chief Burkholder tucked it into his inside jacket pocket. "Thanks, Larry."

"No problem, Tom. Let me know if I can help you in any way. I hate to think this is happening to our people."

The chief nodded, his mouth set in a grim line. "You and me both." As soon as they exited the judge's home, Chief Burkholder handed the document to Nick. "Go get that file."

In the Jeep, Brenna pressed her foot to the accelerator, slowing only for curves and turns.

Nick sat next to her, holding tight to the handle above his door. "I take it you've driven on wet, icy roads before."

"I cut my driving teeth on these roads. And, if you remember, I was a street cop before I went to work at the bureau. I know my vehicle's limits."

"I'll take your word for it."

She slid around another curve without batting an eyelash, set on getting to the information Mrs. Keckler had before anyone else learned of its existence.

At the next corner, Nick banged shoulders with her. "Do you think that file will have gone somewhere in the past twenty minutes?"

"I don't want to take any chances. We waited too long to get into Dr. Drummond's files. We can't risk losing the backup."

"Agreed." His grip tightened on the handle as he braced himself for the next turn.

Brenna gained a minor amount of enjoyment by shaking up the tough Nick Tarver. Too many times during this incredibly long day, she'd leaned on this man's broad shoulders. A bad habit she had to curtail or he'd think she was incapable of doing her job and boot her off the team. Because this case impacted her hometown and the people she loved, she had to work it and find the bastard. She chewed on her bottom lip. If only she'd gotten that information from Dr. Drummond sooner, she might already have a lead on the maniac.

"Stop it."

She took her foot off the accelerator. "What?"

"Stop second-guessing yourself."

She resumed her speed. "How did you know?"

"You get that look on your face."

"What look?" She dared a quick glance at his face.

"You bite your lip and frown."

"I do not." She bit her lower lip and frowned. "Okay, so I do. It's not a crime."

"Maybe not, but it makes me nervous when you're driving."

Her lips lifted on the corners. "So I've found a way to test the great Nick Tarver?"

"Don't go there."

"Not to worry. I won't do a three-sixty with you in the car. Besides, we're here." She pulled the Jeep against the curb next to a small cottage tucked beneath a stand of trees. The porch light shone brightly and all the windows were lit like a shopping mall.

"Do you think Mrs. Keckler is a bit unsettled by all this?" Nick asked.

"I would be if I were her." Brenna slid from the Jeep and trudged through the slush and water. Her feet squished in her tennis shoes, reminding her she hadn't had a chance to change since her jog. Her toes were past numb.

The curtain next to the window twitched and Mrs. Keckler's face appeared. Two seconds later she flung the door open. "Oh, thank God you're here!" The woman embraced Brenna like a long-lost relative, her thick arms crushing the air from her lungs. When Mrs. Keckler pulled back, she had tears glistening in her eyes.

"Is anything wrong, Mrs. Keckler?" Brenna asked.

Mrs. Keckler dug into her pocket and pulled out a tissue. "No, it's just all that's happened, what with Dr. Drummond's murder and the building burning. I don't know what to do and frankly, I'm scared."

Tears pricked at Brenna's eyes. This was her hometown, too, and it was terrifying to know there was a killer among the good folk who'd lived here all their lives. She slid an arm around Mrs. Keckler's shoulders. "We'll get him."

"I hope it's soon. I don't know if I can live like this. I've been so worried, I couldn't sit still for a second."

Nick handed her the warrant. "Mrs. Keckler, could we relieve you of that backup disk?"

"Oh, yes, please!" She fished in her other pocket and

yanked out a compact disc. "Here. Take this before I have a heart attack or somebody decides he wants it bad enough to kill me, too."

Nick took the shiny silver disk. "Thank you, ma'am." He nodded at Brenna. "Let's go check this out and see if it'll give us a clue."

"The password's Lulu1948." Mrs. Keckler gave them a sad smile. "The doctor was born in 1948 and she used to have a beagle named Lulu. It helped her to remember. Call me if you have any trouble getting into the files."

Brenna pulled a pen from her purse and jotted down the information. "Thanks, Mrs. Keckler." She said her goodbyes and headed for the Jeep.

Once inside, Nick turned to Brenna. "How long has it been since you've eaten?"

Brenna shot a startled look at him. "I don't remember. This morning, maybe?"

"Let's stop on the way and grab a quick bite. I'm hungry and I bet you haven't eaten since yesterday."

"Now that you mention it, I am a bit hungry." She glanced at the digital clock on the dash where bright green numbers flashed eleven o'clock. "Not that we'll have many choices at this hour. This isn't D.C. or Chicago. In Riverton, restaurants close promptly at nine o'clock on weeknights."

"The chief recommended a bar down the street from the police station that's supposed to have the best buffalo wings this side of the Red River."

Brenna's fingers tightened on the steering wheel. She remembered the place. It was the same place she'd met Victor over two years ago. How did she tell Nick she didn't want to go there because of the bad memories associated with the place?

She didn't, choosing to keep her mouth shut and her eyes on the road. Besides, what were the chances of running into her ex-lover on a Monday night?

With an extreme amount of restraint, she managed to drive past the police station without stopping. Her gut told her to pull into the parking lot and let Nick take her car from there. But then she'd have to explain why she wasn't hungry all of a sudden and she wasn't ready to own up to a bad love affair. Especially not to Nick, who'd turned her inside out with just one kiss.

The Rusty Nail Tavern was located a block off Main Street in the older section of Riverton. The building was one of the Historical Society's landmarks. But for as long as Brenna could recall and, as many owners as it had seen, it had been a bar.

Nick held the door for her to enter the dark interior. "Want to sit in a booth?" he asked.

The last time she'd been in the Rusty Nail was with Victor and he'd always insisted on sitting in a dark corner booth. She'd thought he'd just wanted to be alone with her, until she'd learned he was married. "Let's sit at the bar."

Once they were seated, Nick asked her preference and then ordered the spicy wings.

Brenna risked a look around the room, half expecting to find Victor there. When she didn't see him, she relaxed a little, chuckling beneath her breath at the absurdity of her fear.

She hadn't seen him in two years and even if she did run into him, they were no longer an item. After he'd told her he was married, she'd lost all respect for the man. Of course, he hadn't bothered to tell her until after they'd spent the night in his hotel room.

"If you'll excuse me, I want to wash my hands."

Brenna slid from the stool and made her way down a darkened hallway to the ladies' restroom.

Inside, she stared at herself in the mirror. The dark circles, sweat- and smoke-matted hair didn't help her appearance. She never went out looking this shabby. What must the bartender think of her in such a state? What must Nick think? Not that she cared. She was too tired to care about much. Nevertheless she ran her fingers through her hair and splashed water on her face. Once she felt a little more presentable, she left the bathroom and walked straight into a man in the hallway.

"Excuse me," she said and backed away.

His hands went out to steady her. "Brenna?"

What were the chances—in a town with over fifty-five thousand people—of running into an ex-lover? Brenna's luck hadn't been the best lately. She should have known better than to tempt fate. "Hello, Victor."

Chapter Eight

The blond-haired, blue-eyed man blocking her path looked much the same as he had two years ago, with the addition of a few more wrinkles across the forehead and dark circles beneath the eyes.

"I heard you were back," he said.

"Yup, I'm back." Brenna eased to the side, trying to inch past Victor, all the while wondering what she'd seen in him. Besides being classically good-looking, he was too full of himself with the cocky air of a used-car salesman. Nowhere near the ruggedly handsome self-confidence of a man like Nick Tarver.

Nick.

Great. One of the biggest mistakes in her life had to show up at about the worst time he could manage, and he wasn't moving out of her way. She had two choices— knee him where it counted, or ask him to move. Although her first choice would have been more satisfying, she said, "Victor, if you'll excuse me, I'd like to get by."

"What's your hurry?" He leaned close and brushed a hair from her face, the overpowering scent of cheap whiskey gagging Brenna. "You and I used to be good together. Don't you remember?"

"All I remember is that you lied to me."

"What's a little lie compared to what we had?"

"One night in a motel?" Brenna let go with an un-ladylike snort. "Sorry, it wasn't that memorable."

"You should be thankful I wanted you." Victor's eyes narrowed. "What with your...issues. Good thing we did it with the lights off."

"Better if we hadn't done it at all." She crossed her arms over her chest, reminding herself Victor wasn't worth losing her temper over. "Now move."

"You're just like them all. Holier-than-thou. It's people like you that give women a bad name. Think you're all smarter than us dumb, stupid men." Before Brenna knew what was happening, Victor shoved her against the wall. "You're not smarter than me, you know."

He held her arms so tightly she knew she'd have bruises where his fingers were. And she sure as hell didn't have to put up with this. With a jerk, she kneed him in the groin. When his grip loosened on her arms, she shoved her hands up between them and brought her fists together and down over his head.

Victor crumpled to his knees, moaning.

When Brenna moved to step around him, he grabbed her ankles and yanked her feet out from under her. She crashed to her knees, wincing as they hit the hard tile.

Crawling up her body, Victor straddled her, sneering down into her face. "Bitch."

Brenna spat in his face. "Get off me or I'll scream."

Victor raised his hand to strike her.

Closing her eyes, she struggled to get her hand loose to block the blow, but suddenly Victor's body was hauled off her.

When she opened her eyes, the first thing she noticed was Victor dangling from Nick's very strong arms. "Want to apologize to the lady?" Nick asked, his voice a snarl.

All Victor could do was blink. The fist clenched around his vocal cords cut off any words he might have said.

Nick shoved him to the wall and held his collar tight against his throat. "Get started with your apology."

"I'm sorry, Brenna," Victor muttered.

"That's better." Nick turned to Brenna. "Special Agent Jensen, you want to press charges against this man?"

"No." Her face burned as she climbed to her feet.

Nick scowled at Victor. "I don't like a guy who beats up or takes advantage of women. So don't piss me off." He jerked his hand loose and Victor all but crumpled at his feet.

"I could press charges," Victor said, shooting a look of loathing at Nick and then Brenna.

"I could tell your wife." Brenna climbed to her feet and fixed Victor with a cold, direct stare. "Everything."

Victor's mouth opened, but nothing came out. "This ain't over."

"Wanna bet?" Brenna brushed the dust from her sweatpants, the way she'd brushed him from her life two years ago.

The blond man straightened his collar and ran a hand through his hair, glancing from Brenna to Nick as if they might jump him before he got away. Then with a grunt, he turned and limped away, a little bent at the middle from Brenna's knee connection to the groin.

Brenna watched until Victor left the bar, avoiding any further conversation with Nick, hoping he wouldn't ask what she knew he would.

Once the other man was out of the building, Nick turned to her. "Care to explain?"

"Not really."

"Then humor me and do it anyway."

As her father would say, a good defense was always a good offense. Brenna summoned all the rightful or unjustified indignation she could muster and answered with an attack of her own. "Look, why do I have to tell you anything? You practically know my life history, whereas I know nothing about you."

Before Nick could open his mouth to rebut, Brenna jumped in again. "Not to mention, I'm exhausted and starving." She stopped him with a look and dared him to say anything else about Victor.

"Fair enough." He took her elbow and steered her toward the bar. "I had them bag our wings so we can take them back to the room. After we eat, you can tell me all about the man who was getting the better of you."

"He was not. I was doing fine before you got there."

Nick smiled. "Do you always argue? Or is it your hunger making you so cranky?"

Brenna grabbed the bag of food from the counter. "I'm not answering any more questions until I've had at least six wings and a soda."

"Deal. Then I'll insist on full disclosure."

Despite only three hours of sleep and being knocked on her butt both mentally and physically all in one day, Brenna's feet felt lighter as she walked to her vehicle. Perhaps she was dizzy from low blood sugar. Or maybe it was because Nick Tarver was teasing her.

God forbid she should make the mistake of falling for a man like Nick.

RAIN HAD STARTED FALLING by the time they got back to the hotel room. When she pushed through the suite door, Brenna wasn't as upset about Nick sharing the set of rooms as she had been at first. With the death of Dr. Drummond and the subsequent office burning, she was glad she wasn't alone. Whoever was doing this thought he was smarter than the best that North Dakota and the FBI had to offer.

That he'd felt the need to torch the doctor's office was an indication he might be getting nervous. But they were one up on him. They had the backup disk.

While Nick set the food on the table, Brenna pulled out her laptop and plugged it into the wall.

The scent of spicy chicken wings wafted across the little table in the sitting area. Her stomach rumbled in response. "Wow, that really smells good." She set the laptop on the table and reached into the bag for a messy wing. "You want to pop that disk in?" she said, licking her fingers.

"Sure." He did as she asked, then keyed in the password when prompted. "We're in."

Brenna breathed a sigh and leaned over his shoulder. "Bring up the list of patients."

He clicked on a file named Patient Info and a list of names appeared. "Recognize anyone?"

She ran her finger down the screen and stopped. "That one."

Nick leaned close and read aloud, "Greeley, Victor?" He glanced up at her. "You know him?"

"Yeah, he was the guy we ran into at the bar a few minutes ago." She sat in the chair beside him and took off her wet tennis shoes and socks. "He's a jerk, and a real slimy character, but I'd never peg him as a murderer."

"Got to look at all angles. I'm sure nobody pegged the BTK killer as a murderer, either."

"And we let him go." Brenna popped up from her

seat, pacing barefoot across the carpet. "We need to find him. If he's the killer, he might strike again. Tonight."

NICK NOTED HOW BRENNA TWISTED the hem of her sweat jacket and the way she paced. She was nervous and he wanted to know why. "How do you know him?"

Brenna's face reddened and she turned away.

Interesting. For a moment, he thought she wouldn't answer. When Nick had the next question poised on his lips, Brenna turned and faced him.

"We had an affair a couple years ago."

The announcement hit him in the gut. Not that Brenna was any more than a stranger to him. They'd met less than twenty-four hours ago. Not enough time to form an attachment. And Nick wasn't one to believe in love at first sight. Now, lust was an entirely different matter.

Seeing Victor Greeley straddling Brenna in the bar had been another blow to Nick's control, but he accounted for his reaction as what he'd do if he found any woman being overpowered by a man. Another thought occurred to him and made a cold lump form in his gut. "You said something about telling his wife. Is the guy married now?"

"Yeah. And he was married then."

Nick pushed back from the laptop and stood so fast, the chair fell over backward. Without stopping to set it straight, he strode to the window, pictures of another time playing through his memory like a slow-motion film. He'd arrived home early to surprise his wife, Trish, with the news he'd gotten the job with the FBI. He could still picture himself hurrying through the house to find her and the look on her face when he had.

"Nick?" Trish had called his name. "Nick?"

Only it wasn't Trish calling him now.

He shook his head to pull his mind out of that bedroom where he'd found Trish with a man he'd once trusted. A fellow cop, partner and friend—until he'd climbed into Nick's bed, and between his wife's legs.

"Agent Tarver?" Brenna stood across the room, her arms crossed over her chest, her lips pressed in a hard line. "I'm sorry if that disappoints you. But I can assure you my shortcomings in my personal life don't interfere with my job."

"Huh?"

Color spread from her cheeks to the tips of her ears. "The jerk failed to fill me in on all the little details. I don't normally sleep with married men." Her chin tilted at a defiant angle and she straightened her shoulders as if preparing for his censure.

Nick pushed his hands through his hair and looked at her. Really looked at her. "I believe you."

She stood still for a moment longer before her shoulders relaxed. "Good."

He walked back to the computer and stared down at the screen. "Were there any other names on the list you recognized?"

"I don't know. Let me look again." She had to pass in front of him to get to the laptop. The dark circles beneath her eyes caught his attention.

"Wait." He put his hand out and caught her arm. "You look ready to drop. You can have the shower first. We'll pick up on the rest of this after we get a few hours sleep."

"Are you sure?" She looked up into his eyes. "If something happens to someone tonight, I won't be able to live with myself."

"You'll fall flat on your face if you don't get some

rest. And we won't catch a killer if you're in a hospital from exhaustion."

Her gaze drifted past him to the screen. "I'll agree to a shower, but then I'm going over the rest of the list before I go to sleep."

He frowned, but nodded. She was dedicated, and she had the right to be. This was her hometown. Her family lived here. "I'm going to the vending machine for a soda. You want one?"

"Bottled water for me." She yawned and covered her mouth, her eyes widening. "Guess I'm sleepier than I thought."

"Go on. I'll only be gone a minute."

Brenna was halfway to her room when Nick left the suite. What he needed was another jog around the city to work off the events of the past two days and to drown the memories of his lousy marriage in the runoff from melting snow. But if he left Brenna for more than five minutes he'd be on edge wondering if the killer would make his move.

No, he couldn't get away from his memories any more than he could walk away from one hardheaded yet vulnerable criminal investigator.

On the walk down the hall, he made note of all the stairwells and exits. He had to keep his mind clear and alert for danger. Brenna's life might depend on it.

Armed with a soda and a bottle of water, he returned to the room to hear the shower running in the shared bathroom. He kicked off his damp tennis shoes and pulled off the soaked socks he'd been wearing for the past four hours. With a longing glance at the bathroom, he sank into the chair in front of the laptop and clicked on Victor Greeley.

In the file was basic information—name, age, marital status and reason for visit. Marriage counseling.

Surprise, surprise.

Nick clicked on the last set of notes for a session only a month prior and read, *G.G. expressed suspicion of husband's infidelity. V.G. denied. Body language indicates otherwise. V.G demonstrated open hostility at accusation.*

"So, he's still up to no good," Nick muttered.

"What's that?" Brenna's voice behind him made Nick jump.

"Greeley and his wife were in marriage counseling with Dr. Drummond."

Brenna snorted and bent at the waist to unwrap the towel from her hair. "Like that was going to help. The man doesn't understand the meaning of fidelity." When she straightened, her hair fell in wet lengths around her shoulders, dampening the gray tank top she wore with a pair of navy-blue flannel pajama bottoms.

Without makeup and her hair a mess of tangles, she was still a beautiful woman. "I can see why Greeley would find you attractive. I just can't understand what you saw in him."

Hugging herself around the middle, Brenna rocked back on bare feet. "As he would put it, I have 'issues' of my own."

What kind of issues could she have? Then he remembered her story. "Do your issues have to do with the fire?"

Her lips pursed and she nodded, her gaze finally connecting with his.

"How long were you in the hospital?" he asked.

"A month."

"And the burns?"

Brenna tossed her towel over a chair and answered in what sounded like a conversational tone, "Third degree over thirty percent of my body."

"Greeley was referring to your burn scars, wasn't he?" Nick's hands bunched into fists. "Bastard."

When Brenna's lip slipped between her teeth, Nick reached for her bare shoulders. "All I see is a beautiful woman standing in front of me."

"It's what's beneath the clothes that turns men off." With a shrug, she grimaced and moved away. "It doesn't matter."

"You're dating the wrong men."

She barked a short, nervous laugh. "That's what my sister said."

"You're sister's right."

She spun and walked halfway across the room before she faced him again. "It's easy for you and my sister to say that. But it's not so easy to live with the scars."

"Why?" He stalked across the room and stood toe-to-toe with her.

Brenna backed away. "You have to ask?" She flung her hand to the side. "In a world full of supermodels and perfect people. I'm imperfect."

He lifted her hand and threaded his fingers with hers, liking that hers were small and pale, yet strong and supple. "You seem fine to me."

"Because you haven't seen all of me," she whispered, staring down at where their hands joined.

"Are any of us perfect?" With his thumb he tipped her chin.

As she looked into his eyes, her brows furrowed. "Yes." She tried to jerk free, but Nick refused to let her hand go. "Look at you—perfect hair, perfect skin. You even have perfect eyes."

A smile tugged at the corners of Nick's mouth. So she'd been thinking about him. The idea of Brenna Jensen noticing him warmed his insides—a place that had been cold for too long. Until Special Agent Jensen had shown up, coming home to Riverton to solve a murder. This was her turf. When he left, she'd stay. It was the story of his life, being always on the go. It was also the reason his marriage had failed.

"And I had the perfect marriage, until my divorce. Just because a person's appearance is perfect doesn't make them perfect inside. If I had been perfect, my marriage wouldn't have fallen apart." He dropped her hand and hurried toward his bedroom. "I'll be in the shower. Don't open the door for anyone."

Nick stood in the shower for a long time with the hot spray pelting the stiffened muscles of his neck and shoulders. He knew better than to get involved with a team member. Get in, solve the crime and leave. Period. No long goodbyes, nobody gets hurt. Yet, he could feel it happening and he had to put a stop to it soon.

Then why did he get the feeling he was in line for a lot of hurt in this situation?

Brenna Jensen. Tough, yet vulnerable; all about the job, but always considering the people and town she cared about.

When was the last time Nick felt like any town was home? He had a place in Norfolk, but that was all it was—a place to live. Why hadn't he purchased a house and grown roots? Even when he'd been married, he'd only rented, as if he hadn't expected to stay long. Maybe that was what his wife had figured out before he did. He hadn't been rooted in their relationship. He hadn't had any skin in the game.

He hadn't really loved Trish with that deep committed love that makes a man crazy. The kind of love that makes a guy follow a woman to a godforsaken town in the frozen north because it'll make her happy.

Brenna was the kind of woman who could inspire that kind of love. She deserved that kind of commitment. Not a used-up, rootless FBI agent who'd seen one too many horrors to believe in humanity. For a woman with low self-esteem, she had a boatload of guts and chutzpah.

When the hot water turned tepid, Nick shut off the shower and toweled dry. A clean body and dry clothes went a long way toward reviving him. Now if he could get a few hours sleep, he'd almost feel human.

Slipping into a pair of shorts, he opened the door to the sitting area.

The computer monitor was the only light glowing in the room. Brenna lay slumped over the keyboard.

His heart stuttered as he raced to her side. "Brenna?" Had someone gotten in while he'd been taking a leisurely soak beneath the shower? Fear sliced through him, cutting deep.

Her cheek lay against the keys, her breath blowing a drying strand of hair across her hand. Special Agent Brenna Jensen was fast asleep.

Nick drew in a deep breath and almost laughed out loud. Then he collapsed in the chair beside her and dropped his head into his hands. How could he keep his eye on her at all times? Unless he stayed with Brenna every second of every day, she would remain at risk.

In the meantime, she needed to rest. The stress of driving in a blizzard, finding a body beneath the ice and witnessing a building burning had taken their toll on her.

Nick stood and, without weighing his options, slid an arm beneath her legs and lifted her into his arms.

The scent of herbal shampoo and soap filled his senses. Her sandy-blond hair spread across his chest and arm, the silky strands tickling his skin. He leaned a cheek against the top of her head, giving in to instinct.

Brenna nuzzled closer into the crook of his neck, her mouth touching his skin.

The tender texture of her lips sent his nerve endings into overdrive and Nick sucked in his breath. Jeez, the woman was sexy even while she slept. He held that breath and willed his body not to react, but it was a losing battle. All the blood in his head dove southward, filling his loins, making him tight and needy.

It was a good thing Brenna was asleep. Nick could imagine how pissed she'd be if she could feel the evidence of his arousal. They were strangers, for Pete's sake.

Nick hefted her up a little, marveling at how solid she was. Her thigh muscles were soft but firm beneath the flannel pajamas. His gaze traveled the length of her legs to trim ankles. This tough-as-nails agent's one claim to femininity was her pink toenail polish.

He smiled as he carried her to her room and laid her on the bedspread. Immediately she turned to her side, her hand reaching across the empty bed, a frown gently dipping between her eyes. The tank top did little to disguise the turgid peaks of her breasts.

Like a teenage voyeur, Nick couldn't help himself. He drank his fill of the sight of Special Agent Jensen, the satisfaction he gained far outweighing the guilt. If he wasn't careful, he could fall for this woman. And where would that get him?

Fatigue pulled at his eyelids, but Nick couldn't leave her in here and he didn't feel like sleeping on the couch in the sitting room. Too tired to care about consequences, he lay down beside her, determined to leave the bed before she awoke the next morning. What she didn't know couldn't hurt him.

Chapter Nine

The sound of an electronic chirp stirred Brenna from a wonderful dream in which a strong, sexy man held her throughout the night, keeping the bad guys away.

Faint fingers of light slipped in the sides of the curtains, letting morning inch its way into a room she didn't recognize at first. When the electronic chirping persisted, Brenna rolled to her back, memories of all that had occurred over the past few days flooding her mind. Where was that sexy stranger of her dream to rescue her from this nightmare?

"About time you got up." Nick strolled into her room, wiping residual shaving cream from his chin with a hand towel.

"What time is it?" she croaked.

"Six-thirty." He sat at the edge of her bed. "That was Melissa. She's at the station going through the newspaper files."

How could he look so awake and perky, not to mention incredibly sexy with his bare chest and clean-shaven chin? She, on the other hand, probably had a terrible case of bed hair. Brenna wanted to slide farther under the sheets. "Could you call her back and tell her to look for any articles pertaining to the victims?"

"Sure. I'm done in the bathroom. It's all yours."

"Thanks." When she slid out of the bed, she noted that both pillows were dented. Had her dream been more than a dream? Her heart skipped into overdrive as she gathered toiletries and clean clothes.

Nick stared out the window, his cell phone pressed to his ear.

Not like Brenna would ask him if he'd slept with her. A girl should know these things, not guess or ask. For that matter, she didn't recall getting herself to bed. She glanced at the laptop. The last thing she remembered was going over the list of names in the files.

With a glance her way, he nodded then turned back to his conversation. "Hey, Mel, while you're looking for articles on arson, Special Agent Jensen wants you to look through the archives for any reference to our victims. Apparently, one of them was in the news recently. Pull anything you find. We'll be there in forty-five minutes."

Brenna shrugged aside her dream and trudged into the bathroom to repair her face and hair and scrape the layer of morning breath off her teeth and tongue. Ten minutes later, she stepped out from the bathroom.

With her hair pulled back into a neat ponytail, and wearing black jeans and a black pullover sweater, she felt more presentable and less the tumbled bed head. Not that she cared what Nick Tarver thought. They were here for the job, nothing else.

Heading straight for the coffeemaker, she stopped to glance at the notes she'd made prior to falling asleep. Some of them she could read, others were scribbled and indecipherable. Her eyes had crossed with fatigue before she'd gotten halfway down the list of patients.

But there was a star next to one of them. She leaned

close. Klaus. Her sister's married name. There were probably a dozen or more Klauses in the German-Scandinavian town of Riverton. The name was as common as Smith or Jones in English.

"Anything interesting?"

Brenna jumped and fell back against a hard chest.

Nick's strong arms came around her. "Sorry. I didn't mean to startle you." His voice rumbled against her ear and the tantalizing scent of aftershave blended with coffee-flavored breath.

A gulp of air caught in her throat. These were the same arms that had held her yesterday when she'd thought she'd fall apart, and they felt like the same arms that had held her in her dreams. Her world rocked and it took a full five seconds before she could pull herself together and out of Agent Tarver's grasp.

"Interesting? No, not yet." And really, she hadn't found anything that jumped out. "This'll take time. We don't really know who or what we're looking for."

"I'd start with any names you might recognize. The killer knows you."

"Yeah, but there's no guarantee I know him."

"True." He nodded at the laptop. "You want to bring that with us to the station?"

"You betcha. I have a lot more work to do and I'm not letting that disk go up in smoke like Dr. Drummond's office before I get a thorough look." As Brenna gathered her computer and slid her arms into her jacket, she summoned the courage to say, "You know, I don't remember getting from the computer to my bed last night. I must have been really sleepy." There. If that wasn't fishing for answers, she didn't know what was.

"Yeah, you must have been really tired." He headed for the door, no expression whatsoever on his face.

What was that supposed to mean? Did he see her go to bed or not? Brenna counted it off as not and breathed a sigh of relief. She'd hate to think he'd picked her up and carried her into her room while she'd slept like a baby. Not that he would, since it wasn't part of his job.

Without waiting for Brenna, Nick pulled the door open and walked out first. "By the way, you snore."

"What?" Her short-lived relief kicked up into a swarm of butterflies in her stomach.

"You heard me." He didn't slow down, just kept walking.

Brenna hurried to catch up, all her concerns about this stranger burbling up inside.

Snore?

"I do not."

"HEY, BOSS, AGENT JENSEN." Paul climbed out of his car at the same time as Nick and Brenna.

"Find anything at the doctor's office?" Nick didn't wait for his response as he hurried toward the station.

"Fire chief said there was some kind of electrical device in the plug with the computer. And, get this." Paul opened the door for them. "It triggered a short in the circuit that started the fire."

Nick stopped short. "Sounds like our guy knows a little about electronics." Interesting. He glanced at Brenna.

"I'll add that to the list of things to look for in that patient file. I'm not sure the doctor would have made note of something like 'not afraid to use knowledge of electricity to torch buildings,' but you never know." Brenna stepped around him and continued down the hall to the war room.

Nick followed her, liking the way her black jeans swayed side to side. Familiarity with the muscles beneath didn't help his concentration. She'd probably be furious if she knew he'd carried her to bed last night. Not to mention having slept most of the night with her curled up against him.

No, Agent Jensen would not be happy. But Nick had slept a whole lot better knowing she was in the same room. Now, if he could just get the curve of her hips off his mind and get back to the business of finding one psychotic murderer.

"Nick, you gotta check this out," Melissa called from the computer in the corner.

Nick, Paul and Brenna gathered behind Melissa and stared at the screen.

"I didn't find any recent arson cases, but I found something more interesting. I did like you asked and searched on the victims' names, starting with Dr. Gomez. Look at this." Melissa clicked a button and the screen displayed an online newspaper article with a picture of a smiling Dr. Gomez. The header read Riverton Women In The News.

Nick's stomach clenched. "Any clues in the article?"

"None that I could tell, but wait, there's more." Melissa rolled the mouse over a saved Web-site icon and clicked. A picture of Dr. Drummond flashed onto the screen. "You see what I'm seeing? Riverton Women In The News."

Brenna leaned closer, her face pale and her eyes intent on the picture. "You think he's targeting these women because they were in the news?"

"I don't know, but it looks awfully suspicious." She looked back at Nick.

"What about Michelle Carmichael?" Paul asked.

"She's in there, too, a week after Gomez." Melissa clicked and Carmichael's photo appeared. "It gets worse."

Nick was almost afraid to ask. "What do you mean?"

She clicked on another icon and a short list of names appeared with dates next to them. "These are the other articles under the same series." She clicked again and Brenna's picture appeared.

Nick's chest tightened and his glance shot to Brenna.

With her bottom lip caught between her teeth, she lifted her gaze to his.

"Sorry, Brenna." Melissa reached out and touched her arm.

"For what?" Brenna attempted a smile. "This is probably the biggest break we've had yet. Good job." She leaned close to the screen. "Who are the others?"

Before she could answer, Chief Burkholder walked in. "I'm glad you all are here."

"What's wrong, Chief?" Brenna asked.

"Might be better to ask what's right." He sighed and held out another evidence bag. "Two things. You got another letter, Brenna."

The letter was one, but not what had the chief worked up. "What else?" Nick asked.

"We had another woman go missing last night."

Heat of anger spread through Nick's body like liquid silver and he clenched his hand to keep from slamming a fist into the wall. "Damn."

Brenna raced from the room and returned with gloves and a mask. "Let's look at that letter." She pulled on the gloves and mask and reached for the evidence bag.

Inside, the letter looked like the previous ones—innocuous and so normal anyone could have sent it from anywhere in the city. As she took the knife Paul proffered, a chill skittered down her spine. What horrible things would he say this time? With a deep breath, she glanced up at Nick.

"Want me to do it?"

"No." *I want you to hold me again.* The only place she'd felt safe in the past forty-eight hours was in Agent Nick Tarver's arms. The unbidden thought jolted Brenna back to reality and the room full of expectant law-enforcement personnel. She dug the knife into the end of the envelope and ripped it open.

Her hands trembling, Brenna removed the sheet and read, "'Think you're smart? But I know more. Won't be long to number four.'" Brenna's face paled and she shook her head. "He's going to kill her if he hasn't already."

Nick's gut clenched into a hard knot.

"Who was the latest missing person?" Melissa asked.

The chief walked to the whiteboard and lifted a marker. "Willa Stinson, a local chemist at the Biolab."

"Damn." Melissa shook her head, staring at the computer screen. "Look at this."

She clicked the mouse and Willa Stinson's face appeared in the Riverton Women In The News column. "If you follow the dates of the articles, he's moving in order of appearance. And there have been two more articles since Willa's."

"Oh my God." Brenna sank into the seat beside Melissa. "Who's next?"

She clicked the next article in the list and a young woman's face appeared. "Robin Rutledge, senior at Riverton University, and all around perfect student."

"He's going to kill a kid." Paul's mouth twisted into a snarl. "The bastard."

"No, he's not." Nick banged his fist on the desk and the computer rocked. "We're going to put twenty-four-hour protection on the girl and find the son of a bitch before he hurts anyone else."

"I'll assign a patrol to the girl." Chief Burkholder hurried from the room.

"Paul, get out there and interview everyone in Ms. Stinson's neighborhood. Note anything, even the most minute and trivial recollection. Ask them if they'd seen anyone coming, going, lurking or casually strolling past the woman's house in the last week. And find out where Victor Greeley went after he left the Rusty Nail last night."

"Who's he?" Paul asked.

"He's one of the guys in Dr. Drummond's files. We ran into him at the bar and grill around the corner." Nick's gaze sought Brenna's.

Hers was intent, waiting. Did she think he'd tell the others all about the little scuffle? He broke eye contact a little disappointed she didn't trust him. "Melissa, work with the chief to warn Robin Rutledge. I don't want to lose another woman to this psycho."

"Yes, sir." She went back to the computer and clicked several keys. As the printer beside her engaged and several sheets of paper emerged, Melissa turned back to Nick, her gaze darting from him to Brenna. "Something else you need to know." She lifted a sheet and crossed the room to hand it to Nick. "Special Agent Brenna Jensen is the last one in the group of articles." Her lips twisted. "Sorry, Brenna."

"Don't sweat it. I'm not. We knew I was in his cross-hairs from day one." Her chin tipped up. "I'm not running scared from him. I'm going to work."

Nick almost smiled at her back as she walked to her laptop.

"The lady has spunk," Melissa murmured.

"Yes, she does." And Nick was getting too familiar

with it, along with those smooth curves, tight muscles and—

An elbow to his gut made Nick grunt.

"Oops, sorry," Melissa said, her look implying anything but an apology. "Careful, Nick. She's likely to crack that I'm-all-about-the-case veneer. How long has it been since Trish?"

Nick frowned. "None of your business."

"Still, it's about time you thawed a little and gave yourself another chance."

He tore his gaze from Agent Jensen and straightened. "It's not in the job description."

"Sometimes you have to say 'what the hell' and go with your gut."

Nick rubbed his belly where Melissa had elbowed him. He couldn't remember when his gut had been more knotted and he had a feeling it all had to do with one North Dakota criminal investigator. But he wasn't ready to admit to that.

Melissa dropped into the swivel chair. "What's wrong, Nick? Worried you'll fall like a ton of bricks?"

"Shut up, Melissa."

She smiled and turned to the computer. "Just calling it like I see it."

"Stick to the work, Bradley. You're not ready for a career in counseling."

"Chicken." Her lips curled in a knowing smile.

Nick turned his back on her and hurried from the room. He needed coffee. Lots of coffee.

THE FILES WERE CRYPTIC and Brenna had difficulty deciphering some of Dr. Drummond's notes, but with a few calls to Mrs. Keckler, she learned enough to get a picture of each patient's concerns and diagnosis.

One by one she worked through the male names first, scanning for any clue. She didn't know what she was looking for, but maybe something would jump out.

When Brenna got to Klaus, she opened the file. The notes indicated a couple seeking marriage counseling. Brenna stopped when she got to the couple's names— Stanley and Alice Klaus.

Brenna sat up straighter. Could it be? Her sister and brother-in-law had the perfect marriage. Why would they have sought counseling? No, surely this troubled couple was another by the same name. She clicked on the address to be sure, her hand shaking as she moved the mouse—214 West Nodak Street. Her sister's home.

Wow. Her sister's perfect marriage wasn't so perfect after all.

Instead of being elated by this little piece of information, she felt her stomach roil as if it fought to digest a lump of clay. All these years, her mother had told her Alice's marriage was perfect and it wasn't. Alice was human like Brenna. Instead of vindicating her, the knowledge led to another conundrum. What did Brenna do with this information? She didn't like prying into her sister's troubles, but if Alice was having difficulties, maybe she needed her sister's help, a shoulder to lean on.

How could she bring up the subject with her sister if she was never supposed to know anything was wrong? Patient confidentiality was sacred and her sister's marriage had nothing to do with the murder case.

Still…

Brenna glanced over the notes, guilt weighing like a lead blanket on her chest. She had no right to pry into her sister's private life.

She closed the file and moved to the next one.

After several hours poring over cryptic notes and

psychiatric jargon, she had only two names that stood out. Victor Greeley and Jason Conlin. Both had been Dr. Drummond's patients; both had notes in their files about potential violence; and both rang a bell with Brenna.

She found Nick in Chief Burkholder's office using the computer. "I have a couple names we should check out."

"Okay, shoot." He stood and stretched. The circles under his eyes were more pronounced than earlier this morning. Nick Tarver hadn't gotten much sleep last night and, the way things were going, wouldn't until they solved this case.

Brenna had a sudden urge to reach out and smooth the lines across his brow, but resisted. "As you know, Victor's wife accused him of going out every night and fooling around on her. However, she also complained of the occasional smacking around."

"So your friend likes to hit other women, not just you?" Nick asked.

Brenna frowned and started to say something.

But Nick went on, "Paul reported in twenty minutes ago. He said Victor didn't go straight home last night, and he doesn't have any witnesses who can vouch for him. Bears looking into. Who else?"

"Bart Olsen was not in the database, but he's been locked up for the past twenty-four hours."

"I think that rules him out. With our chemist's disappearance last night, that puts Bart in the clear. No doubt he's been released."

"Then there's a young man, Jason Conlin. He knows Robin Rutledge. Seems he beat up on her once during college. I also had a run-in with him a couple years ago when I pulled him over for DUI. Definitely another worth looking into."

"I'll have Paul and Melissa take Jason. You and I are going after Victor. Are you up to a little stakeout?"

"On Victor?"

He nodded.

Victor, the lying sleazebag? "You betcha."

Chapter Ten

A champagne-colored Suburban pulled up as Nick and Brenna stepped out into the parking lot. Nick moved in front of Brenna, his hand reaching for his gun in the shoulder holster beneath his jacket.

Brenna laid a hand on his arm and smiled. "I don't think I'd shoot her. She's the president of the PTA."

The window slid down and a woman with a mild resemblance to Brenna smiled and waved. "Brenna! I'm so glad I caught you."

"Alice, what's up?" Brenna stepped around Nick and stood by the vehicle.

"I should be asking you that." Alice glanced over Brenna's shoulder with raised eyebrows. "Who's the hunk?"

Nick enjoyed Brenna's visible discomfort at the woman's comment and fought to keep a smile from lifting the corners of his mouth.

"This is Agent Nick Tarver." She turned to Nick, her brow twisted into a wry frown. "Agent Tarver, my sister, Alice Klaus."

"It's a pleasure, Ms. Klaus." He held her hand briefly and then dropped it.

With a down-sweep of her long lashes, Alice grinned. "Now I see why you can't take time out to come by."

"I can't come by because we're trying to solve a murder and several kidnappings." Brenna's tone was flat.

Alice's smile sank. "I know. Terrible, isn't it? I was just trying to get your goat."

With a twisted grin, Brenna shrugged. "Consider it gotten."

"I dropped by to see if you'd like to come for dinner tomorrow night. Stan and I would love to have you over."

Brenna shifted from one foot to the other, apparently unaware she stood in a rather large slushy puddle.

Nick couldn't help wondering why her sister made her nervous.

"Maybe after we solve the case," Brenna said.

Alice was undeterred. "You have to eat sometime, so why not at my house? You don't have to stay long. And I understand about the case and all." Her face brightened. "Hey, Stan knows loads of people from all the business he does in town. Maybe he could help. I'll even make sure he comes home on time, for once, so he'll be there."

"I'll think about it," Brenna said. "But my number-one concern is the job."

"Well, I'll cook and if you show, great. If you don't, I'll understand." She reached out and squeezed Brenna's shoulder. "Lord knows, I don't feel safe with that guy loose on our streets."

"Exactly." Brenna's shoulders straightened. "We have to catch him soon."

Alice's lips twisted. "With all the scare about the women missing, I didn't even realize the river's nearing flood stage. I'm on my way to a meeting at the church. They're organizing sandbag teams to shore up the levy on River Road."

"Sandbag teams? Is it that bad?" Nick asked.

Alice shrugged. "There's still plenty of snow on the ground and the weather is getting warmer."

"Just like in ninety-seven." Brenna glanced at Nick. "We had a major flood on the Red River. Shut the city down for months."

"But it hasn't been raining," Nick said.

"All it takes is a bumper snowfall year and a quick melt." Brenna turned to her sister. "Where are the boys?"

"Stan's got them until after the meeting. He took off early since he was out on a troubleshooting call last night. Such is the life of a man who owns his own business. If he can't get someone else to do the work, he ends up doing it himself." Alice waved and smiled at Nick. "Nice to meet you, Nick. When Brenna comes to dinner, please come with her. Our mother would love that." She winked at Brenna and drove away.

Brenna's ears turned red and she chewed on her lower lip. "Don't mind my sister. She likes to push my buttons."

"She does it well." As he headed for his rental car, Nick fought that grin. "We'll take mine."

Brenna climbed in, staring straight ahead.

"Your sister younger?" he asked.

"No." Short, to the point and uncommunicative. When Brenna Jensen didn't want to talk about something, she didn't.

To Nick, her silence was a challenge. But first they needed food to carry them through what looked like a long night on stakeout.

Clouds hung low over the city, holding in the daytime heat and keeping the ground from refreezing during the night. Cold air had long since seeped through the windows and floorboards, and Brenna's breath came out in tiny puffs of fog.

"Chief Burkholder said you're up for a job with the Minnesota Criminal Investigation Division." Nick stared through the windshield at Victor Greeley's home several doors down from where they sat.

The question caught Brenna off guard and she glanced up to search Nick's face in the dim lighting from the corner streetlamp. They'd been sitting in the dark for the past two hours. Brenna rubbed her hands together to keep them warm. "Yeah, I am."

"What can you do there that you can't do in North Dakota?"

Brenna glanced out the window. She'd asked herself that question countless times and it all boiled down to the simple fact that she wanted to get farther away from home. "North Dakota usually isn't overrun with crime and criminals. I guess I was looking for more of a challenge."

Nick shook his head. "Doesn't make sense for someone who clearly loves her hometown."

"I love it here, but I don't want to live here."

"Because of Greeley?"

"Not just." She twisted her fingers around her seat belt. "I love my family, but they drive me nuts."

"I can relate. My brothers and I were always in competition growing up. When we all went into law enforcement, it didn't stop." He laughed. "A little competition was good in some cases, but a lot could get in the way."

"Exactly. Besides, I'm not my sister."

"So she's the older one?"

"Older, prettier, more popular and has everything. A husband who supports her, a house in a good neighborhood and two wonderful children."

"Are you jealous of her?"

"No." She wasn't jealous of her sister and she'd never consider a man like Stan as husband material. In fact, she'd been the only one who didn't like him.

"Then what's your problem?"

"My mother." Once she said it, the bad taste of guilt burned the back of her throat. Her mother couldn't help her disease or the things she said. But the remarks hurt, nonetheless.

"Ahhh." Nick nodded as if he could see inside her head.

The thought didn't make Brenna any more comfortable. "What do you mean by 'ahhh'?"

His lips twisted into a crooked grin. "I have a meddling mother, too. Let me guess, she thinks you should have it as good as your sister and every time you're with her she asks why you aren't married."

"Yeah." The man truly could read her mind. But why was she telling him her secrets? What was it about Nick Tarver that made her want to bare her soul?

"And is that what you want?"

Was that what she wanted? Did she envy her sister's ideal life? "Someday." Then again, her sister's life wasn't so wonderful if she'd found the need to go to a marriage counselor.

"In the meantime you like chasing bad guys."

"Right." She turned in her seat and pinned him with her own stare. "What about you, Mr. I'm-all-about-the-job Tarver? Did your divorce turn you against having a wife, a house in the suburbs and two-point-five children?"

"Hey, this wasn't about me." He held up his hands as if to ward off her attack.

Good, Brenna wanted him on the defensive after

putting her through her paces for the past four minutes. "You've been grilling me. Now it's my turn."

"Shouldn't we be watching for Greeley?" Nick asked, pointing toward the large white-sided house with the black shutters.

"Well? What about it, Tarver?" She crossed her arms over her chest and waited. At first she didn't think he'd answer.

Nick sighed, running his finger down the curve of the steering wheel. "I had all that, minus the two-point-five kids."

"And you can't have it again?"

"I had a wife, an apartment and I thought I had a good marriage." His jaw tightened, the only display of emotion reflected in the light from the dash.

"But…?"

"Like you said, I was all about the job. Home late every night, away on assignments too often… You know the drill."

"Didn't your wife know about your work before you married her?"

He snorted. "I guess not."

Brenna already felt like a heel for prying, but she couldn't help asking, "So she left you?"

"No, I left her."

His admission was not what Brenna had expected. She sat forward. "Why?"

Nick glanced her way. "I left her after I caught her in my bed with my partner."

"Oh." She clapped a hand over her mouth. She'd certainly opened a can of worms. "I'm sorry. I shouldn't have pushed you into that."

With a shrug, he looked back out the window. "It's okay. That was two years ago. I'm over it."

Brenna doubted that.

By the tone of his voice and the way he didn't meet her eyes when he spoke the words, Agent Nick Tarver wasn't over his wife's betrayal.

Then another thought occurred to Brenna. "And I slept with a married man," she said. "I guess that makes me as bad as her."

Nick shook his head and turned to look at her. "No, Brenna. You were duped. I don't see it the same at all."

"Whew!" She slid a hand over her forehead. "I'm glad of that. Can't imagine you having a lower opinion of me than you already did."

His emerald-green eyes flashed in the little light shining through the window. "I don't think bad of you at all. On the contrary, I think—"

Brenna wouldn't find out what he thought because a car backed out of Victor Greeley's driveway. "He's on the move."

Nick shoved the gear into Drive and followed at a distance with his headlights off for several blocks until Victor pulled onto Lincoln Street heading south. Out in traffic, Nick switched his lights on and blended with the surrounding vehicles, keeping a car between them and Victor at all times.

They followed him through town and across the interstate, where Victor pulled into a trailer park.

"We're on foot from here." Nick parked the car across from the trailer park in an auto-body repair lot.

The cold night air had a bite, but not enough to freeze the adrenaline coursing through Brenna's veins. She followed Nick across the street and ducked between the mobile homes with their picket fences half-buried in dirty snow. The going was wet and sloppy and at times treacherous.

Victor's car was parked near the rear of a dull gray mobile home with an old barbecue grill listing to the side on the tiny wooden porch. Lights shone through the bent slats of window blinds that had seen better days.

"Have the station run a scan on who lives at this address," Nick said.

Brenna slid back the way she'd come until she stood several trailer houses away and out of hearing distance. Then she opened her cell phone, hit the speed dial for the Riverton Police Department and relayed her request.

As quickly as she'd gone, she hurried back. Nick stood on a concrete block, peering through the blinds to the little room behind.

"What are they doing?" she whispered.

"He's doing a lot of fooling around and she's giggling."

"Think he'll hurt her?" She danced around in the slush, wishing Nick would climb down from the block so she could get a look.

"I don't think so. If this girl is one of the women on the hit list, I say we go in."

"Let me have a look to see if I know her."

"It's all yours." But when he stepped off the block, it tilted to the side and he crashed into Brenna, bumping her into a half-melted bank of snow and ice. Nick struggled to keep his feet beneath him, but the slick ice proved his undoing.

Brenna braced herself for his landing. On her.

Nick's chest hit hers, knocking the wind out of her lungs and keeping it out as he lay on top of her from shoulder to toe. When he finally moved, Brenna lay in stunned silence, as much stunned by the blow to her body as by the sensation of having Nick Tarver lying on top of her.

He leaned up on his arms. "Are you all right?"

No, she wasn't. The gorgeously perfect Agent Tarver was practically lying all over her. She couldn't breathe, even with him off her, and she didn't want him to move. Hell, no, she wasn't all right! "Yes…yes, I'm fine," she managed to say.

As Nick rolled to his side, his butt hit the cold, wet slush for only a second before he sprang to his feet. "Give me your hand."

Without hesitation, Brenna responded to his command and stuck her hand out.

When her palm hit his, he jerked her to her feet and into his arms. "I'm sorry. You must be freezing."

Liking the feeling of his arms around her too much, she couldn't think straight.

A loud bang sounded from inside the trailer and the girl inside screamed.

Brenna ducked into a crouching position. "Gunfire?"

A giggle sounded from within, followed by a male voice.

Shaking her head, Brenna jumped up onto the concrete block and, standing on her tiptoes, stared through the blinds.

Victor Greeley and a woman Brenna recognized stood with a bottle between them as he poured liquid into two glasses.

"Get down." Nick caught her around the waist and pulled her off the brick and back into his arms. "You want to get killed?"

The feel of his arms around her could be addictive, if she didn't get her mind back on her work. "Only way I'll be killed by one of them is if I get hit by the cork."

An Important Message from the Editors

Dear Reader,

Because you've chosen to read one of our fine romance novels, we'd like to say "thank you!" And, as a **special** way to thank you, we've selected <u>two more</u> of the books you love so well **plus** two exciting Mystery Gifts to send you — absolutely <u>FREE</u>!

Please enjoy them with our compliments...

Pam Powers

Lift here

Peel off seal and place inside...

How to validate your Editor's "Thank You" FREE GIFTS

1. Peel off gift seal from front cover. Place it in space provided at right. This automatically entitles you to receive 2 FREE BOOKS and 2 FREE mystery gifts.

2. Send back this card and you'll get 2 new Harlequin *Intrigue®* novels. These books have a cover price of $4.99 or more each in the U.S. and $5.99 or more each in Canada, but they are yours to keep absolutely free.

3. There's no catch. You're under no obligation to buy anything. We charge nothing—ZERO—for your first shipment. And you don't have to make any minimum number of purchases— not even one!

4. The fact is, thousands of readers enjoy receiving their books by mail from The Harlequin Reader Service®. They enjoy the convenience of home delivery...they like getting the best new novels at discount prices BEFORE they're available in stores... and they love their Reader to Reader subscriber newsletter featuring author news, special book offers, book reviews and much more!

5. We hope that after receiving your free books you'll want to remain a subscriber. But the choice is yours— to continue or cancel, any time at all! So why not take us up on our invitation, with no risk of any kind. You'll be glad you did!

GET TWO *Free* MYSTERY GIFTS...

SURPRISE MYSTERY GIFTS COULD BE YOURS **FREE** AS A SPECIAL "THANK YOU" FROM THE EDITORS

DETACH AND MAIL CARD TODAY!

Yes! I have placed my

Editor's "Thank You" seal in the space provided at right. Please send me 2 free books and 2 free mystery gifts. I understand I am under no obligation to purchase any books, as explained on the back and on the opposite page.

382 HDL EFVS   **182 HDL EFZS**

FIRST NAME	LAST NAME

ADDRESS

APT.#   CITY

STATE/PROV.   ZIP/POSTAL CODE

(H-I-08/06)

Thank You!

Accepting your 2 free books and 2 free mystery gifts places you under no obligation to buy anything. You may keep the books and gifts and return the shipping statement marked "cancel." If you do not cancel, about a month later we'll send you 6 additional books and bill you just $4.24 each in the U.S., or $4.99 each in Canada, plus 25¢ shipping & handling per book and applicable taxes if any.* That's the complete price and — compared to cover prices starting from $4.99 each in the U.S. and $5.99 each in Canada — it's quite a bargain! You may cancel at any time, but if you choose to continue, every month we'll send you 6 more books, which you may either purchase at the discount price or return to us and cancel your subscription.

*Terms and prices subject to change without notice. Sales tax applicable in N.Y. Canadian residents will be charged applicable provincial taxes and GST. All orders subject to approval. Credit or debit balances in a customer's account(s) may be offset by any other outstanding balance owed by or to the customer. Please allow 4 to 6 weeks for delivery.

She didn't add that he could let her go now. She liked how warm he was compared to her wet clothing. Then her phone vibrated against her hip.

Nick dropped his arms and stepped away, running his hand through his hair.

On the third vibration, Brenna flipped open her cell phone and answered in little more than a whisper, "Yes?"

"This is Sergeant Putnam at the station. That address you asked for?"

"Let me guess…Greta Farley?"

"That's right. Guess you didn't need us after all."

On the contrary, the call had saved her from Nick Tarver's arms for the second time in so many minutes. "Thanks, Sergeant." She closed the phone and brushed the slush from her pants, the cold and dampness sinking through her skin to her bones. A shiver shook her frame.

Nick's brow furrowed. "Was Greta Farley one of the women on the list?"

"No."

"But you know her."

"Yes. I went to high school with her. Let's just say, she had a reputation." She glanced toward the trailer that was rocking now.

"Looks like she still does." Nick grinned. "Think we should stick it out?"

"I think we should have a cop keep an eye on Victor, but I wouldn't bet my paycheck on Greta being a target for the killer."

"Why not?" Nick asked.

"Her reputation wasn't for her intelligence. And she surely wasn't on the Who's Who of Riverton Women."

"Then come on." He brushed the slush from his own pants. "Let's get back to the hotel and out of these clothes. We can check in with Paul and Melissa and see if they've come up with anything on Jason Conlin."

"Sounds like a plan." She looked forward to a hot shower and warm, dry clothes.

A loud thump sounded from the trailer, stopping Brenna in her tracks. She locked gazes with Nick.

A giggle erupted and the little mobile home rocked again.

That was Victor, up to his old tricks. Glad she was over the creep, Brenna realized she'd never been in love with him. The more she thought about it, the more she admitted to herself she'd been in love with the idea of being loved.

She followed Nick out of the trailer park and back to the car, enjoying the view from behind. Here was a man who carried himself proudly and admitted when he was wrong in a relationship. He'd never stoop to sneaking around, never betray the woman he loved.

What would it be like to be loved by Nick Tarver?

Brenna's breath caught in her chest. *Get those notions out of your mind right now, girl.* Nick Tarver would never look at her any differently than he did Melissa or Paul. She was only a part of the team, nothing more.

Brenna drew in a deep breath and climbed into the car next to Nick, suddenly shy and too aware of his physical attributes and her shortcomings.

Would a man like Nick look past her imperfections to the person beneath the scars? She shook her head. *Why set yourself up for disappointment?* As Victor had put it, she wasn't even pretty.

"You're doing it again."

Brenna jumped. Then she took a deep breath and asked as casually as she could manage, "Doing what?"

"That lip-biting thing. What are you second-guessing now?"

As if she'd tell him! How pathetic would that be? Poor little Brenna Jensen mooning over handsome FBI Agent Tarver. As if she had a snowball's chance with him. "I was just trying to think of what we might have missed."

"In what?"

"The patient files, the notes, a connection to the women." She was getting really good at dodging her feelings. The case was more important anyway. *Stay on track, Brenna.*

"All the women were in the newspaper lately so the guy obviously gets the newspaper."

"Or reads the online copy. Either way, he reads the paper along with probably every other adult male in Riverton. That should narrow it down to about twenty thousand." Brenna tapped a finger to her lip. "Victor said something about me not being as smart as he is. He said it twice. I just can't remember anyone being angry at me for being smarter than them."

"Anyone you put behind bars would be."

"Yes, but we've already gone through that list. Unless we missed someone." Brenna banged her fist into her palm. "We have to nail this guy. I can't stand the thought of another woman murdered while we chase empty leads."

IT WAS WELL AFTER MIDNIGHT when they reached the hotel suite, and Nick was exhausted, but he let Brenna have the first shower. "I'm hitting the snack machine. Want anything?"

"No, I'm good. I just want a hot shower and warm clothes." Her body trembled as if to emphasize her point.

"Take your time."

Fifteen minutes later, and several trips up and down the stairs and halls, Nick returned to the room.

Brenna was out of the bathroom and back in her room. She stood by her queen-size bed, tugging a brush through her long, wet hair. "It's all yours. I'm going to get some sleep."

Something about that soft gray tank top and the navy-blue flannel pajamas that bunched at her feet because they were too long had Nick's heart racing behind his ribs. Or maybe it was the vulnerability in her eyes, or the way she'd coaxed Dean Helmke into talking with them.

Despite his cold, wet clothing, heat rose from his body. The thought of a hot shower dwindled into the need for a cold one to keep the testosterone in check.

Brenna reached back with the brush to untangle the back of her hair and, in the process, the tank top stretched tightly over her breasts.

Nick picked that moment to beat a hasty retreat to the bathroom and a lukewarm shower. Last night he'd made the error of sleeping with Brenna, unbeknownst to her. He couldn't repeat the same mistake.

Could he? And get away with it?

Did she even have a clue he found her desirable? Probably not and he'd better leave well enough alone. As a member of his team, she was off-limits.

Nick stripped to the skin and stepped beneath the shower spray, willing his body to relax and his desire to abate.

By the time he shut the water off, he had the temperature to refrigerator cool. No amount of mental flaying helped; only the shock to his system could tame his erection.

Shivering, he toweled dry and slipped into boxers, preferring to sleep naked but making this one concession to his roommate's sensitivities. Hopefully, Brenna would be sound asleep and he could convince his body to loosen up enough to allow him a little of that elusive energy restoration called sleep.

Only the light over the computer in the sitting area remained on when Nick made his rounds. Brenna had thrown the bolt on the door and the safety latch over that. All the windows were secure in Nick's room and the sitting area. Which left Brenna's room.

He'd saved her room for last to make sure she was asleep before he slipped in and checked the windows.

Brenna lay on her back in the big bed, her face pale in the muted light from the other room. Her chest rose and fell in slow, even breaths. Blond hair spilled out across the pillow in a fan of golden silk, like an angel's halo.

Nick reached out to touch the fine strands and as he did, she shifted, rolling onto her side and over his hand, trapping him.

Great, now all he needed was for her to wake up and find him taking advantage of her in her sleep. Nick tugged at his hand, easing it from beneath her velvety soft cheek. As he slipped it past her mouth, she pressed a kiss against his fingers.

That tender touch to the sensitive tips of his fingers shot a bolt of lightning through his body and he stood shaken in the shadows. This woman, without even being aware of it, had taken him from numb feelings to full-blown sensations in just two nights. And the thought of her being a target of a psychopathic killer made Nick's gut clench.

Dare he go back to his room and sleep with the very

slim chance of a killer sneaking into her room and doing to her what he'd done to Dr. Drummond?

As if she were clued into his internal dilemma, Brenna rolled to her back again, her head tossing from side to side. A low moan escaped her lips and her fingers clenched the blanket's edge. Was she having a nightmare about the killer?

Torn between leaving her to sleep it off and the desire to soothe her fears away, Nick stood in the shadows and waited for the dream to end. But the longer Nick waited, the more agitated Brenna grew. Her forehead creased in a deep frown and her mouth formed soundless words.

Nick almost left the room, guilt nudging him toward the door. He had no right to watch her while she slept. Then he reminded himself he had a responsibility to protect her and he stopped.

About that time, Brenna sat up straight in bed and sobbed in ragged, strangled breaths. "Fire…can't get…out." She coughed as if smoke filled her lungs. "Help me. Please, help me."

No longer able to stand by and watch her, Nick lunged for the bed and pulled her into his arms. "It's okay, Brenna." He stroked the back of her head, pressing her face into his shoulder, holding her close and safe in his arms.

"Too much smoke…can't see…" she muttered against his skin, her fingers curling into his chest hairs.

Nick wasn't surprised that Brenna was dreaming about the barn fire. With Dr. Drummond's office fire the previous evening and the strain of a killer stalking her, it was only a matter of time before her sleep was impacted.

Her shoulders shook and tears dampened Nick's

chest. The face of her fear, the screaming and terror were one thing. But the quiet tears broke his heart, and Nick couldn't take it anymore. "Wake up, Brenna. It's a dream."

Chapter Eleven

Flames licked at her clothing; smoke obscured the light creeping through the cracks in the old boards and seared the inner lining of her lungs. Brenna coughed and dropped to her knees, crawling across the dirt in the direction of the door.

"Help! Please, help!" she cried, her lungs filling with suffocating smoke with each breath. Pulling her shirt up over her mouth, she dragged herself farther, fear clutching her heart. Smoke stung her eyes and she clenched them tightly closed, feeling her way across the barn.

She bumped headfirst into a wall and scrambled for the doorway, her fingers feeling their way upward to the handle. At last, freedom from smoke and the fire moving swiftly through the hay bales, lighting them like giant torches.

As she shoved hard on the door lever, fire leaped onto her back and ate hungrily through the thin fabric of her blouse to her skin.

Pain seized her and she screamed, slapping at the angry fire, unable to extinguish the blaze. She had to get out. Had to get help. Then she realized the lever wouldn't lower the way it had the twenty or more times they'd been through the door that day playing hide-and-

seek. Excruciating pain raced across her shoulder blades and down her backside. Fire surrounded her, overwhelmed her, consuming the skin on her back and legs. She fought against waves of dizziness and screamed as loud as her tortured lungs could manage. She couldn't die like this. She wouldn't. But no one came. No one heard.

"Brenna, wake up!"

Hands gripped her arms. Someone shook her.

"Have to get out. Have to breathe." She struggled against the arms holding her in the hellish place of dark and smoke, fighting to reach the light and clean, fresh air. "Let me out!" She pummeled the door, sobs racking her body. "Let me out! Oh, please."

Lips descended on hers, briefly stemming her pleas for help. Then gentle words were spoken against her cheek. "Please, Brenna, wake up. Everything will be okay. Just wake up."

Clawing her way out of the smoke and fire, Brenna opened her eyes and stared around a room completely smoke free. She gulped in air, tears streaming from her eyes.

"It was only a dream," someone murmured against her ear. Those strong arms now held her in a warm embrace. Not warm like the scorching heat of a fire, but warm like a blanket on a cold day.

A gentle hand curved around her jaw and turned her face to look into the intense green eyes of Nick Tarver.

"What happened?" Still unable to comprehend her surroundings, Brenna clung to him, her savior from burning to death. "Where am I?"

He fingered aside a hair plastered in the tears on her face. "You had a really bad dream."

She released a heavy sigh and sagged against him. "Thank God." Her arms circled his waist and she pressed her face into his chest, reveling in the hairs tickling her nose. "It was only a dream." Images of fire climbing the inside walls of the barn flickered across her memory and she shuddered. "It seemed so real."

"But it was only a dream. You're here with me. There's no fire, no smoke. Just me." His arms tightened around her and he rested the side of his face against her hair, his hands stroking her back.

How long she sheltered in his arms, she didn't know. But his tender, soothing fingers eased the tension from her shoulders, massaged the length of her spine. Nestling deeper into his arms, she inhaled the woodsy scent of his aftershave and the clean smell of freshly washed hair. With her cheek pressed against his nipples, her hands skimmed across his back, the feel of skin against skin at once grounding her from her dream and spinning her in a different direction altogether. Forcing her body not to react, she allowed her fingers to test the firmness of his muscles. They climbed up his ribs, to the skin that felt warmer around his heart.

Nick's hands stopped moving and his body tensed. "Brenna, are you awake?"

Yes, she was. Would he believe she was still dreaming if she pressed a kiss to his nipple? How would he react if she told him she was awake and wanted to make love to him? Would he insist on lights? And would he recoil in horror when he saw the scars covering her back?

Could she handle his rejection?

Tears leaked from the corner of her eyes. "Hold me?" she asked tentatively. Maybe that was all she needed, the reassurance of another living soul in the same room to dispel the terror of her lingering nightmare.

"I don't know if I can," Nick whispered against her hair.

Brenna held her breath and then let it out slowly. He couldn't hold her. He didn't find her in the least attractive, and all his tender care was nothing more than he'd give to a child in distress. How pathetic was she to want more? "It's okay. You don't have to."

Instead of letting go, his arms tensed. "I'm afraid if I hold you much longer, I'll forget myself."

She managed to force air past her constricted vocal cords. "How?"

"Right this minute I want to kiss you."

Her heart stopped and she stared up into his face.

Nick continued, "And I'm afraid I won't stop with a kiss."

Joy warred with fear, pressing against lungs, making her words even more difficult. "Who said I'd stop you?"

"You're suffering the effects of a nightmare. I'd be taking advantage of the situation."

Brenna reached out and slid her fingers around his neck, pulling his face down to hers. "My eyes are wide open." Then she kissed him. She pressed her breasts against his chest in an attempt to get closer, immediately regretting the shirt that kept her from the skin-to-skin contact she craved.

Nick pulled back, his lips hovering over hers. "Are you sure?"

"Yes," she said on a sigh, her fingers digging into his shoulders, loving the feel of the taut muscles beneath bronzed skin.

Nick's arms wrapped around her, pulling her against him, and he took her mouth in a savage kiss, no holds barred. His tongue pushed past her teeth to war with hers, tangling, teasing and tasting of mint toothpaste and Nick.

The dream pushed to the farthest corner of Brenna's mind as her head spun in the rapid bombardment of sensations.

His hands slid up her back and inside her shirt, kneading the flesh and scar tissue.

Brenna stiffened and pulled her mouth from his. "No."

Eyes glazed, Nick sat back on the bed, his hands resting on her back. "What? Am I going too fast?"

"No, you're not." She reached for his hands and moved them around the front where scars weren't an issue and more pleasure would be gained. "I'm just… reticent about certain things."

He stared down at where she'd moved his hands, and his lips pressed together. Gazing into her eyes, he trailed his hands around to where they'd been. "I'm not bothered by your scars, Brenna. They are a part of you and what makes you beautiful."

Tears welled in Brenna's eyes and she blinked to clear them away before he saw. "You don't know what you're talking about. You don't have to live every day of your life knowing you're damaged goods." She pushed at his hands but his grip tightened. "You haven't even seen them."

In a soft, persistent voice, Nick said, "Show me."

"No," Brenna said, her voice strangled in tears. All her thoughts of making love to Nick were crushed beneath the overpowering desire to hide. Hide from Nick, from the kids who'd teased her in school, from Victor who'd told her she wasn't pretty and from her mother who wanted her to "settle" for someone. "I can't," she said, lowering her head.

With one hand, he cupped her face and tilted her head up until she was forced to look into his eyes. "Then I'll help you."

His gaze locked with hers as his hands pulled the hem of her tank top up and over her head. He leaned forward and kissed one breast, twisting his tongue around the nipple until it hardened into a beaded peak.

Brenna moaned and locked her hands behind his head, holding his mouth to her while he laved attention to first one then the other aching breast. She could handle this as long as he didn't pay attention to her back and the wretched scars there.

Nick laid Brenna against the pillows, branding a trail of kisses from her breasts down her rib cage, delving into her belly button. His hands worked ahead of his lips, moving lower to where her pajama bottoms rode her hips.

With her breath caught in her throat, Brenna waited for him to push aside the fabric and continue on his downward path. She wasn't disappointed. His fingers eased the elastic down over her hips, exposing inch by sweltering inch of her to his gaze, his tongue and the coarse tips of his long fingers. When the elastic reached the top of her curly mound, she moaned and her hands reached down between them to help the situation along. Her body burned for him, wanted him inside her, filling her completely.

He laughed, his breath soft against her skin, only making her hotter. "Are you in a hurry?"

"Yes!"

"Then by all means." With one strong tug, he yanked the pajamas the rest of the way down her legs and tossed them into a corner. Now, with nothing between them but one pair of boxers and a minuscule scrap of lace panties, Brenna writhed on the bed, her knees falling open to him.

Nick slid his body between her legs and pressed a

kiss to the lace, a smile curving his lips. "Black lace? Amazing secrets you North Dakota agents hide."

"So, I like pretty under things. Is it a crime?"

"On you? Maybe. But I'm not complaining." He tongued her through the lace.

The wet heat pierced her like a bolt of electricity and sent her nerve endings skyrocketing. She wanted the rest of her clothing gone and him inside her, but she was too afraid to say so. A sudden case of shyness rendered her incapable of speech. Why now? Why when she wanted so much? But what did she want from Nick Tarver? A one-night stand? A quick tumble and goodbye?

"What do you want, Brenna?" He spoke her jumbled thoughts aloud, his breath hot against her most intimate place, his hands splayed out over her thighs. His fingers hooked into the elastic around her hips, tugging the panties downward until his mouth had full access to her.

Brenna's body screamed for him to take her, fill her and love her until she couldn't move. "I want you," she gasped.

In one smooth glide he pulled her panties past her knees, kissing the inside of her thigh as he moved lower. When the last of the lace cleared her ankles, she sighed.

A gleam flashing in his eyes, Nick slid his boxers off and stood next to the bed in all his naked glory, fully erect and pulsing in the faint light from the study.

Brenna's eyes widened at his length and girth, her legs parting automatically.

"Wait," he said and jogged out of the room.

"Wait?" Brenna sat up. "Wait? You've got to be kidding." Her body was on fire and he wanted to wait? Had he changed his mind? No! Please, not now.

Within moments, he returned sporting a square, foil

package and an apologetic grin. "Sorry. But I thought you'd want protection." He tore the packet open and eased the sheath down over his erection.

Brenna fell back against the pillows, relieved but with her passions a bit cooled. Was she making a mistake? Would sleeping with Nick change everything? She bit on her lower lip.

"Don't start second-guessing now," he said, leaning over her to press his lips to hers. His kiss slid along her jawline to the sensitive spot behind her ear.

"How did you know?" She turned her head to the side allowing him more access, her desire leaping back to fever pitch with just one touch of his lips.

When his hand slid down her belly to bury itself in the mound at the juncture of her thighs, she arched up to meet him.

Nick nibbled at her lower lip. "You were biting your lip."

"Umm. I like it better when you do the biting."

"Me, too." Nipping at her neck, Nick pushed his fingers lower, sliding inside to find the special place between her folds. That place that vanquished her mind of all thoughts except Nick and the wonderful things he was doing to her.

Tension built, tightening her muscles, until Brenna clutched at Nick's shoulders. "Now. I want you now!"

With a lingering kiss pressed between her breasts, Nick settled himself between her legs. "I want you, too." Then he kissed her full on the lips and slid inside her, easing his way into her slick channel and back out.

Her muscles constricted, holding him within. But she wanted more, faster. Brenna raised her knees, planted her feet on the bed and met him on his next thrust and the next until they rocked in rhythm, climbing higher until Brenna burst over the edge, her body shuddering her release.

Nick thrust one last time, deep and hard, then went still as his climax rocked him and he dropped down on her, his breath coming in ragged gasps against her throat.

She welcomed his weight, loving the feeling of his naked body stretched over hers from cheek to toe, glistening in sweat. Even the way he crushed the air from her lungs made her smile.

Then Nick rolled to the side, taking her with him, never losing the intimate connection. With his hand resting on her hip, he kissed her. "You're beautiful, Brenna. Don't let anyone tell you different."

Lying in the warmth of his arms, Brenna feigned sleep, praying he wouldn't want to talk. Her emotions raw from what she'd just experienced, she didn't want to put words to how she felt.

Nuzzling his face into the side of her neck, Nick pulled her close, chest to chest, and draped a leg over hers. Not long afterward, his eyes drifted shut and his breathing deepened.

Brenna relaxed and opened her eyes, her gaze filled with Nick in all his naked glory.

Broad, muscular shoulders narrowed to a trim waist, a tight butt and rock-hard thighs. The man was truly blessed. A dark lock of hair fell over his forehead adding mystery and vulnerability to an already perfect picture.

When Brenna reached out to brush the hair off his forehead, Nick's arm tightened around her waist, his hand splaying over her back where the scars stretched tight and ugly.

He'd told her she was beautiful. Yet, he hadn't seen

her in the light. Brenna knew his opinion would be different once he did. And she couldn't bring herself to let that happen.

Chapter Twelve

When the alarm blasted through Nick's sleep, he rolled to his back and opened his eyes. For a moment, the strange room and furniture disoriented him until he remembered he was in a suite with Special Agent Brenna Jensen and they'd had the most incredible—

He sat up straight. The sheets beside him were tangled but empty. Brenna was nowhere to be seen. Tossing the bedclothes aside, he pulled on his boxers and raced through the door. "Brenna?"

Fully dressed, her hair pulled back in a tight ponytail, Brenna turned from her seat in front of the laptop. "Yes, Agent Tarver?"

He stopped in mid-stride, his heart slamming against his chest. "You weren't there. I thought you'd—"

"Gone?" She smiled, although the smile didn't reach her eyes. "I'm checking online news articles trying to see if there's something we missed."

"How long have you been up?"

"Does it matter?"

So this was the way she wanted it? Brenna would pull back into her shell and pretend last night hadn't happened.

Nick knew better. Hell, yeah, he knew better. "Brenna—"

"I called the station. The autopsy report is complete on Dr. Drummond. I'd like to take a look at what they found as soon as possible." The glance she shot his way was as emotionless as a stump. But the added color in her cheeks gave her away.

"You can duck the issue this time, but we *will* talk," Nick said.

The red flags in her cheeks faded to white and her eyes widened. "What do we have to talk about?" She turned back to the computer.

"You are not going to shut me out."

"Last night…" She pressed a hand to her mouth. "Well…we shouldn't have. It was a mistake."

Nick grabbed her arms and turned her around, chair and all. He placed one hand on each wooden armrest and leaned over her until his nose was within inches of hers. "Not for me."

Brenna stared down at her hands. "I'm sorry if you feel that way."

"Brenna, look at me and tell me to my face that last night didn't mean anything to you."

Her head remained down but her hands trembled in her lap.

With the tips of his fingers, he tilted Brenna's chin up. "Tell me."

"I—" Tears welled in her eyes.

A cell phone rang, vibrating the tabletop beside the computer, and Brenna grabbed for it, blinking several times before she flipped it open.

Nick swore under his breath and backed away.

"Agent Jensen," she said, her voice cracking on the first word. As she listened, she sat up straighter. "Thanks, Sergeant Koenig, we'll be in right away."

Brenna stood and straightened the hem of her black turtleneck sweater. "I'm going in to the station."

Nick stared at her, his eyes narrowed. If she wanted to withdraw, so be it. Maybe he needed time to cool down and think about what had happened before he tried to shake a reaction out of her anyway. "You're not going without me."

Her chin tilted upward, an obstinate frown denting her brow. "And why not? It's daylight. The bogeyman won't try anything in broad daylight."

"We don't know that, and bogeyman or not, if you remember, your car is still in the station parking lot." He had to repress a satisfied smile as Brenna's face fell.

At the very least, he would have her with him until they reached the station. And if he had any say, which he did as team lead, she would be by his side at all times. "I'll be ready in five. Don't go anywhere." He spun toward his room and, before he shut the door, he turned back to her. "That's an order."

BRENNA MAINTAINED HER SILENCE all the way to the station, refusing to talk about anything. Especially last night. What was there to talk about? She'd experienced the most incredible sex ever. But, in the light of day, she knew nothing could come of it. They were two people caught up in the adrenaline rush of a case. When they captured the killer, they'd go their separate ways, Nick back to Virginia and Brenna on to Minneapolis, with any luck.

Despite her attempt to be nonchalant about a one-night stand, Brenna couldn't stop feeling as gray as the overcast sky.

Paul met them at the door to the war room. "Look at

this." He shoved Dr. Drummond's autopsy report in Nick's face.

Brenna leaned over Nick's shoulder to read it.

"Death by strangulation. The coroner believes the cable used to bind her hands and feet was the same kind used to strangle her," Paul said, before Nick or Brenna could read down to that part.

"What kind of cable?" Nick asked.

"Ethernet cable," Paul responded.

Brenna cringed, imagining how painful it must have been to be strangled by such thin wire. "Was it hers?"

"I have a man swinging by the doctor's place to check." Paul paced across the room and back. "I don't know that it makes a difference."

"What about the Conlin kid?" Nick looked up from the report. "Anything on him?"

"Melissa and I did some asking around. You might find this interesting in light of the cable evidence. He was a computer lab tech at the same college with Dr. Gomez. Robin Rutledge also goes to that same college. We staked out his place, but he didn't come out all night."

"I take it you two didn't get much sleep."

"Only in shifts, while we waited for something to happen," Melissa said from her position at the computer. "How about you two? Victor Greeley pan out?"

Nick didn't answer so Brenna spoke up. "Not really. He had a rendezvous with his latest mistress."

"He's married, isn't he?" Paul asked.

"Yeah." Nick's lips pressed together.

"Scumbag," Melissa muttered.

"So you guys got about as much sleep as we did." Paul yawned. "Very little."

Brenna's face warmed all the way to the tips of her ears. "I'm going for coffee." She spun on her heel and marched away before anyone could read into her red face something she'd rather not get around.

As she left the war room, she could hear Paul ask Nick, "Did I say something wrong?"

Brenna didn't wait to hear his response, mentally kicking herself all the way down the hall to the coffee-maker. How could she allow herself to react in front of the rest of the team? Would they read into her dash out of the room, put two and two together and come up with the fact she and Nick had made love?

How mortifying if they did. They were professional FBI agents. How would it look for one of their own to make it with a local? How would she look as the local who made it with the big bad FBI team lead?

Brenna stood before the coffee machine, her hand shaking so badly she couldn't pour a cup.

"Excuse me."

The voice behind her made her jump and she turned wide-eyed toward the one person she didn't want to talk to. Nick Tarver.

"If you want coffee, you have to pour it into a cup." Nick gave her a lopsided smile and took her trembling hands in his. Warmth flowed from her fingertips to her heart. "Hey, if it helps, we can pretend nothing happened."

A tear slid from the corner of her eye down her cheek. "If only it hadn't."

Nick winced.

"Not that you weren't...that I didn't..." She pressed her eyelids together to shut out the hurt look in Nick's eyes.

He squeezed her hands and let them go. "Come on, Jensen. We have a killer to catch. Are you in or not?"

Brenna squared her shoulders. She had a murder to

solve and she couldn't allow her own lapse in reason to get in the way. "Hell, yeah. I'm in."

Nick lifted the carafe, poured coffee into a foam cup and handed it to her. "Then get going. I want to interview Conlin sometime this morning."

Cradling the steaming brew in her hands, she sniffed the fragrant aroma, focusing on the coffee instead of the man following her. As she marched back to the war room, she set her poker face firmly in place and prepared to find a killer.

"MR. CONLIN, I'm Special Agent Jensen with the North Dakota Bureau of Criminal Investigations. We have a few questions we'd like to ask."

Jason Conlin stood in the doorway to his apartment, wearing faded jeans, zipped but not buttoned, and a dingy white T-shirt that looked slept in. His dark brown hair didn't look as if it had been combed in days. Rubbing the sleep from his eyes, Conlin frowned. "Why do you want to talk to me?"

The young man had just enough of a whine to his tone that grated on Nick's nerves. Here was a guy who'd harassed a young woman to distraction, going so far as to hit her. As far as Nick was concerned, any man who hit a woman was pretty low on the food chain and didn't deserve any respect.

"FBI Agent Tarver and I are investigating the murder of Janine Drummond and the disappearance of three other women."

Conlin leaned against the doorjamb. "What's that got to do with me?" His eyes widened and he straightened. "You're not accusing me, are you?"

Nick had to give Brenna credit for maintaining a

calm, professional tone. "No, we aren't. But we have a few questions for you regarding the case."

"I didn't kill no one and I don't know nothin' about them." Conlin stepped back and tried to close the door.

Before he got the door half-closed, Nick stepped in. "Mr. Conlin, it would be in your best interest to cooperate with us. If, as you say, you aren't involved in the murder, your answers might assist us in determining who might be."

Jason's eyes narrowed to slits and stared from Brenna to Nick and back to Brenna again. "Don't I know you?"

Brenna nodded. "I used to be a police officer in Riverton."

"Yeah, you're the she-cop that gave me that DUI." Jason crossed his arms over his chest. "I lost my job at the university over that."

"Driving under the influence is illegal, Mr. Conlin. I was only doing my job."

Jason's lip curled into a snarl. "You cost me my job."

Brenna stood taller, her expression one-hundred-percent professional. "You're lucky you didn't cost someone his life."

Nick almost smiled as Jason studied Brenna for a moment and then turned to him. "What do you want to know?"

"Let's start with where you've been since last Wednesday night," Brenna said.

Giving Brenna the side of his face, Jason spoke to Nick, effectively telling Brenna he didn't want to talk with her.

The only sign of annoyance was a slight tightening of her lips. If Nick hadn't been so familiar with those full, luscious lips, he wouldn't have seen it.

"I worked Wednesday and Thursday until six, came

home and watched television. Friday, I ordered out pizza and watched a video by myself."

"Did you have anyone with you during any of that time? A friend, a girlfriend?" Nick asked.

Jason ran a hand through his hair, making it stand up even more than it already had. "No." His tone was abrupt.

"Did you leave your apartment Wednesday evening for anything?" Brenna asked.

"I went down to the Valley Dairy convenience store for a six-pack around ten or so. I don't remember exactly." Jason shot a glare at Brenna. "And no, I didn't drink and drive."

"Jason, did you know Dr. Drummond?" Nick asked.

"Yeah. She was the shrink the court ordered me to see."

"For DUI?" Nick asked, although he already knew it was because of the assault on Robin Rutledge.

"Yeah." Jason said, his eyes shifting back and forth between Nick and Brenna. "Is that all you want to know, because I have to get ready for work."

"Not quite," Brenna said. "You still haven't told us where you were the rest of the days."

Jason inhaled and blew out a hard breath. "I don't believe this. Did you just come to harass me, or what?"

"No." Nick gave him a hard look. "We only want answers."

"I worked at the Computer Store Saturday all day, came home and watched a football game on TV the rest of the evening. Sunday, I didn't do anything but watch sports. Too damn cold to get out. Monday and Tuesday, I worked, came home, watched TV and went to bed." Conlin shifted from one foot to the other and his eyes never made direct contact with either agent.

Nick would have bet his paycheck Conlin was lying or omitting a lot of the truth.

"Is there anyone who can verify you were at work and who would know you were in your apartment during those times?"

"My boss could verify the work. But I was on my own at night. Is this going to be a problem? Are you going to hit me up with murder charges because I don't have an alibi?"

"Only if you're guilty, Mr. Conlin." Brenna raised an eyebrow. "Only if you're guilty."

"This is bullshit." Jason Conlin got ready to slam the door in their faces.

Nick stepped forward. "Mr. Conlin, have you ever harmed a woman in any way?"

Jason sputtered and his face turned red. "That's none of your goddam—"

Raising his hand, Nick stared hard at Jason. "Mr. Conlin, just answer the question."

"She put you up to this, didn't she?" Jason jammed his hands into his pockets, a frown wrinkling his forehead.

"Who put us up to what?"

"That bitch, Robin." He glared at Brenna then Nick. "She sent you here to harass me, didn't she?"

"We don't know what you're talking about." Brenna's brows rose, her tone calm and cool. "Maybe you'd care to elaborate?"

"I got nothing more to say. If you want me to answer any more questions, you'll have to go through my lawyer." Conlin stepped back and slammed the door with a resounding thud.

Nick rubbed his hands together and walked to the steps leading down. "Where to next?" He stopped and waited for Brenna to precede him off the metal-and-concrete landing.

"We check in with Robin Rutledge," she replied, her voice soft yet firm.

When they reached ground level, he gripped Brenna's elbow and assisted her over a patch of slushy ice. As soon as she could, she pulled away from his grasp and completed the rest of the short walk to his car on her own.

Nick opened Brenna's car door. "I think our Mr. Conlin wasn't telling us everything." He rounded the car and slid in next to Brenna.

"Me, too." Brenna clicked her seat belt in place.

She was too quiet and entirely too rigid for Nick's liking. His fingers itched to massage the stiffness from her shoulders and smooth the frown from her brow. He shifted the car into drive and jammed his foot onto the accelerator, spinning melting snow out from under his tires. With a soft curse beneath his breath, he let off the gas and eased out of the parking lot. How could he stand to be near her and not touch her? All the more reason not to get personal with a team member.

When Nick glanced toward Brenna, a smile twitched at the corner of her mouth.

The little bit of humor made his heart race at the same time it made him angry. "What are you laughing about?"

"Nothing."

"No, really." He stopped at the exit to the parking area and frowned at her. "What are you laughing about?"

She sighed and shook her head. "You. Me. The situation."

His frown deepened. "You find it humorous?"

With a shrug she said, "In a sad sort of way."

"I don't understand."

"We're trying so hard to pretend nothing happened last night that we're only making each other miserable." Her eyes glistened with moisture.

"I'm not the one trying to pretend," Nick said softly.

"I know." She stared out her window, her face half-turned away, the smile completely wiped from her face. "I'm sorry."

"Look, Brenna." He reached for her hand lying in her lap. "Last night meant something. I don't know what, but it meant something." His fingers tightened around hers.

"Thanks," she said. "It's just—"

A horn blared behind them. Being interrupted in the middle of talking with Brenna was becoming a recurring nuisance.

"Damn," Nick cursed softly. "Promise me we'll talk later?"

Another honk sounded and Brenna jumped. "Okay. But you better get moving before the guy behind you decides honking isn't enough."

As Nick eased out onto the busy street, hope soared in his heart. At least she'd promised to talk with him about what had happened. Problem was what would he say? What could he say? They'd only just met, and they were hardly at a point in their relationship to make any lasting commitments.

Nick heaved a sigh. He'd deal with it later, after they talked with Robin Rutledge.

Chapter Thirteen

"I knew Jason was seeing Dr. Drummond, but I don't know if he had a connection with Dr. Gomez or Ms. Carmichael. And I can't imagine how he'd know the woman at the Biolab." Robin Rutledge sat across the glass-topped table from Brenna and Nick at the Riverton Bistro, where she worked part-time while completing her degree at Riverton University.

Careful not to reveal any information from Jason's patient file, Brenna asked, "During your relationship with Jason, did he ever display any tendencies toward violence?"

Robin shifted in her chair, her finger swirling along the rim of her water glass. "Jason and I dated for three months during the spring of my junior year. He liked to take me out to the levy overlook and just talk. At first it was nice and peaceful. But the more we dated, the more possessive he got. I finally called it off and told him I didn't want to see him anymore."

Brenna glanced across at Nick, waiting for Robin to continue.

"We were at the levy when I told him I wanted to break up." He went crazy." Robin lifted her glass and swallowed a sip of water, setting the glass back on the table before she continued. "He wouldn't accept the breakup. So I avoided him, hoping he'd take the hint and leave me alone. That's when he started stalking me."

Nick leaned forward. "Did you notify the police?"

Robin nodded. "One night, I came home from working at the Bistro and he was waiting for me in the parking lot of the apartment complex where I lived. I hurried up to my apartment to get inside before he tried something. But just as I inserted my key into the lock, he came up behind me and began shouting and pushing me against the wall." Robin took another sip and set the glass down, her hands trembling. "I was so scared."

Brenna reached across and covered the younger woman's hand. "You had every right to be."

"Thanks." Robin gave Brenna a weak smile. "My neighbor came out and witnessed it all and called the police. When I pressed charges against Jason, the judge issued a restraining order and mandated psychiatric treatment with Dr. Drummond." Robin looked up into Brenna's eyes. "Do you think he killed Dr. Drummond?"

"We don't know and we don't have enough evidence to point to Jason." Brenna tapped her pen to the pad of paper in front of her. "Did Jason stop bothering you after the court decree?"

"If you mean, did he push me around again, no. But he still followed me, although at a distance."

"When was the last time you noticed him following you around?" Nick asked.

"I can't swear to it, but I think I saw his truck behind mine on Friday when I was on my way home from work. And I think he followed me to church on Sunday." Tears welled in Robin's eyes. "I just ignored him and hoped some day he'd get on with his life and leave me alone. That is, until Dr. Drummond was murdered and the city cops started guarding my door-step." She shivered. "It gives me the creeps. I feel like I can't walk out in the open without an armed guard anymore. Why am I a target? Is it because of Jason?"

"We don't know for sure, Miss Rutledge," Nick said. "But we're trying to find out."

"Robin. Call me Robin." She lifted her glass to take another sip, but it was empty. She jumped up from the table and straightened her uniform apron. "I need to get back to work." She sighed. "I'm here till closing tonight and my feet already hurt."

Her feet aching in empathy for the woman, Brenna asked, "What time do you close?"

"Two. The place gets busy around nine and stays that way until after midnight."

"One more thing, Robin." Nick pushed his chair back and stood. "Do you own a computer?"

"Yes. What college student wouldn't?" She smiled. "I'd be absolutely lost without it. Come to think of it, Jason was handy to have around if for only that reason. Anytime I had a problem with it, he'd fix it."

"But you could hire a repairman for less trouble, right?" Brenna smiled.

Robin's lips twisted. "Yeah."

This young woman had been through enough with Jason. And now she had to worry about a murderer on the loose. The desire to jump from her seat, charge out into Riverton and find the culprit was a physical need burning in Brenna's belly. But part of her job was to fit the pieces together and, somehow, Robin was one of the pieces.

The younger woman smoothed the front of her apron again. "Can I get anything else for you two?"

Brenna tipped her coffee mug to stare down into a half-full cup. "Not for me."

"I could use a top-off," Nick said.

"Coming up." Robin raced off for the coffee carafe and returned in less than five seconds to refill Nick's cup. She smiled at Nick, making Brenna's chest tighten.

When Nick smiled back, the tightening eased lower to Brenna's gut. Not that she had a claim on the sexy FBI agent, but they had made love less than twenty-four hours ago. Wasn't there a polite time limit a man should wait before he flirted with other women?

Brenna sank lower in her seat, her brow wrinkling over her eyes, feeling like a heel for even thinking such thoughts.

Nick's gaze followed Robin all the way back across the room. Not until she pushed through the swinging kitchen doors did he turn to face Brenna. The smile he'd maintained now slipped. "What?"

"I'm just thinking." Even to her own ears, her voice sounded grumpy. What was this man doing to her mental wellness?

"Stop it." Nick reached out and touched a finger to her lip, calling attention to the fact she'd been chewing on it.

"Stop thinking? Or stop chewing on my lip?"

"If you're thinking about the case, knock yourself out. If you're thinking about us, stop thinking and biting your lip. What's done is done. You can't take it back."

"Who said I wanted to take it back?" she tossed at him, aiming for flippant, but falling painfully short.

"You were second-guessing again."

"How do you know I was thinking of us? I could have been thinking about the case."

"Possible, but not likely."

"Well, as far as I'm concerned that's what I'm thinking of now." Brenna sat up straight. "Do we have enough to bring Jason in for further questioning?"

"No, but we definitely need to keep a close eye on our bully." Nick drummed his fingers on the table. "I don't trust him."

"Nor do I." Brenna noticed his fingers were long and tapered. They'd certainly done amazing things to her last night.

"So what exactly do we have?"

Nick's question shook Brenna from a dangerous detour down a dead-end road. "We have a suspect with a history of stalking and violent behavior."

Nick continued the list of clues. "He's a former patient of the deceased and could know the professor from working at the university. But I don't see a connection to Carmichael or Stinson."

"I'll review Dr. Drummond's file again for any clues. Maybe he dated Stinson, picked her up at a bar or something. Although, that doesn't explain Michelle Carmichael. She seemed much older than Jason," Brenna said. "Could just be the newspaper articles that link them."

"Having been the computer lab technician at the college, he knows his way around equipment. He could have planted that device in Drummond's office to start the fire. I just can't believe he'd be stupid enough to leave a signature with the Ethernet cable."

"He didn't strike me as overly bright," Brenna said. "Belligerent and hotheaded, yes. Calculating and sneaky…I don't know."

"The victims could have known him through his work with the computer store. Maybe they trusted him enough to let him in."

"He had a history of violent behavior." Brenna shook her head. "I can't see Dr. Drummond willingly letting him into her home. She was a smart woman and knew the risks."

"You have a point and her house was least disturbed, like she knew who it was and trusted him."

"I think we're still missing something."

"Is this a gut feeling, Jensen, or do you have something solid?"

"Gut." She stood, needing to flex her muscles and clear her head. She'd gone too long with too little sleep. "Can we go back to the office and get my car?"

"Yes. But I don't want you going anywhere without me."

"I promised my sister I'd have dinner with her tonight. I don't suppose there's a chance you'd let me go alone?"

He crossed his arms over his chest and shook his head. "Not a chance."

Great. Dinner at her sister's with a man her mother would try to have her married to before the night was over. Maybe the flood would come and sweep her away before dinnertime. A flood sounded more palatable than any food served with a heavy dose of advice topped with a heaping of why-can't-you-be-more-like-Alice. Sometimes her mother's disease really got Brenna down. But she couldn't stop loving the woman who'd raised her, loved her and cared for her all her life. "The upside to having dinner at my sister's is that she's a good cook."

"Good. I haven't had home cooking since the last time I visited my folks in Virginia."

Brenna found herself wanting to know everything about this stranger she'd let into her bed and who would make inroads into her heart if she weren't careful.

When she stepped out into the late afternoon sunshine, she stretched and turned her face to the sun, absorbing the warmth.

But no matter how rejuvenating the sun could be, too

much of a good thing could be worse than winter. If the ground didn't refreeze and the snow melting continued at the pace it was going, Riverton could be in deep trouble and even deeper water.

Brenna almost laughed at the irony. The longer they worked at the case, the more chance of the murderer making the list of victims deeper. The more she was around Agent Tarver, the deeper her emotions ran and the more likely she couldn't swim her way out of certain heartache. She almost laughed, but tears flooded her eyes and she tripped on her way across the parking lot.

Nick's hand steadied her before she wiped out in an embarrassing heap in the middle of a sludge pile of melted snow and dirt used to sand the icy streets.

Water ran through the parking lot an inch deep to the streets where it pooled at flooded storm drains.

What were they missing? What clues still remained beneath the surface?

As soon as Nick entered the war room, he shot a question Paul's way. "Anything on the Ethernet cable?"

"Dr. Drummond's cable was still attached to the computer. So the cable used to bind her wasn't necessarily hers."

"Think there's anything on her computer?" Nick hung his leather jacket on the back of a chair and pushed a hand through his hair. "What about a chat buddy gone berserk or an e-mail from her attacker?"

"I tried to get on. I could get the computer to boot, but I couldn't get the Internet to connect to check her chat room and instant-messaging buddies. Items stored on her computer, like her e-mail in-box, sent files and deleted messages, had all been cleared."

"That's strange," Nick said. "What about the recycle bin?"

"Nothing."

"Send it to the crime lab. They're better equipped to recover data."

"Already done. I sent a car to Bismarck an hour ago with the computer, monitor, keyboard and mouse."

"Good." Nick walked to the whiteboard on the wall and studied the time line.

"What did you find out from Jason Conlin?" Paul asked.

"He's a bully, but I'm not sure he committed the crimes," Nick said. "He had a connection to Dr. Drummond and possibly to Dr. Gomez. Robin Rutledge confirmed she'd dated him. But we don't have a connection between him and the Biolab lady or the real-estate agent. Unless they've had computer problems lately. Paul, will you check with the Computer Store records to see if any of our victims have been there recently?"

"Yes, sir." Paul lifted the telephone book and thumbed through.

"Could be a chance meeting in a bar." Melissa swiveled her chair toward the center of the room.

"Maybe." Nick tapped his finger on the whiteboard. "Dr. Drummond disappeared on Wednesday night. Gomez on Friday night, Carmichael on Sunday. A pattern of every other night up to that point."

"Until Stinson disappeared on Monday night." Brenna moved to stand beside Nick at the board.

The warmth of her body next to him derailed his concentration for a moment and he forced himself to move past it and onto the task at hand. "He missed last night and my bet is we're due another kidnapping."

"And if we go in order of the news articles," Melissa

said from her perch on the conference table, "that would put the college student at the top of the list."

Nick shook his head. Robin Rutledge had been scared when he'd talked to her. Imagine if she knew the rest of the story and that she was prime for the next target on the killer's list.

"I know, I know." Paul stood. "Increase surveillance on her. Melissa and I can pull the first shift tonight."

"Good. She works at Riverton Bistro until 2:00 a.m." Nick glanced down at Brenna. If he didn't go back to the hotel room tonight, he wouldn't be tempted to take Brenna back in his arms and make love to her. "I'll take over from midnight until dawn."

"And you'll sleep when?" Melissa asked.

He jammed his finger against the board. "When we apprehend the killer."

"I feel a caffeine attack coming on." Melissa hopped off the table. "Coffee, anyone?"

"I'm with you," Paul said. "Make mine a double. It's going to be a long night."

Melissa and Paul exited the war room leaving Nick and Brenna alone. All Nick could think about was pulling her into his arms and kissing her until the morning.

"I'm coming with you," Brenna said.

"No, you're not." With the thoughts he had bumping around inside of his head, he didn't need her any closer than she already was. "You need sleep."

"I'll catch a nap before I go to my sister's for dinner. I don't need much sleep." The dark circles beneath her eyes belied her words.

Nick wanted to tuck her into bed and kiss her to sleep, and a lot of other non-sleep-related things. "You'll sleep all night."

Her brows rose. "In the hotel room, without a guard?"

Nick frowned and his lips pressed into a tight line. He couldn't leave her alone and it wouldn't be fair to Paul and Melissa to keep watch over her after pulling a late shift. "You'll come with me."

"Right." She turned away, a slight smile playing with the corners of her mouth.

Melissa entered the room balancing a steaming cup of coffee in one hand. "Filled it too full." She blew at the steam and sipped. "Mmmm, you don't know what you're missing."

Paul entered carrying two cups.

The aroma of coffee filled the air, warming the room and tempting Nick. "Special Agent Jensen and I will take the midnight to dawn shift."

"Sounds good." Setting one of the coffee cups on the table, Paul sipped at the other.

Brenna glanced at her watch, her brow twisting into a frown. "I need to make an appearance at my sister's house for a quick dinner." She looked up at Nick. "Really, I don't need you to come with me. I'll be at her house the entire time. I can give you the address and everything."

"I'm coming," he said, his voice brooking no argument. "And don't worry, your mother won't bother me. I'll just pretend she's my mother."

Brenna smiled. "Oh, she'll love that."

"It'll be fine. We could use a break from the case, and a home-cooked meal is just the ticket."

Paul's head came up. "Home-cooked meal? Where?"

"Yeah, where?" Melissa chimed in.

"My sister's house," Brenna said.

"Forget it." Nick gave Paul and Melissa a narrow look. "I'm taking her."

"You get all the cushy assignments." Melissa

glanced at Paul. "Heads we call out for pizza, tails we go for Chinese."

"I'll flip." Paul pulled a coin from his pocket and tossed it into the air. Then he slammed it against his wrist. "Damn. I'm going to have heartburn the rest of the night."

Melissa grinned. "Pizza, it is!" She moved toward the door. "We'll be positioned outside the Bistro. If you need us, you know how to get us." She patted the cell phone on her hip and turned to Paul. "You buyin'?"

Paul raised his hands. "No way. I'm all over women's rights. Besides, I don't pay for heartburn."

"You're just sore you didn't win."

Brenna chuckled as the two exited the room to make the call for their pizza delivery.

The sound left a warm feeling inside Nick's chest. "You should laugh more often."

Her chuckling ceased and a frown settled over her forehead. "If I had more to laugh about. Come on. We'd better get moving, I don't want to be late to my sister's. She and Stan are into punctuality."

"What did you say your brother-in-law does?"

Brenna shrugged into her coat. "He owns a communications firm and he's the deacon at their church."

"And your sister?"

"She's a stay-at-home mom and perpetual volunteer."

Nick loosened his collar, already working on his departure speech for right after dinner. "Sounds like an interesting couple."

"You'll love them," Brenna said, her tone flat. "They're perfect."

"That's what I was afraid of." He slung his jacket over his shoulders and shoved his hands into the sleeves. "Maybe they could shed a little light on the people they know."

"Actually, we should ask Stan about the Ethernet cable. He deals in that kind of stuff. He might have an idea where we should look."

Chapter Fourteen

"So, Nick, where did you say you live?" Alice asked as she sliced into a portion of the steaming chicken cordon bleu she'd served on china.

He swallowed the bite in his mouth, savoring the creamy sauce. "I've spent most of my life on the east coast. I have an apartment in Norfolk, Virginia." He stuffed another piece of the chicken into his mouth and hoped Alice wouldn't ask him another question while his mouth was full.

Brenna sat at the edge of her seat, pushing the food around her plate and glancing at the clock on the wall every two minutes. She hadn't said more than two words to Alice or Stan since their initial stilted greetings. Or anyone else for that matter.

"You should be married." Marian Jensen pointed her fork at Nick for the twentieth time. "Brenna needs a husband. You should be married."

Brenna's cheeks reddened and she sank lower in her chair. How many times had her mother said the exact same thing in the past hour? Nick hid a grin at Brenna's obvious discomfort.

Alice smiled and patted Nick's hand. "Don't pay her any mind. She doesn't mean anything by it."

"May we be excused?" asked Brandon, the older of Alice's two children. He sat with his hands in his lap, his hair combed neatly and his shirt tucked into khaki slacks. He hadn't wiggled once at the table and he'd displayed surprising table manners for a six-year-old. If one of Nick's nephews sat at the table, he'd have fallen out of his chair at least three times by now trying to slip scraps to a persistent pooch beneath the chair. Even the younger boy, Luke, was well behaved.

"I don't know how you do it. I've never seen little kids with such good manners," Nick commented.

Sitting closest to Brandon, Brenna ran a hand through his hair and smiled down at Luke, her love for her nephews obvious in the way she'd hugged them and gotten down on the floor to play with them before dinner.

But little boys needed to let loose, whoop and holler. These guys were too quiet. Must be their company manners, Nick reasoned.

"It's a matter of expectations," Stan said. "You let them know their limits and you enforce them. I think too many people allow their children to behave badly." He glanced at Brandon. "You and Luke may be excused."

"Thank you, sir." Brandon climbed down off his chair, gathered his plate and cup and carried them into the kitchen. The smaller child slipped out of his booster seat and followed suit. As soon as they'd deposited their dishes, they left the room and climbed the stairs to their rooms.

"Stan's been very hands-on with the boys. Everywhere we go, people comment on how well mannered they are." Alice smiled at her husband. On the surface, Alice Klaus appeared the happy, supportive wife to an enterprising, if a little overly disciplined, husband. She kept a spotless house and a neat and orderly life. Apparently a life Brenna's mother wanted for her youngest daughter, regardless of whether it was right for her.

Nick set his fork on the table, his plate clean. "Thank you for an incredible meal, Mrs. Klaus."

"Please, call me Alice." She stood and collected his plate. "How about some dessert? I baked a chocolate cake this morning."

"That would be wonderful." He patted his belly wondering where he'd find room for more, but willing to risk the added pound for homemade cake.

Brenna rose from the table. "I'll help you with the dishes. Then we'll have to run."

"You need to be married, Brenna. Have a family like Stan and Alice."

Brenna leaned over and kissed her mother's cheek. "Yes, Mom."

The simple gesture and agreement warmed Nick's heart. Brenna knew her mother wasn't in her right mind, but she didn't hold it against her.

His gaze followed her through the door into the kitchen. When the door swung closed, he realized he was alone for the first time with Brenna's brother-in-law and her mother. He wondered what was between Stan and Brenna that made them uncomfortable.

"Stan, Brenna tells me you're in the communication industry." Nick smiled, reminding himself he wasn't supposed to be in interrogation mode, just friendly curiosity. "What exactly does that mean?"

Stan pushed his chair back and folded his napkin on the table. "I own a business that supplies sixty percent of Riverton's cable television, telephone and Internet."

Nick sat forward. "Do you keep a store of supplies on hand for your customers?"

Stan's face registered mild surprise. "Well, yes, of

course. I have a warehouse full of supplies. My customers trust me to give them sufficient and timely support. If it goes down, I'm there."

"That kind of work must keep you pretty busy, huh? Seems like my Internet back home is always going down." Nick lifted his water glass and sipped.

Stan's chest swelled. "My company prides itself in the backup systems and the redundant servers we have in place to ensure uninterrupted service." The man was proud of his business and quick to warm to the subject.

"What would you say is the leading cause of a customer's downtime?" Nick asked, not really caring about the answer, but wanting to fill dead air. Marian Jensen sat silent in her own world.

"Operator error," Stan said without hesitation. "Most people don't know any more about their computers than they do about their cars. Some have trouble locating the on-off switch."

"Ever have any supplies pilfered from your warehouse?"

With a frown, Stan asked, "You going somewhere with this?"

"Just curious. Seems like computer parts can get expensive."

"Yes they can. That's why I had a security system installed at the warehouse. Only authorized personnel can enter."

"How many people are authorized?"

"Me and the four repairmen I have on staff. Why do you ask?"

"I guess you've heard on television we found Dr. Drummond."

"Yes, I'd heard." Stan frowned. "Tragic, isn't it?"

"Yeah." Nick laid his napkin on the table. "The interesting thing is, her hands were bound in Ethernet cable."

His face paling, Stand leaned back in his chair. "You don't think I had anything to do with it, do you?"

"Not at all," Nick hurried to assure him. "I just wondered where a killer could have gotten hold of Ethernet cable."

"You can buy it at any store that carries computer hardware supplies. It's easily available." Brenna's brother-in-law shook his head. "I find it hard to believe this is happening in Riverton."

"I know. Don't worry. Like I said, I'm curious."

"Have you found any of the other missing women?"

"Not yet. We're still searching."

"Good God," Stan said quietly. "We can't even be safe in our own backyards."

"Do you know any of the missing women?"

"Only from church. Dr. Drummond occasionally joined our Sunday-school class."

"She was a member of your church?" Nick's attention perked. "Did you ever have an opportunity to speak with her on a more personal level? Did she mention anyone who might have been bothering her?"

"No." Stan shook his head. "I should have called the other deacons to notify them of a death in our church family when I learned about it. We have a phone chain we use to notify other members when something of this nature occurs. I've been remiss." He stood. "If you'll excuse me, I think I'll do that now."

"Certainly."

Stan left the room and walked into the entrance hall.

Alone now with Marion Jensen in the tastefully decorated dining room, Nick pushed to his feet and walked around the room, studying the framed prints of Victorian settings. Not a frame was crooked or off-centered. He reached up and nudged one and it tilted to the right.

Nick fought a smile. Stan Klaus seemed a bit uptight and would probably go nuts with a tilted picture. Besides, anyone who made Brenna tense couldn't be all good, despite what her mother thought.

As if on cue, Marian asked, "Are you going to marry my daughter?"

"I don't know, Mrs. Jensen." Having been burned by marriage once, Nick wasn't anxious to jump back into the fire. But the old woman's question made him think.

"Damaged goods, that's what she is."

"Excuse me." Nick shook his head. Had she said what he thought she'd said? At moments she seemed lucid; at others it was as if her mind took a hike.

"Can't get a man because she's damaged goods." Marian dug her fork into her food and twirled it around. "What man can love a woman with ugly scars? Damaged goods. Should never have let her play in that barn. It's all my fault."

"I'm sure it was an accident." Nick took his seat next to Mrs. Jensen. "You shouldn't blame yourself."

"One of those neighbor kids did it. Damn pyromaniac!"

Nick's heart skipped a beat and he leaned forward. Was Mrs. Jensen recalling what really happened, or had she slipped into the imaginings of her warped mind? "What neighbor kid?"

"Had to have been one of the neighbor kids." Marian set her fork on her plate and rocked back and forth in her chair, tears welling in her tired blue eyes. "My poor baby. So much pain. Now she can't be loved."

Nick didn't want to add to the woman's grief but he couldn't help asking, "Why can't she be loved?"

"Damaged goods. All those ugly scars."

Reaching for Marian's hands, he held them in his. "Brenna is a beautiful woman, Mrs. Jensen. Any man would be lucky to have her."

"Damaged. Scars are so ugly. My beautiful baby." Her fingers clutched at his with a bruising grip.

What could he say to her that would break through her grief? The only thing that might soothe her guilt would be an admission to loving her daughter and regarding her as beautiful despite the scars.

Nick couldn't do that. He didn't know what he felt for Brenna and was afraid to ask himself. He did know he admired her for her dedication to her home and family and her abilities as an investigator. But love? After knowing her only a few days?

Not possible.

Why the hell didn't she come out of the kitchen so they could get going?

LIFTING THE GLASS cake cover, Alice asked, "Is Nick your own personal bodyguard now?"

"I wouldn't call him that. It's more like he's guarding a body of evidence."

"Yeah," Alice said as if she believed Brenna's nonchalance. She slid a serrated knife into a beautifully decorated chocolate cake that looked as if it came from a bakery.

Brenna almost put her hand out to stop Alice from cutting into the work of art.

"And it doesn't hurt that he's an absolute babe, huh?"

Brenna shrugged. "He's okay."

"Okay?" Alice stared across the island countertop at her sister, her eyes narrowing. "Is there something you want to tell your big sis?"

"No." Brenna's face heated and she could have

stomped her own foot for responding too quickly to her sister's question. With her cheeks burning, she knew she gave herself away.

Alice's narrowed glance widened and a grin spread across her face. "You did it! You slept with him, didn't you?"

By now Brenna's face burned all the way out to her ears and she couldn't help glancing back over her shoulder to make sure the door remained closed between the kitchen and the dining room. "Shhh! It's not like you think."

"Oh, come on." Alice laid the knife on the cake plate and rounded the counter to take Brenna's hands. "How long has it been since you've let someone in your bedroom?"

"Not that long." Brenna stared down at their hands. Alice's were slender and manicured, while her own nails were clipped short, giving her fingers a masculine appearance in comparison.

"Bull. You haven't been with anyone since Victor. Am I right?" She squeezed Brenna's hands gently. "That bastard made a mess of you, didn't he?"

"No. I did it to myself."

"And with Nick?"

Brenna pulled her fingers loose and turned away. "I don't know. We've only known each other a couple days. I have no idea what I was thinking...why I let him...oh hell." Her shoulders sagged. "What am I doing?"

"You like him, and from what I can tell, he likes you. Sounds like you're grabbing for a little happiness."

Brenna swung back toward her sister. "I'm in the middle of a murder investigation. I have no right to grab for happiness when women are dying."

"Honey, there will always be another investigation,

another murder to solve. When will you make time for you?" She slid her arm around Brenna's waist and hugged her.

Brenna leaned into her sister, cherishing the comfort of the closeness she'd missed since Alice's marriage. "It's not like he'll stay."

"So you'll have a little fun while he's here. Who said you had to marry him?"

Brenna doubted she could be so superficial. She'd taken two years to get over Victor, and he wasn't even worth shedding a tear over. With Nick… She glanced toward the door standing between him and her. It might as well be a solid rock wall. They could never have more than a quick fling. Once they solved the case, he'd go back to Virginia and she'd return to Bismarck or move on to Minneapolis. Once again, she'd pick up the pieces and march on. Alone.

Alice stepped back and looked her in the eyes. "You really like him, don't you?"

More then she wanted to admit. "I'm afraid to fall for him."

"I know. Love can be a scary thing. You never know if it'll last."

"What do you mean?"

Alice shrugged and went back to cutting the cake. "Just that you've only known each other a couple days. It's hard to tell at this point if the attraction will last." Her words came out quicker than casual conversation and her hands shook as she laid a slab of cake on a plate.

Brenna bit into her bottom lip. Now was the time to ask Alice about her marriage. But how, without letting her know she'd seen Dr. Drummond's records? "Alice, are you happy?"

"Who, me?" She didn't look up but slid the knife

into the cake again. "Of course I'm happy. Why wouldn't I be?"

"Are you and Stan doing okay?"

"Now, don't try to turn this conversation away from you. I won't let you." Alice shook a finger at her sister and jerked a drawer open.

"Sometimes I worry about you."

"Don't be silly. Stan and I have a good marriage. He provides for us and we want for nothing."

"Nothing, huh?" Brenna almost snorted, but held back at the last minute.

"Stop." Her sister stared across the counter, her smile gone. "I know you and he don't get along, but that doesn't mean we can't still be friends. And stop worrying about me. I'm fine."

"Do you have any regrets?"

Alice reached up and pushed a lock of her golden-blond hair behind her ear, smearing chocolate icing on her cheek. "No. I can never regret Brandon and Luke. And Stan takes care of us."

"Do you love him?"

She gave a shaky laugh and lifted two plates of cake. "Of course I do. Now, take this out to your man before he thinks we took the cake and ran with it."

Brenna grabbed the plates, but looked into her sister's eyes as she did. "You know I'm always here if you need someone to talk to."

"I know, sweetie. I know." Alice smiled her normal smile. "You shouldn't be worrying about me. You have a murder to solve."

"Right." So her sister didn't want to talk. Brenna swallowed her disappointment. Now might not be the time, but she would make the effort before she left Riverton. "I hope you won't be insulted if we cut loose right after dessert. We have to get some sleep before we go on duty tonight."

"You're working a night shift?" Alice's brows rose. "I thought only cops worked all-nighters. You're an investigator, why can't you keep normal hours?"

"Because psycho killers don't." Brenna smiled at her sister and backed into the swinging door. "Come on, this cake smells delicious."

As she laid the cake in front of Nick, she plastered on her best poker face, hoping he hadn't overheard any of their conversation about him in the kitchen.

Alice looked around the corner of the dining room. "Where'd Stan go?"

"He went to notify the church of Dr. Drummond's passing…. Something about a phone chain," Nick said, his breath a soft puff against Brenna's arm.

Her hand jerked and the plate teetered as she set it on the edge of the table.

Nick grabbed her wrist and helped the plate to a safer resting place. "I like to eat my cake, not wear it." He winked up at her.

Brenna backed away and carried her plate to the other side of the table, her gaze locked on the cake, her concentration on reducing her heartbeat to a normal pace.

How could a man she'd only known for two days turn her into a jittery idiot? Taking her seat, she inhaled and exhaled slowly before she lifted her fork and dug into her cake.

"I saw that about Dr. Drummond," Alice said between bites. "Very sad news. They also reported another woman went missing since we last talked, but they wouldn't release names until the families were notified. Anybody I know? Or are you allowed to discuss this?"

"I don't know if you know any of them. They were new to me," Brenna said. "Dr. Deborah Gomez from the university, a woman who worked at the Biolab, Willa Stinson, and the real-estate lady, Michelle Carmichael."

Alice's fork clattered to her plate and her face blanched. "Deborah Gomez and Willa Stinson?"

"You know them?" Brenna touched a hand to her sister's.

"Yes, I do." She pressed a hand to her mouth. "They sat a few pews over from us in church. Dr. Drummond was in my Sunday-school class. And come to think of it, Michelle Carmichael was a member of the congregation as well, although she didn't come as often because of her work."

"You knew all of them?"

"Yes. I worked with Deborah and Willa on the annual charity auction last spring." Alice's brows knit together. "Are they dead?"

Brenna shook her head. "We don't know. We haven't found bodies yet."

"But…you think you will." Alice stood, pressing her hands to her cheeks. "I need to call someone."

Seeing her sister's reaction to the news made Brenna's stomach clench. She set her fork aside and stood, the cake forgotten. "I'm sorry, Alice. I didn't know you were friends."

"We're not, more like acquaintants." She shook her head again. "Wow, this is getting scary. So close to home."

"Are you okay?" Brenna put an arm around her sister's waist.

"I'm okay. Shocked, but okay." Alice pulled herself up straight. "Do you mind? I feel like I ought to call the pastor or someone. Or maybe the prayer group."

"It's okay. Agent Tarver and I have to get back to

work, anyway," Brenna said, sorry she'd even shared the little bit of information with Alice. Had she known she'd be so shocked, she'd have waited until another time. As it was, her appetite was spoiled for the beautiful cake and, from Nick's expression, so was his.

"You ready to go?" she asked him.

"Absolutely."

Alice, her socially conscious sister, walked out of the room without saying goodbye, as if Brenna and Nick had already left the house.

"Remind me not to talk shop at the dinner table," Nick said as he slipped into his black leather jacket.

"Me, too."

"What say we drop by the station before we head to the hotel?"

"I'm game." Anything to delay being in a hotel suite alone with Agent Tarver.

The trip to the station was accomplished in silence, with Brenna lost in her thoughts. So all the victims were members of Alice's church. Could the killer be someone in their church?

Chief Burkholder met them at the door to the war room, his face as gray as the few hairs left on his head. "I'm glad you're here. We found another body."

Brenna's heart bumped against her chest. "Where?"

"A farmer down by the river went out to check his fields because of the flooding and found a body."

"Gomez?" Brenna asked. "Carmichael?"

The older man shook his head. "Stinson."

Chapter Fifteen

FLOODLIGHTS SHONE DOWN on Willa Stinson's body as it lay on its side in the slush. She'd been dumped behind a huge pile of dirt and snow on the edge of Olaf Oland's farm field half a mile away from the swollen Red River. Her naked body was tied at the ankles and wrists with Ethernet cable just like Dr. Drummond.

The difference in this killing was instead of strangling her to death, the murderer had chosen to asphyxiate her. Her horror-filled face was clearly visible through the clear plastic bag tied over her head.

Brenna had seen her share of murders, some of them strangulations, but never had she seen the victim's face frozen in such a frightening expression as Willa Stinson's.

Having always been empathetic to others' pain, Brenna could imagine the terror this woman had felt at slowly losing consciousness while her executioner stood by and watched.

"This man is…" Brenna couldn't think of a word to describe the killer.

"Not a man at all," Nick said. "He's an animal to put a person through something so awful."

Chief Burkholder stood beside them on the edge of the embankment. "There were footprints from the road up to the body, but with the recent rain, the forensic team won't have much to go on."

Although she'd guess the other missing women were most likely dead, the actual evidence was much harder to stomach than Brenna had anticipated.

"Same MO with the bindings," Nick noted. "Different choice of death."

"Do you think he's experimenting?" Brenna asked.

"Whatever he's doing, he's killing innocent people." The chief jammed his hands into his pockets, a shiver jerking his shoulders beneath his winter coat. Although warm enough to melt the lingering snow, the temperature hadn't risen above forty-five.

"So, what do we have?" Nick asked aloud. "We have a killer who likes to use Ethernet cable to bind his victims. So far, he's used two different methods to kill them."

"Could be more victims." Chief Burkholder stared down at the dead woman. "We haven't found Gomez or Carmichael, yet."

Brenna pressed a gloved finger to her lips and then dropped it to her side. "Let's hope we don't find them like Stinson. He's also not above a little arson to keep his identity a secret and he likes flaunting how smart he is compared to me."

"Don't take it personally, Jensen," the chief said.

Brenna couldn't help but take it personally. The notes came directly to her.

"A sociopath who likes variety in his killing," Nick murmured.

"Yeah, a sociopath." Brenna closed her eyes and pictured the book she'd read on serial killers. All had been sociopaths who walked among society undetected. "A man like Ted Bundy who blends in with the crowd. Liked by his neighbors and a member of a church." She opened her eyes and stared across at Nick. "An upstanding citizen by all outward appearances. Impossible to discern."

"No." Nick lifted one of her hands. "Not impossible. Even sociopaths are human."

He squeezed her fingers through the gloves. "Humans make mistakes. We just have to dig beneath the surface of the evidence and find his mistake."

The pressure on her hand gave her hope. "In the meantime, we watch out over his next potential victim."

As they walked away from the site, Brenna glanced farther up the road, the familiarity sinking in even in the dark. "My grandmother's house is about half a mile north of here."

"The same grandmother with the burning barn?" Nick asked quietly.

"Yeah." The old barn was long gone, but Brenna could still smell the smoke in her memory.

"Does it bother you to go there?"

Nick's words broke through her thoughts, pulling her back to the farm field and the road running alongside. "No, not really," she lied, glancing down at her feet before she forced herself to meet his gaze. "I visited my grandmother's house after the fire with no problem. Seems the only time I recall the incident is during times of stress."

"Like now." He stared across at her, as if seeing through her fib.

"I suppose." Brenna climbed into her Jeep. "Ready?"

"Do you mind swinging by your grandmother's house?"

Brenna darted a look at Nick. "Why? Can't see much in the dark."

He adjusted his seat belt. "Just curious."

Brenna shrugged. "We still have a few minutes to spare. Why not?"

As she drove up the road, Brenna could see glimpses of the levy, imagining the swollen waterway churning huge clumps of ice and muddy water in a thrust to move downstream. "I'm surprised the mayor and FEMA haven't ordered a mandatory evacuation yet."

"Do they do that often?" Nick's gaze drifted toward the levy.

"After the flood of ninety-seven, they haven't hesitated to clear the town when the river gets this high. It's probably only a matter of time and they'll have the emergency management teams issuing the mandate."

Nick stared out the side window. "That'll make our jobs a lot harder."

As Brenna neared the simple two-story white house, with the wide, welcoming front porch, she looked at it with a critical eye. It needed paint and the corner of the porch sagged. "My grandfather farmed this land all his life."

"Does your family still own it?"

"No." A cold ache of regret rode hard in her stomach as she neared the driveway leading up to the house. "My father was their only child and he had no desire to go into farming, preferring a career in law enforcement."

"Didn't his father try to convince him to stay?"

"No. My grandfather didn't want to force my father to do something he didn't want. 'If you don't love farming, you'll never be good at it,' he'd tell us."

"So they sold?"

"When my grandfather was seventy-two, he and my grandmother sold the farm and moved to Florida." She remembered standing with her mother and father on the porch of the empty house, waving goodbye.

"Are they still alive?"

"No." She hadn't realized how much she missed them until she stared out at the white clapboard house visible in the headlights. The new owner had built a cavernous metal barn to replace the old wooden one that had burned. It looked new and modern, a stark contrast to the century-old home.

"Who lived in those houses?" Nick pointed farther up the road where lone security lights marked the driveways of other homes scattered along the road.

"My grandparents' neighbors." She smiled. "We'd stay out here for a couple weeks in the summer and play with the kids who lived up the road."

"Do you remember any of them?"

"Yes." Brenna's lips twisted. "One of them married my sister. My brother-in-law used to live in the house next door."

"Were they farmers, too?" Nick glanced at her, a little bit of a smile lifting the corners of his mouth.

Brenna liked talking with him about her past. His smooth baritone lulled her into recalling memories she'd thought long forgotten. "I think his father farmed, but he died in a freak farming accident when Stan was really young. His mother sold the land but kept the house. She was a hard woman. I guess having to raise a son alone can do that to you." Her mouth pressed into a tight line.

"You don't like Stan?"

She thought about lying, but figured Nick would see through her. "Not really."

"Why?"

"I don't know." Brenna shrugged. "Maybe it's

because I think my sister could have done so much more with her life if she hadn't married Stan. She could have had a career."

"Maybe that wasn't what she wanted."

"I suppose." She tapped her thumb against the steering wheel. "Alice is a beautiful woman and she was always the best at everything in school. She could have done so much more."

"But she chose to stay in Riverton and be a full-time wife and mom."

"Yeah." Now that she looked back, it all sounded silly. But Brenna had looked up to her sister and had higher aspirations for her than Stan Klaus.

"And you resent Stan for that?"

"I suppose I resent him for asking her to marry him when she hadn't had a chance to explore what the world had to offer."

"Not everyone wants the same things."

"I know." Brenna shifted the SUV into Reverse. "But that's in the past." She should have let go of her resentment a long time ago.

Nick's cell phone rang on his hip. He unclipped it and flipped the phone open. "Tarver."

Brenna's hand hovered over the gearshift. Had they found Gomez? She strained her ears to make sense of the voice she could barely hear, finally giving up.

"Do you need us to help?" Nick listened to more talking Brenna couldn't understand, and then nodded. "We'll see you in a few. If anything comes up, let me know."

Nick flipped his phone shut. "That was Paul. He and Melissa are positioned outside the Riverton Bistro where Robin Rutledge works."

Brenna nodded. "You know it's crazy, and I don't

wish anything bad to happen to Robin, but I'm hoping our killer tries something tonight."

Nick stared straight ahead into the dark night. "Careful what you wish for."

"WHERE'S OUR GIRL? It's after two," Nick said, pushing the light button on his watch for the tenth time in the past fifteen minutes. Patience had never been one of his strengths and waiting for Robin Rutledge to get off work wasn't the easiest task considering he hadn't had a decent night's sleep in several days.

"She should be out any minute, I guess." Brenna sat as far away from him as she could get in the tight confines of the sedan, avoiding conversation through the past two hours since they'd assumed the watch from Paul and Melissa.

The outside lights blinked out and still Robin didn't exit the front or side doors.

"Do you think she went out the back?" Nick tapped his fingers against the steering wheel.

"Robin promised Paul earlier this evening that she'd come out the front door so they could watch everyone entering and leaving. And Adam, the plainclothes policeman, is inside, so nothing should happen."

"She should be out by now. I'm going to check. Stay here and don't get out of the car."

"Bull." She opened her door. "I'm coming with you."

Nick grinned in the darkness, glad she chose to stick with him. He'd rather keep an eye on her in case the killer was stalking them using Robin as his decoy.

They circled the building in time to see a man wearing a white cook's apron locking the back door with no sign of Robin.

All systems on instant alert, Nick hurried forward. "Sir!"

The man's hand jerked, he dropped the keys and lifted his hands high as if he were at gunpoint. "Wh-what do you want?"

Nick held his badge up. "FBI Agent Nick Tarver and Special Agent Jensen. Who are you?"

"Ray Svendsen." His gaze darted from Nick to Brenna and back. "What do you want?"

Brenna stepped forward. "Sir, we're looking for Robin Rutledge."

The man's eyes narrowed as he concentrated on Nick's credentials in the light shining down over the back porch. When he was satisfied, his frown cleared. "You just missed her. She left with her boyfriend not more than two minutes ago."

"What do you mean she left with her boyfriend?" Brenna asked.

"That guy that hangs around all the time. I don't remember his name. She left without saying anything and when I came out back, I saw her get into a truck. I recognized the guy because he used to come in a lot."

"Do you know if the man was Jason Conlin?"

Svendsen nodded. "I'm pretty sure that's the name Robin mentioned. Can't keep up with the young people and their on-again-off-again boyfriends." He turned to fit the key in the lock again. "All I know is I'm tired and want to get to bed."

"Can you describe the vehicle?"

"Sure, it's a late-model white Chevy truck with a lot of rust."

Nick remembered seeing the truck in Jason's apartment parking lot.

Brenna touched a hand to Nick's arm. "What about Adam?"

"Sir, do you mind if we take a quick look inside?"

The man's hand stilled on the key in the lock and he heaved a sigh. "Why did I know you was gonna say that?" He pulled the door open and waved them in. "Help yourself."

"I'll take the office and the ladies' room," Brenna said and dashed down the dark, narrow hallway.

Nick made a quick pass through the barroom and the men's bathroom. Nothing.

"Nick!" Brenna called out from the hall. "Get an ambulance."

"What have you got?" Nick flipped his phone open and pressed 911 as he crossed the barroom.

Brenna moved back to let him see into the bathroom, where Adam Weinheimer lay sprawled across the tile. "He's unconscious. Looks like someone hit him in the back of the head."

Nick dropped to his haunches and felt for a pulse as the phone made a connection. "This is Nick Tarver, FBI, working the Drummond murder. Send an ambulance to the Riverton Bistro. We have an officer down, unconscious, but breathing. And put an APB out on Jason Conlin. He's driving a white Chevrolet pickup."

"What the hell's going on?" Mr. Svendsen appeared in the doorway.

"Don't you check all the rooms before you lock up?" Nick asked.

"The ladies' room is Robin's job. I assumed she did it."

"She probably did." Brenna stared down into Nick's gaze, her lips tightening into a thin line. "We need to find Robin. Now."

Adam stirred and groaned, his eyes opening. "What happened?"

When the cop tried to sit up, Nick placed a hand on his shoulder. "Lie still until the EMS gets here."

"But the girl. Where is she?" He glanced from Brenna to Nick. "The guy who hit me got her, didn't he?" He closed his eyes again and let his head sink back to the floor.

"Yeah." Nick stood.

"Go." Adam eased his eyes open. "Go find her."

Nick frowned down at the cop. "You sure you don't need us?"

"Hell, no." He lifted a hand to his head and winced. "That girl needs you more."

"We're on it." Nick turned to Mr. Svendsen.

"I'll stay with him until the ambulance arrives," the cook said before Nick could get the words out.

"Thanks." Then he turned to Brenna. "Let's go."

Outside, they jogged back to his car and jumped in.

"Where do you think he took her?" Brenna buckled her seat belt.

Nick turned the key in the ignition and the engine roared to life. "I don't think he's stupid enough to take her to his place, and I'd bet he didn't take her home."

"What about the levy overlook Robin mentioned? It was Jason's favorite place."

"Yeah." Nick shoved the shift into Reverse and backed out of the parking lot. "You know where that is?"

"On the north end of town. Take a left at the next street." As the car sped along the dark, wet streets, Brenna prayed they were headed in the right direction. "So, do you think Jason's our man?" Brenna asked.

"I don't know. The other kidnappings were directly from the victims' homes, not work."

"But we've had Robin's home under surveillance," Brenna said. "Maybe he's frustrated and taking a different approach."

"Or maybe he's just a jealous lover." Nick pressed harder on the gas pedal. Something about this abduction didn't smell like the others.

"If he is our bad guy, we have to find Robin before something awful happens to her." Brenna's brows furrowed in the light from the dash. "The levy overlook is about a mile out the north end of town. We should be there in another two minutes."

The headlights shone off the water accumulated in the ditches, giving the slushy road the appearance of a very wet black island.

Brenna touched his arm. "Start slowing down. I'm not exactly sure where the turnoff is."

The heat of her fingers on his arm radiated up his arm. "You know, Brenna, when this is all over…"

Her hand jerked away. "I know. You'll go back to your job on the east coast and I'll be in either Bismarck or in Minnesota." She didn't look at him, only at the road ahead.

His heart squeezed. After the time he'd spent in Riverton, he found he wasn't as anxious to leave as when he'd arrived. The reason for his change of heart sat with her lip between her teeth in the seat next to him. "That wasn't what I was going to say."

"Nick, you don't have to say anything. I'm a big girl. I know what we did the other night didn't have any strings attached. You don't have to worry about the local trying to cling to you when you leave."

Nick ground his teeth, recognizing Brenna's attempt to push him away, most likely to avoid being hurt, and it made him mad. While his fingers tightened on the steering wheel, his foot pressed harder on the gas pedal. "Would you shut up and let me say what I want to say? I want to—"

"Stop!"

Nick jammed his foot on the brake and the car hydroplaned, skidding sideways before it straightened.

"Look. There in the ditch." Brenna pointed and then scrambled for her seat belt.

Nick's gaze followed Brenna's direction. The tailgate of a beat-up white Chevrolet pickup protruded from five feet of inky-black water. All they could see was the truck bed and a corner of the cab sticking up above the water.

Nick felt the cool night air hit him as the passenger door to his car flung open. Brenna leaped out and charged along the road until she was even with the truck, then she disappeared down the embankment before Nick could unbuckle his belt.

"Wait, Brenna!"

She couldn't hear him or she wasn't listening. Nick couldn't tell which; he only knew he had to get to her before she hurt herself.

Making a splash, Brenna plunged into the frigid water up to her waist. She gasped, yet she pushed deeper until she was up to her neck.

Nick grabbed the police-issue flashlight from beneath the seat and raced to the edge of the embankment, descending into the water after her.

When the icy water soaked through his jeans to his thighs, Nick's breath caught in his throat. He tried to reach out and yank Brenna out of the water, but she was out of reach. "Brenna, get out!"

"I can't. They're probably still inside. We have to get them out!" Her teeth clattered, making her speech more like a chattering stutter. Her hands tracing the top of the cab to the passenger door, she reached beneath the surface, grabbed for the submerged door handle and yanked. Nothing happened. "I think it's locked."

Just beneath the surface of the water, a pale, white hand drifted into view against the passenger window.

Brenna screamed and staggered backward. "Oh, my God. Robin's in there and she's still alive. Help me, Nick!"

She renewed her effort to pull the door open, to no avail.

His breath coming in shallow gasps, Nick eased up behind Brenna and grabbed her shoulders. "Move."

"No! We have to get her out."

"That's what I'm going to do." Holding the flashlight for her to see, he climbed into the back of the pickup, Brenna right behind him. "Get back, Robin! I'm going to break the rear window."

The hand drifted into sight again, and then disappeared in the blackness of the water.

"Hurry!" Brenna urged.

Nick tapped the glass on the back window with the battery-laden end of the flashlight. Bunching his muscles, he reared back and slammed the flashlight down with all the force he could muster. The old glass shattered into jagged edges and water rushed in, filling the remainder of the cab.

"There she is!" Brenna cried.

Nick shone the flashlight into the cab.

Robin's face skimmed the ceiling of the truck, her nose just above the water. "Help," she gasped.

"We will, just hold on." Using the flashlight to knock out the jagged edges of the window, Nick called out, "Robin, can you swim over to the back window?"

She shook her head and tried to talk. "Seat belt… jammed."

Handing the flashlight to Brenna, Nick took a deep breath and pushed through the window. A sharp edge tore down his right side through his shirt to the skin, but Nick ignored the pain and moved along the back of the seat to Robin. The cold water numbed his shin and he fought the debilitating tremors, focusing on helping Robin. Unable to see anything in the inky darkness, he groped around until he felt the curve of Robin's shoulder. Then he pushed up to grab a gulp of air at the ceiling.

"Help me. I'm so c-cold." Robin's voice was weak. Her hand reached out, but she couldn't curl her fingers to grasp onto him.

With his mouth in the air pocket he said, "Hang on." His hand followed the seat belt crossing her chest to her hip where the buckle held her in place. Pressing with all his might, he worked to release the latch, but the buckle refused to give.

Then he remembered the pocketknife he always carried. Coming up for another breath of air, he shoved numb fingers into his pocket and pulled the pocketknife out. In the mind-deadening cold, he almost dropped it. After several attempts he managed to open the blade. In a sawing motion, he cut through the thick strap until the final thread gave way.

Robin drifted up in the water, her arms moving in a slow, pathetic attempt to swim out.

With the chill setting into him, Nick dragged in another breath and dove below the surface to grab Robin beneath the shoulders. He pulled her over the top of him and shoved her through the rear window into Brenna's waiting arms.

Back at the air pocket, he gulped another breath before he turned to Jason. The young man was slumped over the steering wheel. He'd been underwater for who knew how long without the benefit of the air pocket Robin had used to survive. It took several attempts to free his body and push him through the rear window, but Nick managed.

Brenna stood at the far corner of the truck bed with Robin in her arms, trying to keep her warm. "I'll need your help to get her back to the car. I think she's in shock."

Nick felt for a pulse on Jason, but between the frigid water and the lack of oxygen, he hadn't stood a chance. Nick pulled him to the high corner of the truck bed. With a quick glance at Brenna and Robin, whose lips were a startling shade of purple, he dropped back into the freezing water. "Can you shove her over the tailgate into my arms?"

"Yeah. I think I can."

Brenna stood and draped Robin over the edge of the tailgate then pushed her over into Nick's arms. Then she scrambled down into the water beside him and took the woman's legs. Together, they managed to get her out of the water and into the back seat of Nick's car.

While Nick cranked up the heater, Brenna placed the emergency call. As the interior of the car heated, Robin drifted in and out of consciousness.

"Robin, can you hear me?" Brenna sat on the edge of the seat rubbing her hands over Robin's.

Robin moaned and her eyes drifted open. "Agent Jensen?"

"It's me, Brenna."

"Jason... Did he hurt the officer?" The young woman's hand tapped against Brenna's arm.

"He'll be okay." Nick leaned into the back seat and draped his leather jacket over Robin. "What happened?"

"Truck smashed into…" Her head dropped against the back seat as if it were too hard to hold it up.

"Yes, the truck smashed into the ditch," Brenna said.

"No. Different truck. Ran us off…" Her voice faded and Nick thought she'd passed out again. But Robin's eyes opened and she said in little above a whisper, "A truck ran us off the road."

Chapter Sixteen

By the time Brenna got back to the suite, she couldn't feel her hands or her feet, and every wet inch of her was beyond exhausted. Nick let her go first in the shower, for which she'd be eternally grateful as soon as she could think clearly.

It had been hours till they'd left the levy, waiting till Robin had been taken to the hospital and Jason's body to the morgue. Then they'd briefed the cops. All the while, Brenna had shivered, despite the blankets given to her and Nick by the emergency medical technicians.

Now, stepping from a hot shower, she wrapped her hair in a towel and climbed into her pajamas. She almost felt normal when she emerged from the bathroom.

Nick stood in his black jeans, his shirt and shoes in a damp pile at his feet. "Did you save me any hot water?"

"Yes, sir." She smiled and a lingering shiver chased down her spine. Brenna couldn't determine whether the shiver was from seeing Nick's naked torso or from the chill she couldn't shake since being in water cold enough to have ice floating on the top. "Hop in while I see if I can't scare up a cup of hot cocoa."

"Sounds wonderful." He passed close by her on his

way to the bathroom and Brenna squeezed her eyes shut to keep from turning to watch him all the way.

When she opened her eyes, Nick's face was in hers, a smile quirking the corners of his lips. "Something bothering you, Jensen?"

"You!" Her face burning, Brenna whipped the towel off her head and snapped it at his retreating figure. The guy had nerve! To think he was in her thoughts when they had a murderer still on the loose was positively ridiculous.

But when the door closed behind Nick, Brenna let the image of his naked torso hover in her mind, and her body heated, her panties suddenly wet.

Would he sleep with her tonight?

Her heart slammed against her ribs.

Did she want him to?

Yes, oh, yes! her wanton inner self screamed.

After they solved the case, he'd be gone. The thought pulled Brenna to the ground with a thump. She drifted into her room and rifled through her suitcase for her stash of hot-cocoa packets. The drink reminded her of the times she'd sat beside her father on the couch in their living room, sipping cocoa and talking about fishing. Did Nick like to fish?

Good, thinking about her father, fish and cocoa would definitely calm her libido and shake a little reality into her system. She shouldn't be thinking about going to bed with Nick when she didn't even like to get naked in front of men.

But, oh, she wanted to get naked with him.

The man foremost in her thoughts emerged from the bathroom in sweatpants and nothing else. His skin glistened where he'd missed a spot drying.

Fathers, fish and cocoa flew from her thoughts and all she could think about was licking that drop of water from his chest. A shiver shook her body from her shoulders to her toenails.

Nick's eyes narrowed. "Are you still cold?" Before she could answer, he was striding across the room toward her, his long legs eating the short distance at an alarming pace.

What should she do? Run screaming or fall into his arms and let nature take its course? Brenna stood rooted to the spot, her options quickly running out.

When Nick stopped in front of her, she swayed forward, metal to his magnet. Who was she kidding? She couldn't resist Nick Tarver to save her life. And after the frightening night they'd endured, all she wanted was to be held. Okay, maybe not all.

Brenna stared up into Nick's deep green eyes. "No, I'm not cold."

His hands remained at his sides. Why wasn't he making a move? Didn't he want her the way she wanted him?

She wished he'd reach out and take her in his arms.

Nick shook his head. "That's too bad, because I'm still chilled."

So, he wanted her to make the first move? A thrill of anticipation shot through her. "I know a surefire cure for hypothermia."

His deep chuckle reverberated in her ears. "In this climate, I bet you do. Okay, I'll bite, what's your cure?"

Throwing inhibition to the wind, she went after what she wanted. "First," she said as she lifted the corner of her tank top and slid it up her ribs and over her head, "you both have to get naked." She tossed her shirt onto a nearby chair and stood there, her breasts bare and ready for the next step in her lesson.

Nick's eyes narrowed and he backed a step.

Oh, no! Brenna's face burned. Had she read him wrong? Had he only wanted a blanket and a warm but solitary bed? Shame made her shoulders droop. Maybe he didn't want to see her naked. The shock of the scars on her back might be too much. Her gaze darted to the shirt she'd so carelessly discarded. "I'm sorry, I didn't... I thought... Just let me get my shirt...."

When she tried to step around him, his hand shot out and captured her wrist.

"No, I don't want you to stop."

What had seemed like a good idea a moment ago now loomed like the giant hand of doom. What had she been thinking? "This is a mistake. You could have any woman you want."

"I choose you."

Panic rose in her at the thought of his ultimate rejection. Better to cut her losses and run. But she didn't want to. "Nick, you're perfect and I'm flawed."

"There lies the error in your thinking." He pulled her closer until her body was an inch from his. "No one's perfect. We all have our flaws."

The warmth emanating from all that exposed skin made Brenna's fingers ache to touch him. "How am I supposed to walk away when you're standing there half-naked?"

"You're not supposed to." He pushed a damp tendril of hair behind her ear. "What are you really afraid of, Brenna?"

Brenna leaned her face into his hand. "I'm not afraid." *I'm petrified.*

His thumb smoothed across her cheek. "Liar."

"Okay, so I'm afraid." She had to inject one last attempt, one last note of reason. "If anything happens tonight, it doesn't have to mean anything."

"Like hell it doesn't." His lips descended on hers, blocking out further protest.

As if the levy burst, all the pent-up emotion of the last few days poured through into that one kiss. Despite her words to the contrary, Brenna knew this kiss meant everything to her. She knew by going into Nick's arms tonight, she'd be opening herself to heartache.

No longer able to hold back, she knew she needed Nick almost more than she needed to breathe. After the chilling bath in the freezing waters of a roadside ditch, the discovery of three dead bodies and the ever-present knowledge she was a killer's target, Brenna wanted some reassurance. Hadn't she given her all to the job? Didn't she deserve a little happiness, even if only for a couple hours in the darkness before dawn? Even if she didn't deserve it, she damned well would take what she could.

And Nick seemed willing, if the hands skimming across her back then sliding beneath her pajama bottoms were any indication. Did he notice the different texture of her scars? Did it repulse him?

Did she care? All she wanted was to be held in his arms and have him climb between her legs and fill her with life.

She leaned against his chest, the friction of his coarse hairs against her bare breasts making her nipples tighten into hard beads. Sliding her hands up his biceps, she reveled in the smooth skin stretched over rock-hard muscles. She loved the power he held in check, and wanted more.

Without turning to expose the scars on her back, Brenna backed toward her bedroom, pulling Nick along with her.

His hands skimmed over her bottom and down to cup her thighs. Lifting her off the floor, he wrapped her legs around his waist and he carried her into the room, never breaking contact with her lips.

"What about protection?" she said against his mouth.

"I've got that covered."

A thrill of anticipation coursed through her veins. This was no chance encounter. Nick had been thinking about this before he'd made his first move. "You're very sure of yourself."

His lips curved into a gentle grin. "No, just hopeful. I haven't stopped thinking about you since last night."

Brenna's heart sang. Gorgeous Nick Tarver had been thinking about her.

Nick kissed the tip of her nose and eased her down onto the bed, laying her back against the bedspread. "Is it so hard to believe I could find you incredibly attractive?"

"Yeah."

"Well, believe it."

"I want to." She turned her face aside, the intensity of Nick's green gaze boring into her soul. "It's hard when I'm not even pretty."

"You're beautiful."

"Only with the lights off." She stared at the nightstand where the light glowed as a testament to the harsh reality of the truth as she'd known it.

"Brenna." Nick lay down beside her on the bed and turned her face to his. "You're beautiful where it counts." He traced a finger over her left breast, his touch sending fire deep within.

"You say that now, but you haven't seen me." Brenna wanted his words to be the truth, wanted to believe him. But she knew better. How could anyone look past the horrible scars? "Will you still think the same when you see all of me?" She pushed off the bed, tears blinding her, and stood with her back to Nick, fully exposing her flaws for his inspection. How could he not be horrified by the wide path of destruction from her shoulders downward? "Do you still feel the same, Nick?" She couldn't turn to see his face. Couldn't bear to witness his disgust and certainly not the pity. Tears flowed freely now, and she stumbled from the room in search of her shirt.

"Brenna!" Nick followed her and grabbed her around the waist before she reached her shirt. "Give yourself a chance."

"I did once, and what did it buy me?" She tipped her face toward the ceiling, willing her tears to dry. "You can't know that feeling of rejection."

"Yes, I can." He pulled her against him and pressed his cheek to her damp hair. "My wife rejected me by sleeping with another man."

"It's different."

"Not so different." His arms circled her, locking her into his embrace. "Trish was beautiful on the outside, but inside she was ugly. Had I looked deeper, I'd have seen it. When I look at you, all I see is the person who cares about others and wants to make them happy. You're loyal and protective of those you love. What's ugly about that? It's what's beneath the surface that counts, not the outer package."

"Even when the outer package is ugly?"

"I don't think you could be ugly in any way." His arms loosened around her and his hands moved to her shoulders. Nick stepped away from her.

Brenna's breath caught in her throat and she stood still. She felt his gaze burning her back, taking in the mottled skin and thick, revolting scars. Would he rethink his position?

Then his fingers skimmed over her shoulders and

down her spine, across the acres of scars. His lips soon followed, pressing little kisses to the damaged skin.

"No." Brenna tried to pull away. The thought of Nick kissing her ugliness tore at her heart. "Please, don't."

"Yes." With one hand at her hip, he stayed her from running and continued his sensual assault on the one area she hated most about herself. His hands massaged her back and shoulders; his lips teased the curve of her neck and inched downward.

The fear melted away, to be replaced by a tension she couldn't deny. When he slipped her pajamas and panties down her legs, she stepped out of them and turned to face him, her skin on fire. "You make it really hard for me to resist."

"Then don't." He pulled her into his arms and claimed her lips, her body and her heart.

Chapter Seventeen

Brenna lay for several minutes in the circle of Nick's arms enjoying the sight of him sleeping, his naked chest rising and falling with every breath. Midnight-black hair fell over his forehead and Brenna longed to brush it aside. But she didn't want to wake him yet.

Her emotions were too raw and she needed time alone to work through what had happened during the dark hours of the morning.

With a glance at the clock, she realized it was nearing noon and the others would wonder where they were.

Although she longed to stay snuggled in Nick's arms, she needed to get away from him and think. Carefully, so as not to awaken him, she slipped from the bed, gathered clothing and left the room. Closing the door behind her, she locked herself in the bathroom, dressing quickly and pulling her hair into a ponytail.

Other than her lips being a little swollen and a bit of beard burn on her throat, she didn't look any different. But she felt as if another woman stared back at her from the mirror.

Blowing out her cheeks, she bent to brush her teeth and left the bathroom without another glance at the stranger in the looking glass.

Nick would be angry she'd left, but she had to get away and think without him in the vicinity. Careful not to make a sound, she tiptoed out of the room and eased the door closed. Not until she was safely out of the hotel did she take a deep breath and run for her car.

When she arrived at the station, Brenna headed straight for the war room.

"Hey, Jensen, where's Tarver?" Paul sat at the computer, a cup of coffee perched on the edge of the desk.

"I left him at the hotel, sleeping."

Paul frowned. "That's too bad."

"Why?"

Melissa walked up beside her, wearing gloves and a mask and carrying an envelope. "You got another one of those letters."

Brenna's gut erupted in a flutter of nerves.

"We didn't think you'd mind if we opened it." Chief Burkholder spoke from the doorway.

"Hi, Chief." Brenna shrugged. "I'm glad you did. I'm tired of the notes. Hell, I'm tired, period. What did he say this time?"

"He didn't say anything," the chief said.

"Huh?"

Melissa held up a sheet of paper. "He sent us a map."

"A map?" Brenna leaned close to the paper. It was a computer printout of an online map with two bright red stars near the center of the page.

"We figure it's the locations of Gomez and Car-michael. He's impatient for us to find his little presents." Chief Burkholder sighed. "I have a forensics team on their way out to both locations."

"What about the map? Can we get any information about it?" Brenna wanted to take the map from Melissa, but she didn't dare without gloves.

"I'm working that angle." Paul sat with his gaze intent on the computer screen. "I have a buddy in the bureau who traced the Maury Travis case in St. Louis. He's already working with MyStreetMapper to pinpoint the IP address."

"How long do you think it'll take?" Brenna asked.

"No telling." Paul tapped a pen on the desk. "It took them four days on the Travis case."

Her chest squeezed tight as she thought about all the people the killer could take out in that time frame. "We don't have four days. This guy tried to kill Robin last night."

"We have two cops on her room at the hospital. He'd be a fool to try killing her after last night." The chief slipped an arm around Brenna's shoulder. "Heard you went for a swim to get her out of that truck."

A chill shivered its way down her spine despite the warmth of the chief's arm. "That's right. Unfortunately, Jason Conlin didn't make it."

A cell phone chirped and everyone in the room glanced down at his or her cell phone. It was the chief's.

"Chief Burkholder." As he listened, every gaze in the room was on him.

Brenna held her breath.

When he finally flipped his phone shut, he sighed. "They found Gomez and Carmichael's bodies."

"Damn." Melissa walked to the whiteboard and made note of the locations and date as the chief told them.

"That wasn't all they said." The chief stared around the room at the assembled team.

"What? Another body?" Paul asked.

"No. The levy is leaking like a freakin' sieve and it's only a matter of time before it breaks. The mayor and emergency management team have issued an immediate evacuation order for the city."

Brenna's heart thumped against her rib cage. "Great. Nothing like a flood to get in the way of catching a murderer." She'd been through the last flood and knew the chaos of a citywide evacuation. "Jeez, he could take out anybody, anywhere, anytime. This is going to be a disaster."

Chief Burkholder shook his head. "And we're going to need every cop on the force to direct traffic out of town. We won't have enough for the evacuation, much less to watch out for every single woman." He hurried to the door and yelled, "Sergeant Behrendt!"

The desk sergeant raced into the room a minute later. "Yes, sir?"

"Mobilize every available man. The city is under a mandatory evacuation order issued by the mayor."

"Yes, sir." The sergeant spun and left the room to carry out the orders.

Melissa stood beside the whiteboard, her gaze on the empty doorway. "Where will everyone go?"

"Bismarck, Minot, and some of the smaller towns in between. The emergency management team will notify nearby towns and cities to expect evacuees." He gave them a twisted smile. "You guys are on your own. Let me know if you need anything from the force. I have a city to clear."

Paul reached for his cell phone. "Time for our fearless leader to come to work."

Brenna's heart leaped into overdrive at the mention of Nick. She wasn't ready to face him after last night. She'd opened up to him more than she'd ever done with any other man. It left her feeling…exposed.

Her phone rang at her side and she pulled it from its

clip, breathing a sigh of relief that it was her sister's number flashing across the screen and not Nick's. "Hey, Alice. What's up?" *Besides the water, a killer and the fact I'm falling for an FBI agent.*

"Have you heard?" Before Brenna could respond, she continued, her voice fast and high pitched. "They're talking about evacuating Riverton."

"The chief just informed us. Are you okay?"

"Yes, a little nuts, but okay." Her normally calm and unflappable sister didn't sound so okay.

Brenna gripped the phone tighter.

"I can't get hold of Stan. He's out on a call and not answering his cell phone. I need help getting Mom loaded into the minivan. I can't do it by myself with the little ones. Can you come for a few minutes? I hate to ask the neighbors when they're all as busy as I am."

Brenna stared around the room at Paul and Melissa. They hadn't found the killer yet and when people started leaving, they may not find him. Her sister never asked for help and had taken on the burden of caring for their mother without complaint. "I'll be right over."

"Thank you." Alice's gratitude came across in a gust of a sigh.

Since Paul was on the phone with Nick, Brenna turned to Melissa, who lounged against the conference table staring up at the whiteboard of evidence. "I need to run to my sister's house for a few minutes. I should be back before Nick gets here."

Melissa pushed away from the table. "I'll go with you."

Paul flipped his phone shut. "Go where?"

"My sister needs my help with my mother. It'll only take thirty minutes tops."

"Good, because Melissa and I just got orders to

round up your brother-in-law's employees for a little questioning about Internet cables before they leave town. That means we have to call them in now." Paul stood and stretched. "Which reminds me, the boss man wasn't happy you skipped out on him."

Her face burning, Brenna turned away on the pretext of slipping into her jacket. "He'll get over it. Besides, I don't need a babysitter."

Melissa touched a hand to her arm. "We know you're not a baby, but that killer has you in his crosshairs and it's just not safe out there."

Brenna glanced at the two agents staring at her with concern in their eyes. "I'll be careful. I'm only going to my sister's and back."

Melissa frowned. "Still, I think I should go with you."

"We need to catch a killer. Questioning those employees is of a higher priority than escorting me. You'd better get to it." Brenna zipped her jacket. "I'll be back in thirty minutes."

Before they could lodge further protests, Brenna swept out of the room and through the station.

Her sister needed her and she couldn't let her down. Besides, what could happen in thirty minutes?

NICK SCRAMBLED INTO JEANS, shirt and shoes, cursing when he stubbed his toe on the metal bed frame. Why the hell didn't she wake him? She knew the rules and she'd gone off without him.

Dread settled low in his gut. After talking with Paul, he knew Brenna was safe at the station, but he couldn't help worrying. With the city in an uproar to evacuate, the killer could capitalize on the chaos and make his move on Brenna. And Nick wouldn't be there to run interference.

He accomplished the trip to the station in less than ten minutes, gripping the steering wheel so tightly at each stoplight he thought for sure the damned thing would break in two. His instinct told him Brenna was in danger and he was running out of time.

After parking in a no-parking zone in the station lot, Nick leaped from the sedan and raced into the building.

Paul met him at the door to the war room, his face excited. "We have an IP address!"

"I thought you were questioning Klaus's employees." Nick pushed past him, his gaze scanning the room's interior.

"We are, or we will be once the police bring them in. But did you hear me? We have an IP address."

When he didn't see any sign of the female special agent, Nick asked, "Where's Brenna?"

"She should be back in…" Paul glanced down at his watch "…fifteen minutes."

"Back?" Nick grabbed Paul's shoulders. "Back from where? The bathroom, the soda machine? Please tell me she's in the station."

Paul's brow furrowed and he shook off Nick's hands. "Get a grip, buddy. She ran over to her sister's house to help with her mother."

"By herself?" He held his breath for Paul's answer.

The other man cocked a brow at Nick. "Yeah. She said she'd be back in thirty minutes. That was fifteen minutes ago. She should be on her way back about now. Is there a problem?"

Realizing he might be overreacting a bit, Nick inhaled and exhaled twice before he spoke again. "I don't know. But you and Melissa knew I didn't want her out there alone."

"She insisted. Besides, it's broad daylight. This guy hasn't attacked in the daytime."

"Not that we know." Nick glanced at his watch. Fifteen minutes seemed like a long time. "What were you saying about an IP address?"

"Like I told you over the phone, I had a buddy of mine run a scan on the MyStreetMapper database to find the IP address of the computer that generated the map we received in the mail this morning. Anyway, we got a hit. Thank God this is a small town. We should have a phone number and a name in the next thirty minutes to an hour." Paul grinned and dropped down into the seat in front of the computer.

"He's made his mistake." Hope flared in Nick's chest, but his satisfaction was short-lived when he glanced down at his watch. Without Brenna there, he couldn't feel good about anything. He shoved his hand through his hair as he walked over to the whiteboard. "When did she say she'd be back?"

Paul's hands paused over the keyboard. "Who, Brenna?"

"Yes, Brenna!"

"Ten more minutes." Paul's phone rang. "Maybe that's her now." He flipped open his phone. "Fletcher speaking."

Nick's gaze could have bored a hole into Paul's phone but he still couldn't hear the caller's voice.

Paul glanced his way and shook his head, silently telling him it was not Brenna. Then he turned his attention to the caller. "Great. Give it to me." Paul listened, jotting down the information. Then he said, "Thanks, Joe. I owe you one." He hung up and grinned. "We've got him!"

"Got who? What are you talking about?" Nick asked.

Right now, though his eyes stared at the whiteboard details, his thoughts focused on nothing but Brenna.

"The killer. We traced the IP address to the phone number and came up with a name." Paul lunged across the room for the local phone book in the middle of the conference table. "Now all we have to do is match the phone number and name to an address." He riffled through the pages.

"S. Klaus," Paul said, not looking up.

Nick froze as the name crashed through his preoccupied thoughts to his brain. Fear gripped him in its icy clutches, freezing out everything but the words Paul uttered.

"What did you say?" Nick asked, wanting, needing confirmation.

"An S. Klaus," Paul repeated, moving his index finger down the phone-book page. "There are three of them in town."

Nick leaned over Paul's shoulder, seeing a Klaus, Stanley at 214 West Nodak Street. "Where's that phone number you wrote down? Give it to me quick."

Paul raced across the room and snatched the paper from beside the computer, returning in less than four seconds.

It might as well have been a lifetime. Even before he matched up the numbers on the paper with those in the book, Nick knew. Stanley Klaus was the one who'd sent the map and notes.

Stanley Klaus was their murderer.

"Damn!" Nick's fist pounded the conference table.

Paul jumped. "What's going on?"

"Stanley Klaus is Brenna's brother-in-law." Before he finished the sentence, he was halfway across the room, tossing his jacket over his shoulder.

"The man married to the sister she went to help?" Paul trotted to keep up with Nick all the way out to the parking lot.

Nick unlocked the door to the sedan and climbed in, his thoughts on the house on Nodak Street and the woman walking into a possible trap. "One and the same."

Chapter Eighteen

Brenna parked beside Stan's truck, climbed out of her SUV and stared around the neighborhood. People rushed back and forth from their houses packing clothes, food, blankets and treasured memorabilia into vehicles. They hurried to cram in as much as they could as quickly as possible. She felt sorry for those who stood a chance of losing their homes as they had in 1997.

She'd expected her sister's minivan to be parked in the driveway. It wasn't, and Brenna assumed her sister was busily packing it with the garage doors closed. At least Stan had finally shown up to help.

Brenna hurried to the door. Nick would be furious if he knew she'd left the station alone. Too bad. She didn't need a bodyguard during the day. Besides, after she helped her sister get their mother ready to leave, she could get back to the station before Nick arrived.

As she passed the passenger side of Stan's truck, she noticed a long scrape and a dent in the right front bumper. Brenna leaned closer. Had Stan, the perfect driver, had an accident? Part of Brenna was glad he wasn't so faultless. But as she studied the damage, she noted the scrape had white in it, a stark contrast to the dark pewter paint of Stan's truck.

Brenna's heart slammed against her ribs. White paint? Robin's words echoed in her head. A truck had run them off the road. Stan's truck? As one thought led to another, Brenna straightened. Could Stan be the killer?

No. She shook her head. No way. Stan was her brother-in-law. He and Alice had the ideal marriage and two perfect little boys.

Alice. Where was Alice? Brenna ran to the house and burst through the door. "Alice? Brandon? Luke?"

No one responded and the house had that empty, echoing quality as if it had been weeks since anyone had been in it.

Brenna raced through the living room and into the master bedroom. "Alice!"

"She isn't here." Stan stepped out of a walk-in closet behind Brenna, pulling an oversize wheeled suitcase.

Brenna turned to face him. Could this man be the killer? If she was wrong, her sister would never forgive her. If she was right, where the hell was Alice? "Hi, Stan," she said in what she hoped was a normal tone. "I came to help Alice with Mom. I guess you already did?"

"Yes, I did." Stan unzipped the suitcase and laid it open in the middle of the floor. "She should be on her way out of town by now."

"Then they're okay?"

"Of course. Why shouldn't they be?" His slow, methodical movements gave Brenna the creeps. But the creeps weren't evidence enough to point to murder. She had to be wrong. "Good. Then I guess I'll get back to work." And the first chance she got, she'd call her sister's cell phone to make sure they were in fact okay, and that the case was making her delusional.

"Did you ever find your killer?" Her brother-in-law knelt next to the case and unzipped an inner pouch.

Stan's question knocked her delusions out in left field and all her misgivings returned. "Not yet, but we're getting close."

"Oh, you're close all right." He reached into the suitcase and removed a 9 mm pistol. With a click, he slid free the clip.

The air caught in Brenna's throat. All the pieces spiraled into place. The notes sent to her, the Ethernet cable to tie the victims, the location close to his mother's old home. And why the women would let him into their homes without a struggle. Who wouldn't trust the deacon of their church and the man they'd always depended on to fix their Internet service?

Stan stood and gazed at the sleek black weapon. "Never know when you'll need one of these. Especially with a serial killer on the loose." He slammed the clip into the handle. "Tell me, Brenna. Did your killer ever take anyone out with one of these?"

"As a matter of fact, no." And she sure as hell hoped he didn't start now.

He nodded. "Too messy. He hates getting blood everywhere."

The way Stan said *he* sent shivers down Brenna's back.

Stan stood between her and the bedroom door, hefting the gun as if it belonged in his hand.

Without any alternative exit, Brenna knew she had to go around him to get out. She eased slowly to the side as casually as she could, her growing concern leaving a metallic taste in her mouth.

"Do you know the funny thing about a serial killer?" Stan didn't wait for her response. "Once he starts killing, it gets in his blood. He can't stop."

"He can if he wants it to stop."

Her brother-in-law glanced up, his eyes narrowing.

"No, Brenna, he can't." A smile spread across Stan's face. A smile colder than anything Brenna had ever experienced.

She forced herself not to reveal her fear or revulsion. "It's over, Stan. It's only a matter of minutes before the trace on your map query comes through."

He caressed the barrel of the 9 mm. "By then I'll be in Canada. And you—" the nose of the gun turned toward Brenna, and Stan cocked the hammer "—will be dead."

"You won't get away. They expect me back at the station in ten minutes. When I don't show up, they'll put out an APB for you. Don't be stupid, Stan."

As soon as Brenna said the word *stupid,* Stan's face flushed a mottled red. "I'm not stupid. Don't call me stupid." The hand holding the gun shook. "Mother always called me that. But she was wrong." He jabbed the gun toward Brenna. "How many women did I walk right out of their homes without anyone knowing?"

Brenna refused to answer. Instead she assessed her options, which were very few with a gun pointed at her chest.

"Four! That's how many. And why?" He didn't wait for her response. "Because I'm smarter than all their degrees put together. Smarter than you and the freakin' FBI. Isn't that right? The great criminal investigator Brenna Jensen couldn't figure it out. And you didn't think I was good enough to marry your sister. Well, the hell with you."

He swung out to snatch Brenna.

Dropping into a crouch, she lunged for his gut. If she couldn't get around him to get out, she'd go through him. But he was heavier than she was and when she hit him, she felt as though she'd hit a brick wall.

Stan staggered back, quickly regained his footing and slammed the butt of the pistol down onto her temple.

Squiggling light worms and bright stars swirled through her vision. Brenna struggled to remain alert to fight back against the crazy man her sister had married, the man who'd killed four women and who would kill her as surely as she passed out. Another crushing blow turned her world black.

WHEN NICK SKIDDED SIDEWAYS onto West Nodak Street, he dodged another car packed to the rooftop with everything one family could load into one vehicle.

He'd broken every speed limit and driven a few yards on a sidewalk to get from the station to Stan Klaus's house in less than five minutes.

Stan's truck stood in the driveway and the house looked normal, almost peaceful. Yet, deep in his gut, Nick knew he hadn't imagined the danger to Brenna. Stanley Klaus had something against her and he wouldn't stop short of murder to wreak his revenge.

Only Nick would be there to stop him. He had to be there. Brenna needed him and he needed her.

As soon as he slammed the shift into Park, he leaped from the car and raced to the doorway.

"Stan already left," a woman called out from the driveway next door. "Saw him with his suitcase loading up in a black SUV. You just missed him. He can't have been gone more than five minutes." She shoved a stack of blankets and pillows into the back seat of her Suburban.

"Did he leave alone?" Nick asked.

"Yeah, he helped Alice with her mother and the kids. They left about half an hour ago. Well, I better get moving." She hurried into the house for her next load.

A jolting image of Brenna lying unconscious on the

floor in Stan's house flashed into Nick's mind. He forced himself to jog toward the house, dread tugging at his heart. Brenna couldn't die. After the past few days, he knew he wanted to get to know her better, take her on a real date and sit with her in front of a blazing hearth sipping hot cocoa.

The door was slightly ajar, as if Stan had left in a hurry and had no intention of returning. Nick raced through the house, but he couldn't find even a trace of Brenna, Stan or anyone else.

How had he gotten Brenna past the neighbors without alerting them?

The woman next door said he'd loaded a suitcase. Had he packed Brenna in the suitcase and wheeled her out without anyone the wiser?

Where would he have taken her? *Think, Nick.*

He had no idea. Nick wanted to howl his frustration. Instead he climbed into his car and headed back to the station, his heart dragging lower than his knees.

FIGHTING HER WAY BACK to consciousness, Brenna opened her eyes. She had to blink several times to make sure her eyes truly were open. The darkness was so complete, not a glimmer of light penetrated.

Her knees pressed into her chest and her face rested against what felt like canvas. The steady vibration beneath her could only mean she was inside a vehicle. But where? In the trunk of a car or the rear of her Jeep, since she was parked in the driveway?

She tried to move her hands but rubber-coated wire dug into her wrists. She'd bet money it was Ethernet cable. When she tried to stretch her legs out, she couldn't. Stan must have stuffed her into a box…or the suitcase he'd laid out on his bedroom floor.

Hot and short on air, Brenna struggled to loosen her bonds, only managing to make them tighter. A hard knot pressed into her side and she shifted her weight off it. Her cell phone! If she could get to it, maybe she could call for help.

Tugging the edge of her jacket with the tips of her fingers, she inched the pocket closer. After several attempts, she managed to pull the phone free, praying no one would call her. If she were in the back of the SUV, Stan would hear the ringing and take the phone away from her before she could get help. Her best bet was to get hold of someone and try to whisper her location.

Then the thought dawned on her. Zipped into a suitcase, she had no idea where she was.

Flipping the phone open, she felt across the face of the keys picturing the numbers in her mind. She might only have one chance at this, so she better make it good. Her number-one key was a preprogrammed speed dial for 911. Fairly certain she had the right one, she pressed it, sent a prayer heavenward and strained to listen for a response.

Even with her ear four inches from the receiver, Brenna could hear, "Riverton Emergency Service, may I help you?"

"Help," Brenna whispered as loud as she dared, hoping the road noise and the suitcase fabric drowned out her voice to the driver.

"I'm sorry, did you say *help?*"

"Help," she repeated. "Get FBI Agent Tarver at the Riverton Police Department. This is Brenna Jensen."

"I'm sorry, I only caught about half of that. You need the FBI?"

"Yes." Brenna was light-headed from the bump on her temple and the limited air filtering through the thick canvas. She inhaled and tried again. "Agent Tarver at the Riverton P.D., now!"

"Hold please while I transfer."

A few moments later, Brenna could have cried when she heard the familiar voice of the man she'd grown to love.

"Tarver speaking."

"It's Brenna," she whispered as loudly as she dared.

"Brenna! Where are you? Are you all right?"

The concern in Nick's voice made her throat ache. "I'm in a suitcase in a car. I don't know where."

"Does Klaus have you?"

"Yes. My cell phone has GPS. Contact Bismarck and have them locate me. Hurry!"

The vehicle slowed and the sound of water splashing against the wheel wells drowned out Nick's response.

Where was Stan taking her? What was the water sound and why wasn't it dissipating? It was as if he was driving a long way through a stream.

Brenna raked her memory of the area for any such place, but came up blank. Then she remembered the levy had sprung a leak, thus the need to evacuate fifty-five thousand people from Riverton. Had the levy given way? Would Stan toss her, suitcase and all, into the raging Red River?

She closed her phone and stuffed it back into her pocket. If it rang, Stan would hear and might guess she'd managed to get a call through. The North Dakota Bureau of Criminal Investigations was based out of Bismarck and they needed time to pull the information on her whereabouts via the GPS tracking system. She had to keep the cell phone on for them to find her.

A car door opened and slammed shut, rocking the vehicle. Then the metal clunk of the hatch door opening was followed by the whoosh of the hydraulic lifts pushing upward.

The rasp of the suitcase zipper brought a rush of fresh air to replenish her lungs. Brenna inhaled deeply, blinking at the light streaming into the back of her Jeep. A dark figure shadowed her position.

"Ready for the next step, Brenna?" His voice sounded happy, like a father encouraging his child to cheer up over going to the dentist. Only she wasn't a child going to the dentist.

"I take it you're going to let me get out of this suit-case?" Hope sprang in her chest. If she could get out of the confined space, she had more of a chance of fighting her way free of Stan.

"Oh, yes. I have bigger plans for you." His teeth and the whites of his eyes shone in the shadows, an evil combination considering the source.

Like a spider crawling across her skin, a shiver of fear fed its way through her system. She tested her legs, stretching first one then the other over the edge of the case.

"Hurry up. I'm not going to stand here all day." He waved his hand, the gun in it catching a glint of sunlight.

Rocking herself to the side, she pushed up on her elbow and tumbled over the side of the case into the back of the Jeep. "Thanks for the help," she muttered.

"You're tough, you'll manage. Besides, my hands are otherwise occupied."

She snorted and calculated the distance between her feet and his face.

As if he read her mind, Stan stepped away from the back of the vehicle. "Don't try anything or I'll shoot."

"What, and spoil all your fun?" Squelching her dis-appointment, Brenna rolled to the edge of the vehicle and let her feet slide to the ground into six inches of muddy, freezing water. "What's this?"

"The levy burst. We're in the middle of a flood." He nudged her with the tip of the 9 mm. "Move."

When she rounded the corner of the Jeep, she recognized the old farmhouse standing inches above the swirling water. This was the house Stan had lived in with his mother. "Now, Stan, what would your mother say if she knew you were killing women?"

"Ask her when you see her in hell. I killed her, too."

Brenna gasped. "Your own mother?"

"She never loved me. Every chance she got, she called me stupid. But I showed her." He chuckled. "A little rat poison did the trick. Looked like she died of a heart attack."

The grin he threw her way made her belly roil.

"I guess you could say it all started here." He motioned for her to lead the way.

Brenna slogged through the water and up onto the front porch. "What do you mean?"

Stan paused in front of the door. "Do you know how my father died?" he said, his tone conversational.

"I heard he died in a freak farm accident." Brenna wiggled her numb toes inside her shoes while she scanned the horizon, hoping for sight of Nick and the cavalry.

"When I was ten, I was helping him on the tractor, only he wouldn't let me drive it. When he got down to check on a tire, I shifted the tractor into gear. The wheel rolled over my father's head. Do you know what a man's head sounds like when it pops?"

"No." Nor did she want to. Brenna swallowed back the bile rising in her throat.

"Like dropping a watermelon." He stared at the key in his hand for a long time as if lost in his past. "My mother never forgave me. She couldn't even stand to look at me." He barked a mirthless laugh and waved the pistol. "You can't imagine what it feels like to know you're the one responsible for your own father's death."

At once appalled by his revelation, Brenna couldn't help feeling sorry for a little boy who'd grown up with that kind of guilt. "I'm sorry, Stan. I'm sorry for what happened to your father and the way your mother treated you. But you can't keep killing innocent women."

Stan shifted the pistol from one hand to the other, his brows rising with his smile. "I can do anything I want. I've proven I can."

"But why?" Brenna lifted her bound hands toward him. "What did those women do to you?"

His smile disappeared, his mouth thinning into a straight line. "I'll tell you what they did. When Alice saw those articles in the newspaper, she started talking about going back to college. She would have left me, damn it!"

"Alice loves you. She wouldn't have left you." Based on the talk she'd had with her sister, Brenna didn't know whether or not that was true anymore.

He snorted. "What do you know about love?"

Nick's face wavered in Brenna's mind. "More than I thought," she whispered. And she wanted a chance to learn more.

"It's all a lie," Stan said, a sneer lifting the side of his lip. "It's an act people do to make you trust them. Then they stab you in the back."

"Alice would never have betrayed you."

"She went to that damned shrink behind my back, then forced me to go. She signed up for college courses without telling me."

"Did you ever ask Alice how she felt? The kids were in school and preschool. Maybe Alice wanted more.

Did you ever ask her? I know she wouldn't hurt you. She loved you."

"Like my mother loved me?" He snorted.

"Your mother was wrong to turn her back on you. Please, Stan, there are people who could help you."

"People like Dr. Drummond? No thanks." Stan unlocked the front door and pushed her through into the musty old house filled with dust-covered furniture. "Besides, it's too late."

This was it. Stan was going to kill her the way he'd killed his mother, Dr. Drummond and the others. Her lungs constricted. She hadn't had a chance to tell Nick she loved him.

Brenna scanned the room for some way out of this mess. But with her hands tied, she couldn't do much. She'd have to throw herself at Stan and hope for the best.

After a deep breath, she kicked the gun from his hand. Before he could regain his balance, she shoved a foot into his chest and knocked him to the floor.

As Brenna raced for the pistol, Stan swept her legs from beneath her and she sprawled across the floor, the wind forced from her lungs.

Straddling her from behind, Stan yanked her up by the hair. "You'll pay for that, bitch!"

Brenna struggled to breathe beneath his weight flattening her against the hardwood floor. "Get off me." She rocked her body back and forth, her arms trapped beneath her, still tied together at the wrists.

Stan slammed her head against the floor.

Turning her face at the last moment, she missed having her nose smashed, but the hardwood sent pain radiating through her cheekbone, making stars dance in her eyes.

No. Don't pass out now. Must...get...free...stop... Stan.

Darkness claimed her and she sank into oblivion.

Chapter Nineteen

"Get the NDBCI in Bismarck on the phone. Now!" Nick paced the war room, his heart hammering against his ribs, his chest so tight he could barely breathe.

Paul pulled up the online phone directory and clicked on the North Dakota Bureau of Criminal Investigations. He dialed his cell phone and after a few questions, he handed the phone to Nick. "This guy said he's Jensen's boss."

"This is FBI Agent Tarver. The murderer has Agent Jensen, but she's got her cell phone on her. She said something about a GPS tracking. Can you pull her up?"

"Give me ten minutes and I'll have that location."

"She may not have ten minutes." The truth of his words nearly knocked him to his knees. He handed Paul's phone back to him. "Give him your cell-phone number. I want to keep mine free in case she calls back."

"Do you think she will?"

"God, I hope so." He paced the floor like a caged lion ready to rip into anyone who dared poke a finger inside. He'd been back at the station less than two minutes when Brenna's call had come through. At first he'd felt elation, followed quickly by frustration and anger at his helplessness. Now all he could do was wait for word from Bismarck. Nick smashed his fist into his other palm. "Where would he have taken her?"

"Does he have a lake cabin like most of the people around here?" Paul asked. "Or maybe a hunting cabin?"

"Hell, we don't know anything about Stan other than he's Jensen's brother-in-law." Melissa stared up at the whiteboard and pointed at the information about each victim. "Drummond was found on Eagle Lake, Stinson up Highway 7 along the Red River, and Carmichael and Gomez on—"

"Highway 7." Nick pressed his eyes closed and tipped his chin to the ceiling, racking his brain.

"I overheard on the police scanner that they blocked that road due to flooding," Paul said.

"Brenna had a grandmother who lived out Highway 7. Next door to Stan's mother's house." Nick's eyes opened and he ran for the door. "I know where he's taking her."

"I'm coming with you." Paul grabbed his jacket.

"Me, too," Melissa echoed.

"We need something higher off the ground than a sedan." Nick stared across at Paul and Melissa.

"That would be the truck I rented." Melissa pulled her keys from her pocket and tossed them at Nick.

Nick and Melissa climbed in the front seat of the fire-engine-red, four-wheel-drive pickup. Paul slid into the back seat and leaned over the top. "What's with the red pickup?"

Melissa crossed her arms over her chest. "You're not a Texan unless you drive a pickup."

"But you're not a Texan," Paul said. "And we're not in Texas."

Melissa's brow rose. "I'm working on that. I have my paperwork in for my next assignment."

Before Paul could reply, his cell phone rang. He flipped it open and said, "Agent Fletcher." He listened. "Right, we're on our way."

"NDBCI?" Nick glanced over his shoulder.

"Yeah. You were right. The GPS pinpoints her location at five miles north of Riverton on Highway 7."

Nick's teeth ground together as they headed north on Lincoln Street, weaving through traffic bent on heading west away from the flooding Red River.

Water stood four inches deep in some of the streets and by the reports back at the police station, it would only get worse. One breach in the levy system was dumping hundreds of gallons of water a minute into the river district of the city. Those who hadn't gotten out wouldn't without rescue.

By the time they reached the turn to Highway 7, the water was up to six inches and rising.

"Isn't that the levy over there?" Melissa pointed to the right.

Nick's hands gripped the steering wheel as he concentrated on keeping the vehicle between the ditches. "Yes."

"Kinda scary knowing the river is cresting over the levy in other areas, considering the levy rises above this road."

Nick didn't respond. If the levy burst before he got to Brenna, he'd damn well swim the rest of the way. The woman had more courage and gumption than any other he'd ever met. And she loved this town enough to risk her life to save its inhabitants.

Clouds choked the sun from the sky and rain drizzled onto the windshield.

"Jeez, as if there isn't enough water to worry about," Melissa said as Nick switched the wipers on.

Brenna's grandmother's house loomed on the horizon, the house and huge metal barn surrounded by a lake of water.

Plowing through twelve inches of water now, Nick prayed the truck would stay on the road long enough to get to the next house. To Brenna.

"There's Jensen's SUV!" Melissa shouted. "And look, fire!"

Nick pulled in behind the SUV, blocking it from the road. Without bothering to shut off the engine, he leaped out of the truck and raced for the house, yelling back over his shoulder, "You two take the back of the house. Don't let Klaus get away."

Nick didn't wait for Melissa and Paul to take their places at the rear of the building. He knew they were capable as surely as he knew Brenna was inside.

Across the wide wooden porch, a wall of fire burned, the overpowering scent of diesel fuel permeating the air. The smoke rising above the blaze burned black. Stan had doused the house in fuel to burn it to the ground with Brenna inside.

Nick slung his jacket into the icy water around his feet, drenching the leather before draping it over his head and charging through the fire to the front door. Flames licked at his clothes, but he made it to the door. Wrapping his coat sleeve around the door handle, he tried to turn it, but it was locked. With his jacket as a shield, he slammed his elbow through the plate-glass window and reached inside to unlock the dead bolt.

Once inside, he dropped into a crouch. Using his shirt to cover his nose, Nick moved through the room, his eyes stinging from the smoke. He felt his way across the floor until he bumped into an object on the floor.

The lump emitted a soft, feminine groan.

Nick fell to his knees and blinked several times before he could see blond hair spread out on the wood floor. "Brenna!" He rolled her over into his arms, but before he could lift her, a foot came out of the smoke and connected with his rib cage sending him flying backward. His head slammed against a wooden rocker and he struggled to get his bearings, his wet feet sliding on the smooth floor.

Smoke clogged his lungs as he lurched to his feet and plowed back through the thick haze to the man leaning over Brenna with a gun in his hand.

Nick threw himself at Stan Klaus, knocking the weapon free, and the two men crashed to the floor in a tangled heap.

"No! You can't stop me. She needs to die!" Stan screamed.

"Not on my shift." Nick swung a fist with all his pent-up emotions packed behind the punch. Pain sliced through his knuckles when he made contact with Stan's jaw. The killer's head jerked back, bouncing off the hardwood planks.

Nick worried about Brenna lying behind him on the floor. He had to get her out before she died of smoke inhalation.

He cocked his arm, ready to land another fist in Stan's face, when the man twisted and shoved him to the side, rolling out of range.

His feet sliding on the floor, Nick struggled to get up, throwing himself after the serial killer. He caught Stan in the back of the legs and the man fell against the edge of a curio cabinet and lay still.

Pulling his shirt up over his face, Nick nudged Stan with his foot. The man didn't move, didn't respond.

With the fire consuming the dried timbers of the old

house, Nick didn't have time to waste on Stan. He turned back to Brenna and, in one fluid motion, scooped her into his arms and ran for the door.

Flames had climbed into the rafters, eating through the beams like paper. A loud cracking sound rent the air and the porch overhang collapsed in Nick's path. He dodged to the side and leaped off the porch into a foot of freezing water. He didn't stop running until he reached the truck.

Jerking the passenger door open, he gently laid Brenna in the seat, his heart lodging in his throat.

He hadn't stopped to check for a pulse. She hadn't woken up to tell him she was okay.

Now, his hands shaking, Nick touched two fingers to her neck, feeling for life in Brenna's still body.

For what felt like a lifetime, he held his breath until the faintest nudge tapped against his finger, then another, until her pulse beat in a regular rhythm.

Brenna coughed, her eyes fluttering open. "Nick? Oh, God. Nick." She coughed again, and tears trickled from the corners of her eyes, leaving charcoal trails down the sides of her face in the thin layer of soot.

Melissa and Paul waded around from the other side of the house and stood beside the truck. "Hey, boss, that house is toast," Melissa said. "We never saw Klaus, did you?"

Nick stroked Brenna's soft cheek. "He's inside."

"Then he's history," Paul said, gazing back over his shoulder at the fire burning out of control.

"Good." Nick pulled Brenna into his arms, glad he'd found her before Stan could finish what he'd started.

"Well, boss, I hate to break up your reunion," Melissa said, "but the water is rising faster and it's damned cold."

Nick tucked a strand of hair behind Brenna's ear and straightened. "Let's go."

Sliding Brenna to the middle of the seat, Nick climbed in beside her. "Bradley, you drive."

"As they say around these parts, 'you betcha.'" Melissa climbed behind the wheel and turned the truck around in the yard, heading back the way they'd come.

Nick glanced over his shoulder as the roof of the little house caved in, the entire building an inferno. If Stan Klaus survived the fall against the cabinet or the smoke inhalation, the fire burning now would finish the job. Good riddance.

Melissa drove a lot slower in the rising river water on the trip back to town, straining to keep the truck on pavement they could no longer see. "Wow, this might get ugly before it gets better."

"I'm counting on you, Bradley." Nick tightened his hold on Brenna as the truck skidded sideways. "Show us how to drive like a Texan."

And she did, pushing through almost twenty-four inches of water at some points to get them back to the high ground at the police station.

All the while, Nick held Brenna in his arms as she drifted in and out of consciousness. He couldn't lose her now. She was the woman for him. The one who made his life complete. Somehow, he had to convince her to stay with him, even if he had to give up his work with the FBI.

BRENNA OPENED HER EYES and tried to remember where she was. Sterile white walls stared back at her, relieved only by two metal-framed prints of pastel gardens and a television mounted on a stand in the upper corner of the room.

Her throat felt raw and scratchy, and her lungs were tight. Other than that, she was just glad to be alive.

The pungent smell of alcohol and disinfectant permeated the air, stirring memories of her long stay in the burn ward when she'd undergone skin grafting at ten years old. She'd avoided hospitals since and didn't want to stay any longer than she had to now. Tossing the sheet aside, she sat up.

"About time you woke up." Alice rose from the chair beside the bed and leaned over her to kiss her cheek. "I thought you'd sleep the day away."

"Who's watching the kids and Mom?" Brenna asked.

"You'll never believe it. That nice FBI agent, Paul Fletcher, charmed Mom into eating carrots at the shelter. And the kids think he hung the moon."

Events of the previous night flooded into Brenna's mind and her heart squeezed so tightly in her chest she almost doubled over. She reached out and grabbed her sister's hand. "I'm sorry, Alice."

"Sorry for what?" Her sister smiled down at her, tears trailing down her cheek onto their joined hands. "It wasn't your fault Stan killed all those women."

"No, I'm sorry I was right about him." She squeezed her sister's hand.

"I should have known something wasn't right. I should have been able to see through him." Alice pulled her fingers loose and buried her face in her hands. "Those women shouldn't have died."

"As you just told me, it's not your fault Stan killed them." Brenna shivered, blaming it on the cool gust of air rushing in through the gaps in the back of her hospital gown. "He fooled a lot of people, including those he killed."

Alice glanced up, her pretty face ravaged with tears

and guilt. "I lived with him!" She hunched over in her chair, her shoulders shaking with her sobs. "How do I tell the children?"

Brenna slid from the bed, clutching the gown at the back to keep from mooning anyone walking in. Kneeling beside her sister, she took her in her arms. "You don't."

"I can't live here anymore. I couldn't stand for people to stare and point fingers at the woman who was so stupid! The woman who slept with a murdering son of a bi—"

"You can come live with me, Alice. You, Mom and the boys." Brenna lifted her sister's chin and pushed the shiny blond hairs off her tear-stained cheeks.

"Thanks, Brenna." She hugged her close, burying her face against the thin hospital gown. "I can't believe I almost lost you."

"We're family and we'll stick together." Dreams of being with Nick drifted farther out of reach and her heart ached. Not that he'd ever said anything about a long-term relationship. Her family needed her. Nick didn't.

Brenna stroked her sister's hair. The smoke inhalation and the bump on the head were nothing compared to what Alice had to recover from. Her sister needed her now more than ever and Brenna planned to be there for her.

"The police told me Stan's mother's house burned to the ground with him in it." Alice's voice was barely a whisper.

Brenna leaned closer to hear.

"They said he'd started the fire to kill you."

"Yeah, he did." Brenna forced a laugh. "Seems he did carry a grudge about the time I told you not to marry him."

"I never told you, but it was Stan who opened the barn door back when we were kids and you were locked inside, but only after I saw him there. I always thought he saved you from that fire. Until now." Alice stared up at her. "He might have been holding it closed. Brenna, that barn didn't have a lock on the outside."

Brenna squeezed her eyes shut to keep from showing her sister the disgust and loathing she felt for Stan. When she opened them, she smiled down at Alice. "It doesn't matter. It's over and Stan's gone." And it really didn't matter anymore. She was free of him, the fire and the fear of losing another victim to his insanity.

Alice continued, "Not only is the house burned, the flood waters rose and took the rest."

As if God had cleansed the earth of Stanley Klaus.

The two women sat in silence, deep in their own thoughts. After a few minutes, Alice sat up straight and gave a half laugh. "Enough crying. I have two boys to care for and I'm feeling the need for their hugs. I should go, but I promised Nick I'd stay until he got back."

"Don't worry about me. I'm fine." She was even better knowing Nick wanted someone to be with her when she woke. Brenna chose to think it meant something. But she didn't want to see him when she looked like a train wreck. "I'm going to sign myself out and get back to work."

Alice shook her head. "You amaze me."

"Why?" Brenna searched the room for clothing, finding a neat stack of jeans, T-shirt and a jacket in the corner.

"You never stop to think about yourself. You're always thinking about the job or other people. That's why everyone loves you so much." Alice hugged her. "I'll see you later."

"Wait, I need a ride to the hotel." Brenna scrambled into her clothes and left with Alice.

WHEN PAUL RETURNED to the station from helping move Alice, her mother and kids to the shelter in nearby

Roanoke, he gave Nick the news that Brenna had checked out of the hospital and gone to the hotel. Nick wrapped up the reports he'd written and hit the road.

The river had crested during the night, sweeping away many homes along the banks, but thanks to the evacuation plan, no lives had been lost.

With the evacuation complete, there was little traffic on the streets and it didn't take him long to reach the hotel on the dry side of the city.

All the way up the stairs he tried to think of what he'd say to Brenna, coming up blank. His chaotic thoughts kept replaying the scene in the burning house and the emptiness he'd felt when he'd thought he'd lost her. Now that the future loomed ahead of him, what did he have to offer this amazing woman?

As Nick entered the suite, Brenna stepped out of the bathroom, her hair clean and dry and her face clear of all the black soot from the previous evening. Everything Nick wanted to say rose up in his throat to strangle him.

Without uttering a sound he strode across the room and pulled her into his arms, crushing her to him. He stood for a long moment inhaling the fresh scent of her shampoo and feeling the beat of her heart against his. When he thought he had his emotions under control, he stepped back and looked down into her eyes. "I love you, Special Agent Jensen."

Her eyes misted and she smiled up at him. "And I love you, Agent Tarver." Then she hiked her fists onto her hips. "So what are we going to do about it?"

He sighed and shook his head. "I don't have anything to offer you."

"You just gave me everything I ever wanted." She placed a hand over his chest. "You gave me your heart."

"You've had that from the first time I saw you biting your lip." He leaned close and pressed a kiss to that lip.

When he backed away, she pulled the lip between her teeth. "My sister needs me now. She's moving to Minneapolis with me."

"Minneapolis?"

She gave him a weak smile and nodded. "They called a few minutes ago. I got the job."

Clasping her hand in his, he pulled her close. "Then I guess I'll get a transfer to Minneapolis." Somehow, he'd make it happen.

"Are you sure?" Her eyes sparkled with hope.

"Never more sure in my life. I want to be with you."

"And I want to be with you." She snuggled closer, smoothing her fingers over his shirt.

"Will you come with me to Virginia to meet my mother and brothers?" he asked.

Brenna smiled. "I'd love to."

"I'll be on the road a lot," he said against her hair. "Can you handle that?"

"I'm in the same business. Can you handle me being away?" She stared up into his eyes. "Nick, I'm not your ex-wife and I understand the nature of your job. I'll go into this with my eyes open and my expectations clear." She dipped her head. "But what about you? I'll never be beautiful."

"You'll always be beautiful to me, Brenna. Even when we're old and gray rocking on our front porch." He tipped her face up to him and kissed her full on the lips until they both broke away, breathless. "I'll always love you."

"Even with the lights on?" she whispered against his lips.

"Especially with the lights on. I love the way you care

about your job, the way you care what happens to people. I love you, Brenna, no matter what you look like."

"Then what are we waiting for?" Her hands laced around the back of his neck and she pulled his face down to hers.

Nick had come home to the woman for him.

*Experience the anticipation, the thrill of the chase
and the sheer rush of falling in love!
Turn the page for a sneak preview
of a new book from Harlequin Romance
THE REBEL PRINCE
by Raye Morgan
On sale August 29 wherever books are sold*

"OH, NO!"

The reaction slipped out before Emma Valentine could stop it, for there stood the very man she most wanted to avoid seeing again.

He didn't look any happier to see her.

"Well, come on, get on board," he said gruffly. "I won't bite." One eyebrow rose. "Though I might nibble a little," he added, mostly to amuse himself.

But she wasn't paying any attention to what he was saying. She was staring at him, taking in the royal blue uniform he was wearing, with gold braid and glistening badges decorating the sleeves, epaulettes and an upright collar. Ribbons and medals covered the breast of the short, fitted jacket. A gold-encrusted sabre hung at his side. And suddenly it was clear to her who this man really was.

She gulped wordlessly. Reaching out, he took her elbow and pulled her aboard. The doors slid closed. And finally she found her tongue.

"You...you're the prince."

He nodded, barely glancing at her. "Yes. Of course."

She raised a hand and covered her mouth for a moment. "I should have known."

"Of course you should have. I don't know why you didn't." He punched the ground-floor button to get the elevator moving again, then turned to look down at her. "A relatively bright five-year-old child would have tumbled to the truth right away."

Her shock faded as her indignation at his tone asserted itself. He might be the prince, but he was still just as annoying as he had been earlier that day.

"A relatively bright five-year-old child without a bump on the head from a badly thrown water-polo ball, maybe," she said defensively. She wasn't feeling woozy any longer and she wasn't about to let him bully her, no matter how royal he was. "I was unconscious half the time."

"And just clueless the other half, I guess," he said, looking bemused.

The arrogance of the man was really galling.

"I suppose you think your 'royalness' is so obvious it sort of shimmers around you for all to see?" she challenged. "Or better yet, oozes from your pores like… like sweat on a hot day?"

"Something like that," he acknowledged calmly. "Most people tumble to it pretty quickly. In fact, it's hard to hide even when I want to avoid dealing with it."

"Poor baby," she said, still resenting his manner. "I guess that works better with injured people who are half asleep." Looking at him, she felt a strange emotion she couldn't identify. It was as though she wanted to prove something to him, but she wasn't sure what. "And anyway, you know you did your best to fool me," she added.

His brows knit together as though he really didn't know what she was talking about. "I didn't do a thing."

"You told me your name was Monty."

"It is." He shrugged. "I have a lot of names. Some of

them are too rude to be spoken to my face, I'm sure." He glanced at her sideways, his hand on the hilt of his sabre. "Perhaps you're contemplating one of those right now."

You bet I am.

That was what she would like to say. But it suddenly occurred to her that she was supposed to be working for this man. If she wanted to keep the job of coronation chef, maybe she'd better keep her opinions to herself. So she clamped her mouth shut, took a deep breath and looked away, trying hard to calm down.

The elevator ground to a halt and the doors slid open laboriously. She moved to step forward, hoping to make her escape, but his hand shot out again and caught her elbow.

"Wait a minute. *You're* a woman," he said, as though that thought had just presented itself to him.

"That's a rare ability for insight you have there, Your Highness," she snapped before she could stop herself. And then she winced. She was going to have to do better than that if she was going to keep this relationship on an even keel.

But he was ignoring her dig. Nodding, he stared at her with a speculative gleam in his golden eyes. "I've been looking for a woman, but you'll do."

She blanched, stiffening. "I'll do for what?"

He made a head gesture in a direction she knew was opposite of where she was going and his grip tightened on her elbow.

"Come with me," he said abruptly, making it an order.

She dug in her heels, thinking fast. She didn't much like orders. "Wait! I can't. I have to get to the kitchen."

"Not yet. I need you."

"You what?" Her breathless gasp of surprise was soft, but she knew he'd heard it.

"I need you," he said firmly. "Oh, don't look so shocked. I'm not planning to throw you into the hay and have my way with you. I need you for something a bit more mundane than that."

She felt color rushing into her cheeks and she silently begged it to stop. Here she was, formless and stodgy in her chef's whites. No makeup, no stiletto heels. Hardly the picture of the femmes fatales he was undoubtedly used to. The likelihood that he would have any carnal interest in her was remote at best. To have him think she was hysterically defending her virtue was humiliating.

"Well, what if I don't want to go with you?" she said in hopes of deflecting his attention from her blush.

"Too bad."

"What?"

Amusement sparkled in his eyes. He was certainly enjoying this. And that only made her more determined to resist him.

"I'm the prince, remember? And we're in the castle. My orders take precedence. It's that old pesky divine rights thing."

Her jaw jutted out. Despite her embarrassment, she couldn't let that pass.

"Over my free will? Never!"

Exasperation filled his face.

"Hey, call out the historians. Someone will write a book about you and your courageous principles." His eyes glittered sardonically. "But in the meantime, Emma Valentine, you're coming with me."

SAVE UP TO $30! SIGN UP TODAY!

INSIDE Romance

The complete guide to your favorite
Harlequin®, Silhouette® and Love Inspired® books.

✔ Newsletter ABSOLUTELY FREE! No purchase necessary.

✔ Valuable coupons for future purchases of Harlequin,
Silhouette and Love Inspired books in every issue!

✔ Special excerpts & previews in each issue. Learn about all
the hottest titles before they arrive in stores.

✔ No hassle—mailed directly to your door!

✔ Comes complete with a handy shopping checklist
so you won't miss out on any titles.

- -

SIGN ME UP TO RECEIVE INSIDE ROMANCE
ABSOLUTELY FREE
(Please print clearly)

Name

Address

City/Town   State/Province   Zip/Postal Code

(098 KKM EJL9)   **Please mail this form to:**
In the U.S.A.: Inside Romance, P.O. Box 9057, Buffalo, NY 14269-9057
In Canada: Inside Romance, P.O. Box 622, Fort Erie, ON L2A 5X3
<u>OR</u> visit http://www.eHarlequin.com/insideromance

IRNBPA06R   ® and ™ are trademarks owned and used by the trademark owner and/or its licensee.

If you enjoyed what you just read,
then we've got an offer you can't resist!

Take 2 bestselling love stories FREE!

Plus get a FREE surprise gift!

Clip this page and mail it to Harlequin Reader Service®

IN U.S.A.	IN CANADA
3010 Walden Ave.	P.O. Box 609
P.O. Box 1867	Fort Erie, Ontario
Buffalo, N.Y. 14240-1867	L2A 5X3

YES! Please send me 2 free Harlequin Intrigue® novels and my free surprise gift. After receiving them, if I don't wish to receive anymore, I can return the shipping statement marked cancel. If I don't cancel, I will receive 4 brand-new novels each month, before they're available in stores! In the U.S.A., bill me at the bargain price of $4.24 plus 25¢ shipping and handling per book and applicable sales tax, if any*. In Canada, bill me at the bargain price of $4.99 plus 25¢ shipping and handling per book and applicable taxes**. That's the complete price and a savings of at least 10% off the cover prices—what a great deal! I understand that accepting the 2 free books and gift places me under no obligation ever to buy any books. I can always return a shipment and cancel at any time. Even if I never buy another book from Harlequin, the 2 free books and gift are mine to keep forever.

181 HDN DZ7N
381 HDN DZ7P

Name _____ (PLEASE PRINT)

Address _____ Apt.# _____

City _____ State/Prov. _____ Zip/Postal Code _____

Not valid to current Harlequin Intrigue® subscribers.

Want to try two free books from another series?
Call 1-800-873-8635 or visit www.morefreebooks.com.

* Terms and prices subject to change without notice. Sales tax applicable in N.Y.
** Canadian residents will be charged applicable provincial taxes and GST.
All orders subject to approval. Offer limited to one per household.
® are registered trademarks owned and used by the trademark owner and or its licensee.

INTO4R   ©2004 Harlequin Enterprises Limited